CONTENTS

Title Page
Dedication
Chapter 1   1
Chapter 2   11
Chapter 3   16
Chapter 4   28
Chapter 5   35
Chapter 6   48
Chapter 7   57
Chapter 8   68
Chapter 9   73
Chapter 10   86
Chapter 11   94
Chapter 12   103
Chapter 13   116
Chapter 14   129
Chapter 15   136
Chapter 16   144
Chapter 17   152
Chapter 18   160

Chapter 19	174
Chapter 20	184
Chapter 21	193
Chapter 22	199
Chapter 23	205
Chapter 24	214
Chapter 25	221
Chapter 26	228
A Sneak Peek:	235
Thank you for reading	246
Other Books By the Author	247
Copyright	248

THE UNFORGETTABLE QUEEN OF DIAMONDS

Cartwright Ranch Book 1

Nellie K. Neves

To Rebecca- For growing up under your salon chair, to tamales, and everything in between, you've been the best mama bear big sister a girl could ask for.

CHAPTER 1

Kennedy

My heart might break through my ribcage if I keep on like this. I know better than to push my limits, but I need this. If I'm ever going to be anyone, if I'm ever going to prove myself, I have to conquer this.

Sweat beads above my lip. I press them together to dispel the buzz of nervous energy. The spotlight warms my skin, but with anxiety burning from the inside out, it feels like too much. Is it possible to love something and hate it all in the same breath? It has to be. Because there's nothing I want more than to hold this microphone under the lights and sing, but my body acts as though I'm putting it through torture.

The seats are all empty. They have been for years. My fear is irrational. Even if I manage to squeak out a sound, or better, belt out a song, no one would hear me. Other than the doves in the rafters, I'm alone in the old auditorium. I step back, just beyond the ring of the spotlight and the pressure of a thousand bricks lifts from my shoulders. One day, I'll conquer my fear, and at least the mice in the walls will hear me.

That's better than nothing.

I step down from the stage and take the stairs up to the control panel. It's eight switches before the whole place goes dark and the equipment is off. Using the light on my phone, I pick my way out of the old auditorium. We abandoned it once the new one was built. With only one way in or out, no air conditioning, and limited seating, it's basically a dinosaur. I'm surprised dad hasn't flattened it yet, probably just sentimentality that keeps it standing. A nod to the way we started things at Cartwright Ranch.

Cold dew gathers in the air and chills my scorched skin. This is where I belong, in the dark, behind the scenes, not up in the light, star of the show. It's been my place for years. I'm kidding myself to think it'd ever change. The show must go on and all that, but it's not like it'll go on without me there running it.

Lights from the house flicker twice, a message from my dad that he sees me on the path, and he'd like me to come talk. I draw in a breath and let it tumble out with a sigh. Another day, another duty list. It's a good thing I love him. My feet follow the worn trail without so much as a thought, and I make my way back to the house.

Psychologists say that the oldest child is the most responsible. They worry about the family name being upheld and want to protect honor and whatnot. Middle children are supposed to fly under the radar, forgotten.

It's all hogwash if you ask me. I invite someone to come take a peek at the Cartwright family, and maybe they'll have a new case study to blow the rest out of the water. I'm the responsible one, not Victoria, my older sister. I'd love to be the forgotten middle child, but since I turned fifteen, I've been front and center getting it all done. I dream of a life of my own, apart from my family, chasing the dreams I've kept secrets for years, but that's all it is, that's all it will ever be. Dreams.

My mom died when I was young. Car accident. She went fast. It was a head-on collision. I was fifteen, Vic was seventeen, and Hudson, my younger brother, was eight. Vic should have stepped up, taken on the brunt of helping to raise Hudson, but all she took to raising was H-E-double-you-know-what. While Vic hit every party in the county, I helped Hudsie with homework, wiped his tears, and made sure the science fair project didn't explode.

Maybe if mom hadn't died, things would be different. I wouldn't feel the weight of the world on my shoulders. If I didn't have that weight, maybe I could conquer my fear of performing, or take a few lessons, or try something new. But as it stands, I hold the family together. I carry the brunt of the work. I've stepped in to manage the ranch and all the work that goes with it now that dad's health isn't where it should be. I don't have time to chase dreams about stardom or standing in the spotlight. Those are best left for the moments I sneak in the old auditorium, playing pretend at a different reality where dreams are still possible, and I still have freedom to choose my own path.

"Kenny?" My father knows the sound of my steps and stops me in the hall before I can pass his office. "Kennedy, can you come in here?"

Like I wasn't planning on it anyway, but Vic would be the one to say that, not me. I roll over and let it go. That's the only place the psychologists are right with their birth order theories. Middle child: Peacemaker, AKA Kennedy Cartwright.

I lean inside the door and smile at him sitting there. A half-inch of Coke is still in his glass. One oversized, round ice cube still taking up most of the glass. I bought him the specialty ice tray last year for his birthday. At first, he didn't like it. He told me he didn't want ice watering down his drink. Later, when I questioned him, he changed his mind. He said he liked the way it felt to roll the sphere ice cube around, feeling like a big shot. It's dumb that he thinks he has to play at big shot. Not a single person in this county, heck, most of this state, that doesn't know who Ace Cartwright is. He's a legend.

"Whatcha need, Dad?"

"Tomorrow," he taps his fingers against the desk as he speaks, like he's playing a grand piano or something, "I need you to head over to Santos Sound. I've got it set up so you can check out some of their acts for the summer series. Maybe add a few to the event binders for the future."

My gut churns at the thought. Dale Santos owns Santos Sound. He's like that ice cube swirling in my dad's glass—the same width as he is tall, like a sphere with legs. I hate going to see acts with him. He clears his throat every forty-three seconds, I've timed it, and snarfs phlegm from the back of his gullet. When he's meeting someone for the first time, he runs his thumbs along the inside of his belt like they're set on tracks. There's no room there because his belt is too tight, so his fingers turn red when his thumbs get stuck. He makes the same jokes every time I see him, about how my parents thought I was a boy, and how I'm the prettiest boy he's ever seen, built like one too. But the worst is the way his eyes linger, like I owe him something. I never want to know why he looks at me that way.

"I've got a beat on a few local acts already," I say to dad, "maybe we don't even need to go to Santos this time."

"Wedding season is upon us, Kenny. Trust me." He leaves it at that.

"Yeah, I know, you're the boss, Dad. What time is he expecting me?"

"Nine."

I pat the door jamb twice and sigh. I glance up and catch Dad's eye. His smile warms me from the inside out. It doesn't take much from him to convince me. My family loyalty runs deep.

"You know you look more like your mama every day."

I nod but drop my chin to hide because the sting of tears will give me away. Almost a decade later, and it's still too fresh. "I'll get on it tomorrow, don't you worry."

"I never do, not with you, Kennedy."

❊ ❊ ❊

I'm out the door before Dad is out of bed. Now that Hudson can drive himself to school, my days are easier, but I'm prone to wake before the old man anyhow. It's not far to Santos Sound, maybe twenty minutes in small-town traffic. Dale Santos kept his business local, opting to stay on the outskirts of our little town, rather than at the heart of one of the nearby cities.

Dale is technically a recording company. He's got the equipment, the studio, every ability to bring an album to life, but in all the years my dad has been friends with him, I've never heard of him doing that. How he stays in business, I have no idea.

I park to the left of the house. A new luxury sedan up front doesn't escape me, but the lifted black jeep steals my attention. I've never seen either one before, but that's not usual. Santos Sound never seems void of visitors. Dale parks around back most of the time, and he insists I drive to our meetings.

Cartwright Ranch has been working with Santos Sound for eight years now. In the past, Dad went out with Dale and saw whatever new talent he'd dug up. Dad would deem them worthy or not, and Dale would take a cut of whatever money we made from the concerts or wedding reception fees. I gather we're his number one source of revenue. Still, he has a name in the area, and we'd be stupid not to keep the partnership.

When I graduated college, with a major in business, minor in music, dad had me take over the music side of the ranch in addition to my other duties. Last year's concert series was a huge hit, and, for my debut year, it raised a few eyebrows. Ace's daughter hadn't fallen far from the tree.

I pop open my car door and shift to pull myself to standing. My pencil skirt is tight and constricting, but I like how powerful it makes me feel. I need that when I'm around someone like Dale. He likes to make me feel insignificant and small. Last year he snuck in three acts I didn't approve of and proverbially patted me on my head and sent me on my way. It won't happen this year. I refuse to be caught off guard again. I'm ready for anything.

I knock with three crisp taps and straighten my top. The door opens with a whoosh, but it's not Dale Santos. I blink because my eyes have to be playing tricks on me. Easily six-feet tall, with dark, styled hair. The red leather jacket he wears hangs open wide enough that I trace the outline of his chiseled frame through his tight, white shirt. Not burly, but athletic, agile, able. A whimpering sound squeaks from my throat instead of words. I blink again. Dale has either gotten the best plastic surgery that money can buy, or I'm at the wrong house.

"Are you Kennedy?" the stranger asks me. His voice is deep and booming, as if a timpani drum is beating from deep within that chest I can't stop staring at. "Kennedy Cartwright?"

I try again for words, but my noises are incomprehensible, like a puppy whining at the back door. I blink once more.

"Are you having a stroke?" He bends a bit as if to ascertain my health. I shake my head and smile the best I can, so he won't call an ambulance.

"I'm sorry, yes, I'm Kennedy. I'm here to meet with Dale." It's a struggle to keep my words straight, as if I'm in the middle of rebooting my brain.

One of his thick eyebrows juts up as if he's not so sure about the stroke victim, but he extends a hand toward me despite his concerns.

"I'm Roman Palermo. Your appointment is with me. Dale is… indisposed. I've been hired in the interim."

Can I throw my hands up in the air and holler like I just won the jackpot at a slot machine? I suppose that's not professional, is it?

I clear my throat again and straighten my top, despite the fact that it's perfectly straight. "Okay, do you have some acts in mind, or…"

Dale has never let me take the lead. Good looks or not, I doubt this guy will be any different.

"I have leads on a few I'd like to check out. Do you have anything you want to run by me?"

"Not today, I mean, I wasn't expecting to," I clear my throat again because my tongue feels entirely too big for my mouth, "Dale never asks me for any, I mean, in the past…"

"Do you need some water? You seem a little parched." He pulls the door shut behind him and motions for the driveway where I'm parked. "I'll drive. I've got a case of water in the back."

I follow him, still trying to shake the shock from my expression. Is it him, or is it the sheer shock of not going out with Dale?

I mean, anyone is drool-worthy compared to Dale.

Without thinking, I head for the luxury sedan parked at the front and stop by the passenger side. I look up to find Roman is staring at me from twenty feet away. He tips his head to the lifted black Jeep. "This is mine."

Cheeks flushing with embarrassment, I move to join him. The rise into the jeep is a bit more than my pencil skirt will allow. I bend a knee and set it to the floor but know there's no way I can pull myself in gracefully. Turning backwards, I set my rear to the floor and grip the overhead bar, determined to hoist myself up into the cab, but lack the strength to do a pull-up. One little step on the side rail would sure help a girl out.

"Here you go," Roman says, coming around the side of the jeep with the water bottle extended. He catches me with one hand up, bum on the floorboard, and hand bracing against the door. I drop everything and straighten my top again.

"I'm having a little trouble getting in," I say.

"I can see that. Not a lot of give in that skirt, I guess."

His eyes linger on my frame, but not in the way I wish they would. Instead, more like an engineer trying to solve a problem. "You want a boost?"

I'm not sure what he has in mind. Really, I should tell him we can take my car, but curiosity is begging me to find out his plans. I shrug as if it's an answer. Setting my water bottle on the ground, Roman moves closer. His palms grip at the sides of my waist, and, as if I'm lighter than a feather, he pops me up into the cab of the jeep. He snags my water bottle and sets it in my hands. "I'll be right back."

The water is cool, for which I am grateful because my cheeks are red hot. Did dad know about this new, Mr. Roman Palermo? Right on cue, my phone buzzes with a text from the big boss himself.

"You meet Roman yet?"

I stifle the frustration in my chest and type back my reply.

"You could have told me I wasn't meeting Dale."

There's only a brief pause before he types, *"Now what's the fun in that?"*

A thud in the back of the jeep brings my attention back. Two seconds later, Roman hoists himself up to the driver seat and fires up the engine.

"We're going to Jackson first. There's this sibling act, a brother and a sister, that I think you'll like. They've been looking for work locally and have a real down-home sound."

Talking about music settles me. This is what I'm good at. Not climbing in lifted vehicles or talking to handsome men. I've dedicated my life to music, and now to the pursuit of finding talent that would be otherwise undiscovered. It's only a tiny part of what I do at the ranch, but it's the piece of my job that has my heart. My confidence returns as we pass the drive talking about acts we've both seen, music we've fallen in love with, and of course the work my family does at the Cartwright Ranch.

"Do you mind?" Roman reaches for the radio. I shrug to give my consent because life is empty without a soundtrack.

A familiar ballad fills the cab, something I remember from my childhood. I used to sing it at the top of my lungs with Vic and mom pretending to be my adoring fans. Back before everything fell apart and I had to push those thoughts to a backburner. I smile to myself as the chorus swells, remembering when I used to slide across the kitchen floor, hairbrush for a microphone. It doesn't go unnoticed by my companion.

"You like this one?"

"Brings back memories." I hum along with the tunes, unable to stop myself.

"Of high school?"

I frown. "More like elementary school."

Roman casts a quick glance across the cab. "Really?"

"Yeah. Why, how old were you?"

"It's not important." He turns on to a side road and eases his speed. "This is Amanda and Christopher Wakely. They've been going by 'Southern Comforts" when they perform, but I keep telling them they have to change the name."

"I have to agree." I glance over the file on the sibling set, but I keep running over his reaction instead. Why did it matter how old I was when the song came out?

* * *

Roman

I have to admit, I didn't know what to make of her at first. This Kennedy Cartwright, gaping at me on the front stoop like my left ear fell off or something. For as much as I was concerned for her health in the beginning, it doesn't take much to see, other than that introductory moment, she's precise, controlled, and a bit of perfectionist in everything she does.

She smooths every wrinkle from her skirt when she sits down. Her pencil bounces in perfect timing against her notebook while the duo plays their set list. But she's careful not to make a single sound. Even her dark auburn hair, slick, straight, not a curl in sight, stays in perfect alignment. I note early on the way she lists the songs on her notepad, scores each one in five categories, but covers her writing so she won't offend anyone.

Once the shock of not seeing Dale in the doorway wore off, she seemed to get down to business. Maybe she's not one for changing things up. I doubt her reaction could be contributed to much else. As usual, I've slipped into the background, backseat to the singers' performance. Her whole world seems to be music. She doesn't even notice when I slip off to check my leads, disguised as a trip to the restroom. My below the radar appearance serves me well in my work. Other than a slight glance when I come back, she doesn't seem to notice I left.

There was one second, a brief moment, when I lifted her up into the cab, where I felt like we sparked. But then, that was impulsive, and I know better than to try something like that again. Girls like her don't go for guys like me.

It doesn't matter anyway, that's not why I'm here. I have a job to do, and it has nothing to do with music, or a gorgeous talent scout.

CHAPTER 2

Kennedy

I booked *Southern Comforts* for our summer series concerts and agreed to add them to the selection binder for weddings as well. Their bluegrass sound will be popular, even if Amanda goes pitchy in a few places. Hopefully, she'll sort that out before the concert. If anyone knows about nerves messing with their voice, it's me.

My heels clack against the asphalt as we walk back to the jeep. I'm trying to formulate a less embarrassing mode of entry when Roman pulls a step stool from the back and sets it at my feet.

"Thought it might make it easier," he says.

It does. But I must admit I didn't mind him lifting me the last time, at least not too much.

It's a short drive to the next meeting, Joe Fink, but I'm not sold. He's heavy on his guitar strings and lacks the finesse I require. Three more appointments follow and three more disappointments pass.

"You've got high standards," Roman says as we head back for his jeep after the last act.

"You don't?"

"I thought this last group was good. According to his notes, Dale's been considering signing them for a while now."

I have a lot to say, but I've learned to keep my opinions to myself. I rarely win an argument, and I hate ruffling feathers.

Roman slides in on his side but instead of starting the jeep, he waits, watching me.

"What?"

He laughs once, but the smile lingers like his eyes. "What was wrong with this guy?"

"Not my cup of tea."

"And the act before that?"

"They were tap dancing while singing."

"You don't like dancing?"

"Not if it makes their singing sound like they're going over potholes."

That earns me a genuine laugh. "I have to admit, I'm new around here. Maybe I'm too easy to impress."

"You're still doing better than Dale," I say under my breath.

He doesn't miss a beat. "That's good to know. But maybe he wouldn't have shown you any of these acts."

"Maybe not, but he did once take me to see his new favorite barbershop quartet called forties over ninety."

"You gotta be kidding me."

I shrug and fasten my seatbelt. "We booked them, but they never had a chance to perform."

"Why not?"

"Two died before the first show."

"You're making this up."

"Only a little," I say.

He sets the key in the ignition but hesitates. "Where should I go to find good talent then?"

I can't tell if he's just being nice, or he wants to know. I don't want to overstep.

"I'm serious," Roman says, "where should I be looking?"

I chew on the words before I'm willing to speak. "*The Nightingale*. It's open mic night tonight. I usually check out the acts, just to stay on top of things."

Roman nods. It's the only indication I have that he's heard me. He stares over the steering wheel like he's reading the future. Whatever he sees cements his decision.

"What time should I pick you up?"

* * *

Roman

We've got a barebones crew working this case. It's my supervising agent's pet project. He caught wind of something, or someone, called Dark Fox. We're only here because he's got the director's ear and has a little leeway to chase this lead. Dark Fox is barely much more than a whisper, more like a ghost story we've been hearing from the suspects we've brought in. Up until now, it's all been sporadic, bouncing around the country. Weeks ago, the whispers centered on a place called Santos Sound, a nothing recording studio in the middle of nowhere, USA. To the untrained eye, it would look like a washed-out producer trying to sign a couple new acts every so often, but that's the thing, Dale Santos hasn't been as clever as he thought. What originally got flagged by local cops as a scam, has turned into our first lead with this Dark Fox rumor. If we're right, then Dale Santos has been helping Dark Fox launder thousands of dollars for who knows how long.

I enter Santos Sound, careful to close the front door behind me. Two agents are staying at the studio that also doubles as Dale's home, Rick, my supervisor, and Maddox, the other agent. Dale was gracious enough to let us set up camp. Though, being in federal custody has a way of opening doors. He's not talking yet, but at least he's cooperating on some level.

"You find anything?" Jake Maddox asks from the kitchen.

"No, not yet." I drop my keys on the entry table. Takeout boxes litter the counter. I scoop them up and toss them in the trash. I'm glad I don't have to stay here with the rest of them. I have my own apartment to keep up my cover. Rick, our supervisor, has us staying for at least a month trying to sort through this mess and get whatever leads we can on Dark Fox.

"Are the analysts back?" I ask Maddox before he saunters into the room and flops on the couch.

"You that eager to go back to the low life?" He grins, but it's wicked in intent. It's my first time working with him, and I don't plan on being assigned to the same team ever again if I can help it.

"I'm looking for leads, same as you."

Rick must hear our voices because he enters from the back room. "Good, you're back. Can you write up what you found last night in the accounts? I need to show some progress if we plan to stay here any longer."

I start for the command center we've set up. My laptop is linked to Dale's, cross referencing his mountains of handwritten financial notes.

Maddox pulls himself to his feet. "I still don't see why Palermo is the one with the cover. We all know he'd rather be back at base, not out in the field."

I don't rise to the barb, it's not in my nature. But Rick doesn't even need a second to think about his answer. "Palermo blends in, you stand out. I can't have anyone knowing why we're here, not yet." He claps a hand against my back. "Good ol' forgettable over here, he's the one for the job."

He exits while I'm still stinging from the insult he doesn't know he gave me. My average looks, it's what makes me an asset to the bureau. Easier to go undercover when you're not too handsome, not too ugly, just an average white guy who blends into the background.

Still, I can't help but remember the way Kennedy Cartwright looked at me. For once, I didn't feel like I blended in, I felt seen. Noticed. Admired, even. Not great for my work, but my self-esteem sure appreciated the boost.

Maddox waits for Rick to leave but doesn't waste another second beyond that. "You know I requested you to work on this with me, right?"

I heard through back channels that he had. I still don't know why.

He cuts the space between us, poking a finger into my arm. "This is my op, you understand? This is my chance to get in with Rick, impress him and get ahead. I only requested you come along because you've got this reputation for hanging back, letting everyone else take the lead. Am I gonna have a problem with you stealing my thunder?"

I've been dealing with macho alpha types like him since I showed up at Quantico my first day. Since I'm not in it for the glory, I'm more than happy to step aside.

"No, no problem here."

"Good," he claps a hand against my shoulder, "then I'm going out to do some *real* FBI work."

I'm not the average agent, I know that, but what others see as weaknesses, I'm trying to turn into strengths. The boring, lackluster work is what finds leads. All my hours scouring paperwork and financials, that's where the answers tend to hide. Let Maddox lead the charge, without an agent like me behind him, he's running blind.

CHAPTER 3

Kennedy

It's not like it's a date
 It's work.
 That's all it is.
 But I check the mirror once more before I snatch my purse from the bed.
 "Who's the hottie?"
 I turn to find seventeen-year-old Hudson leaning against the doorway.
 "Who said he was a hottie? We're going to watch open mic night so I can build the summer series. It's not a date, Hudsie."
 "I never said it was." He's grinning like there's a joke, and as usual, I'm not a part of it. "And I wasn't talking about the guy. You're all dressed up. Didn't recognize you."
 "I always dress up for *The Nightingale*."
 It's not true, but it's also not a lie. I dress up, but not like this. Not with strappy heels and nails painted black. I don't wear slinky dresses that I know will catch the light and shimmer. Normally, I hide in the back with a notepad and a seltzer water.
 Hudson laughs to himself and backs away. "Whatever you've got to tell yourself, Kenny."
 I snap the latch shut on my purse like a signal that our conversation is over. The doorbell rings and Hudson's smile triples.
 "I think I'll get the door for you." He tears off down the hall,

his stride double my choppy steps as I chase after him. Because of our history, people worry he thinks of me like his mother, but no, not a chance. He's every bit that annoying little brother he's always been.

I'm rushing down the stairs when he whips open the door and stares up at Roman Palermo. With absolutely zero tact, he looks over his shoulder at me to mouth the words, "That's it?"

"Hi," Roman says to my sibling idiot, "I'm here for Kennedy. Is she ready?"

Hudson actually has the nerve to start laughing. "As dressed up as she is, I think I was expecting more, but then Kenny always has had weird taste in me—"

I finish the last two steps and jerk my younger brother back by his collar, effectively silencing the rest of his sentence.

"I'm ready. Shall we go?"

"Are you going to introduce me?" Hudson asks from where he's pretending to recover from his sister-induced injuries.

Roman pauses like he's interested, and, in the name of keeping the peace, I smile even though it hurts a bit.

"This is Roman. Roman, this is the town idiot. We keep him in the barn. He seems to have freed himself." I shoot one last glare at my brother and pull the door shut behind me.

He's enough of a gentleman to wait ten seconds before he asks, "So that was your…"

"Brother," I say. "Younger. He's seventeen."

"Oh yeah, that's an obnoxious age."

"He's certainly proving that to be true."

I'm expecting his jeep out front, but instead the luxury sedan is glistening in the light of the dying sun. He must notice the stutter in my step because he's quick to pull open the passenger door and explain himself.

"Part of the deal. Company car. If I'm expected to save Santos Sound, I should have a few perks, right?"

I save my response and slide in on the leather seat. Gravel crunches as he jogs to the other side to take his spot behind the wheel. The engine purrs like a kitten and inertia presses me back as he heads for the highway.

"You live with your parents?" Roman asks as he takes the final turn to merge with traffic headed for the city.

"Part of the gig," I say, because it's easier than the long answer.

"Because of the ranch?"

I debate whether to tell him more, but his curiosity seems innocent enough. "My mom died when Hudson was young. Dad was clueless and my sister wasn't in any shape to take care of anyone. I took over."

"I'm really sorry. How old were you?"

"A little younger than Hudson is now. I made it work."

The blinker fills the silence as he merges with traffic and lets my words sink in. I shouldn't have told him. People get weird around death. It reminds them that their own time is limited. No one wants to hear that clock tick.

"You had to grow up pretty fast then?"

"That's an understatement. Victoria did manage to cook, she's always loved that, but I made sure he got on the bus and homework was done. I helped him learn his multiplication tables. I did laundry and cleaned the house." A smile teases at my lips. "I made sure he remembered to change his underwear and take a shower now and then. He hates it when I say that."

It lightens the air between us, a warm smile gracing his lips. It pushes his cheeks out and chisels deep lines where his skin used to be smooth. I feel like his smiles are treasures, and I want to find them all.

"Are your parents nearby?"

"Yeah." Roman flips on the radio and thinks about his answer before he adds, "That's part of the reason I took the job. They're getting up there in age. They live in a senior community, and now I can visit more often."

"Do you have siblings?"

"A brother and a sister, but they aren't local. My brother is overseas."

"Older? Younger?"

"I'm oldest." Roman says it like it's admitting defeat. I'm not sure why.

Music fills the silence between us, but because it's music, it doesn't matter. Music is a friend, an old friend that has carried me through the worst of it. I'll never forbid music entrance to my life.

Out of habit, I sing along with the song, soft enough that Roman won't hear me. He taps in time with the beat, fingers drumming the steering wheel. The chorus swells, and my voice follows suit. I feel his eyes find me, and I press my lips together to cut off the sound.

"Do you mind turning it up?" I ask.

"Do I have to?"

"No, I guess not. It's your radio." I point to the exit. "Take this one."

Roman takes the exit and clicks the radio until the volume is another member of the car. He follows my directions until he pulls into *The Nightingale* parking lot. The car eases to a stop, and he twists the key in the ignition. I set my hand to the door latch, but his voice catches me.

"I don't mind the radio, but I preferred hearing you."

He doesn't wait for my reply before he climbs out. I follow suit, the glow of flattery shining in my cheeks. It feels good to be noticed, at least a little bit.

✣ ✣ ✣

Kennedy

He leads me by the small of my back. He's not bossing me around, more like he's directing me as if we're dancing. Slight pressure, only the tips of his fingers, enough to let me know he means to sit in the booth in the corner with a direct view of the stage and three tea light candles for ambiance.

I slide to the back and draw in a deep breath to still my

nerves. It's not a date, so I don't know why I'm feeling this way. Maybe it's Roman, his presence draws it out of me. Giddy feelings burble up inside every time he looks at me, like I might giggle or blush just from his stare. I'm under his spell, that's the only answer.

Or maybe I don't get out much.

That's more likely.

"Your brother called you Kenny." Roman doesn't even glance my way as he says it, but keeps his eyes locked on the empty stage.

"Yeah." I lean out to the aisle to see if I recognize anyone. When I shift back, he's watching me. How did I miss his eyes before? Hazel is the closest color to what I see. Brown at the center, green around the outside but amber in between. I want to stare into them, but he's waiting on me for who knows what.

"That's all you're gonna give me? Your brother calls you Kenny, and I get 'yeah'?" By the glint in his eye, I think he's teasing me. A blush rises to my cheeks again.

I forget people don't know the story. It's such a part of my identity, I guess I figure there's a 'Meet Kennedy' packet that goes out with all my pertinent information inside. As you come into town, all newcomers are given the brochure.

"When mom and dad got together, he warned her that Cartwrights only have boys. All boys club. He said if she wanted girls, she should date someone else. Mom decided to take her chances. She told him she had a plan." He keeps his eyes on mine, listening as if I'm the most interesting person he's ever met. But, for whatever reason, it doesn't unnerve me like it normally would. "When they had Victoria, he was so sure of his heritage they didn't even find out if she was a boy or a girl. She was born, and bam, certain equipment was not where they expected it would be."

Roman laughs and shifts so he can face me. Butterflies surge in my gut at the thought that I'm entertaining him. I lose my nerve and turn my gaze to the center candle instead.

"They named her after my grandmother and went for a second before too much time had passed. Dad doubled down. He said no way would he be wrong this time. He was all out cocky by the time I was born. When the doctor announced me, mom said he looked white as a sheet."

"Two girls for the first time ever, huh?"

"For generations of time. Dad couldn't explain it. He felt like a failure. Mom patted him on the back and said, 'Your genetics may be strong, but my faith is stronger". She claims she prayed for girls and that's why she got us." I glance up to see his reaction, and there's nothing but delight in his eyes. "Dad refused to let her have the last word, so he gave Vic and me boy's nicknames, so we'd carry on the heritage anyway. Everyone in my family calls me Kenny."

"Your dad sounds like a sore loser."

"You have no idea. He'll rig any game to make sure he's champ." I laugh to myself, so he'll know I'm not that serious. Dad is a teddy bear when it comes down to it. "There's no living with him if he loses."

"And yet you do."

I catch his eye, and there's no pity there, no teasing. If I had to label it, I'd say it's admiration.

"It's the gig," I say, hoping to change the subject.

I'm saved by the stage because Nico stands to introduce the first act. I snatch my notebook from my purse and scribble down the name as Nico says it, "Booker Jennings".

I've worked with Booker before, but I'm curious how he stacks up in Roman's eyes, so I keep it to myself. Booker takes his stool at the front, guitar in hand and sets to work. He's got a rock star unplugged vibe I've always liked. He's not much older than me, handsome in that starving artist sort of way. A gravelly voice paired with soft lyrics make a beautiful juxtaposition between music and poetry.

Normally, my eyes are locked on the singer, watching for annoying habits, listening to every note to scrutinize where they'll fit with our line up and clients, but I'm straying tonight. I find myself watching Roman watch Booker. All his weight rests on his elbows, leaning forward and hanging off the sound. His full lips part as if he's drawing air only through his mouth. He's fully enthralled by Booker and for a second, jealousy sparks in my heart. But it doesn't last because Roman's head turns, and all that captivation belongs to me.

Sound swirls between us, twisting, pulling, and tightening the space even if we aren't really moving. Emotionally, we're moving. Emotionally, I'm pulling closer to him with each strum of the guitar. I catch my lip between my teeth, and along with it, his gaze. He focuses on the way I bite down and twist it back and forth with my nerves. The guitar picks up tempo, and my heart follows suit. Unable to keep my anxiety at bay, I duck my head and strands of hair fall forward to give me shelter, like I knew they would. What I didn't predict, what I never would have predicted, was Roman's index finger pushing those strands back and tucking them away to expose my face once more.

Applause surges in the club and Roman backs away to join in. I scribble down a few notes and manage to catch the tail end of the clapping. It might be just enough alibi to hide that what I was feeling was hardly professional.

❊ ❊ ❊

Roman

That was stupid. High grade, fully leaded, one hundred percent stupid. I know better. I was raised better. But what can I do when she looks at me like that?

I'm supposed to be working, but this whole night is a farce, all an excuse to see her one more time. My only hope to stay in control is to not look at her again, and that's not an option either.

I wipe the sweat from my palms on my slacks again. I'd like to pretend that I was innocent coming into this night, but that's not the case. Earlier, that was all work. This here, this is pleasure. She's the reason I took Dale's car. She's the reason I'm wearing cologne. She's the reason I changed outfits five times before I settled on this one, and I'm still not sure it was my best choice.

If that song had been thirty seconds longer, I might have kissed her. Hands down, no question about it, I doubt I could have stopped myself. But it's not possible.

I sneak a glance at her while she's talking to the waitress. They're old friends. From other nights, or from outside work, I'm not sure, but she's laughing with her about some story involving a drink coaster and an emergency room. I smile so I have an alibi to look at her a little longer. Her green eyes took my breath away when I pulled open the door at Santos Sound. I've walked into a disaster there, but she's the light at the end of the tunnel for sure.

Except that light belongs to a train, and I'm gonna get flattened like a penny on the tracks. Average, that's what my younger brother has always called me, average. Not bad. Not good. Background music in an elevator. And Kennedy is anything but average.

"Do you want anything?" Kennedy asks me, pure innocence clinging to her voice. It jolts me from my thoughts, knocking me off balance. I'm thinking 'you' isn't acceptable as far as answers go.

"I don't know, what's good?"

Kennedy faces the waitress again and lists off more food than I think we can eat, but if it will stretch this night out, I don't mind footing the bill.

We're finally alone again. It shouldn't make me this happy. I lace my fingers together to keep my hands to myself. It's too tempting to want more, but I shouldn't.

"So, where's Dale anyhow?"

Relief floods my veins that she's not going to ask what happened during that song.

I barely stop myself from saying, "Detained by the Feds." But that's privileged information, and I almost blurted it out like the weather. What's wrong with me?

"He's got family stuff going on." I should really work on sounding a bit more convincing. Her eyebrow cocks. I try again. "He might have been cooking the books a little. I've been brought in to turn things around."

Her eyes widen. "Really? Like fraud? Are you supposed to tell me that?"

I drag a bowl of nuts closer because I can't be still at this point. "Probably not, but you don't look like the gossiping type." At least I hope she isn't.

Kennedy looks over her shoulder as if we're being watched. She makes me laugh with all her antics. Trying to drag herself into my jeep, picking on her brother, and singing along with the radio, for as much as she tries to be perfect, it's the imperfect moments I want more of. She pulls closer until the heat from her arm is waking me up.

"What's going on? Is Dale okay?"

My focus needs to drift to something other than this beauty sitting less than two feet away from me. I sift through the bowl of nuts and debate the moral issues with telling her what's really going on at Santos Sound. She might have information for me. It might be worth telling her. My cover will allow me some semblance of truth in the name of her inside story.

"He's been laundering money."

"Are you kidding?"

"For his sake I wish, but no, it's looking that way." I spent the last two days looking over books. The evidence is stacking up against Mr. Dale Santos. "Do you know if he's signed anyone to the label in the last couple years?"

Her face contracts and pulls with her disbelief. "Dale? No. He takes me around to meet these groups that he says he's planning on signing, but I've never heard of anyone actually getting a deal with him."

"It looks like he's been claiming to record albums for groups that don't exist. You'd be surprised how easy it is to clean dirty money."

"What's dirty money?"

"Money gained through illegal means, drugs, illegal weapons, prostitution, or counterfeiting." It's my rehearsed answer, but I sound like an FBI agent. I hold my breath, hoping she buys it.

Her brow folds in. "How do you know all this?"

I pop a peanut in my mouth to buy me some time. It's not like I can tell her I'm an undercover FBI agent.

"Okay," the scrawny kid from before takes the stage, "put your hands together and welcome Grayburn and Mimi."

I'm hoping she'll drop it, but when I glance back, she's still staring at me.

"I watch a lot of crime drama on TV. Can't get enough."

I don't watch much TV at all. The reality is, it's Kennedy I can't get enough of.

※ ※ ※

Kennedy

"Who was your favorite?" I ask Roman as we walk back to his car.

"I don't know. They were all great."

"Better than your choices from this morning, I'd wager." I can't help but tease him. I noticed early on that when he blushes, his ears turn red first.

"No contest." He pulls open my door. "You think you have what you need for a good line up?"

"For the most part. I'll have to organize my notes when I get home, make sure I have a good selection for each genre."

"So, you might need some more help?"

Am I mistaken, or is there a twinkle in his eye?

"I might. Are you willing?"

He's willing. I don't know why he's not admitting it, but he's stepping closer.

"Kennedy," he wets his lips and draws in a quick breath, "there's no way to ask this with any kind of tact, but I have to know something."

"Of course," I tell him, worried about what's got him serious for the first time all night.

He looks off into the darkness and then down at his arms where they rest on the door. "How old are you?"

It's not what I expected.

"Twenty-four."

Roman draws in a breath and reverses two steps.

"Yeah, that's about what I calculated, but I was hoping I might be wrong."

"Why? How old are you?"

He shakes his head and moves to the other side of the car. "It's not important. Let's get you home."

※ ※ ※

Kennedy

I've never appreciated being treated like a child. Ever since mom died, I've been acting like an adult. It frustrates me when people act as if I can't handle life, or I'm too fragile to deal. I'm not as tough as Victoria. She fights and shoots, always the tomboy, while I've been more feminine, but that doesn't mean I can't handle a few setbacks.

The way Roman won't even look at me anymore, it speaks volumes. I knew he was older than me, but I didn't care. I've gravitated outside my age group most of my life. He pulls to a stop outside my house. Just as I'm putting my fingers to the door handle, Roman collapses forward on the steering wheel and sighs.

"Thirty-three. I'm thirty-three."

Older than I thought, but still attractive.

"There's a rule," he says, "a rule that says how old is too old."

I've heard it before. My friends in college called it the *Dirtbag Rule*. "Half your age and add seven."

"That's twenty-three and a half."

"And I'm twenty-four."

"You don't see anything wrong with it?"

"I guess I don't." I should probably push it, complain, or argue, but what's the point? He's obviously made up his mind.

"I didn't mean to lead you on or anything, but you're incredibly beautiful. Can't blame a guy for tripping over himself a bit."

I freeze in my seat, even check the back once to make sure it's empty. Did he call me *incredibly* beautiful?

"We should probably keep this professional anyway."

My brain is still stuck back on beautiful, but I shrug and say, "If that's what you want, Roman."

He's thinking about it, debating it. No, I can't read his mind, but his hand washes over his face again, and he shakes his head as if arguing with a voice in his head.

"I'll let you know if I hear about any good groups. Thanks for a fun night."

Leather groans as he leans to give me a hug. At the last second, his lips brush my cheek and hover. His breath flashes warm over my skin. My fingers capture the edge of his jacket to let him know he doesn't have to pull back if he doesn't want to.

"Goodnight, Kennedy," he whispers.

The jacket slips from my grasp as he pulls away.

CHAPTER 4

Roman

It's been two days since I saw her. It shouldn't bother me. I'm not one to fixate on a woman or brood for any length of time. Normally, my work has a way of taking my full focus, but not this time. Kennedy Cartwright holds me hostage, occupying more of my thoughts than she should.

"You got those reports ready for me?" Rick asks as he comes back into Dale's office where I'm working.

I glower at the wood paneling so that I won't glare at my supervising agent. "Not yet. I'm still working through this mess. Who keeps everything on paper anymore?"

I've spent the two days backtracking expenses against accounts, trying to find the holes, but Dale is slippery and every time I've got a grip on his nefarious underworld dealings, I lose the thread. If I'm being honest, Rick is probably more annoyed I'm sifting through the files doing an analyst's work, instead of on my feet chasing leads, but I find most leads are in the paperwork to begin with.

"You have a report ready for me?"

He's talking about the houses I went to with Kennedy. She thought we were listening to local acts, but in reality, I was trying to find more information on what Dale's been up to. All four names came up in his paperwork, but nothing connected. Thus far, I haven't been able to figure out where the dirty money came from.

"More dead ends. I'll keep looking."

"Don't spend all night on it. Maddox might need a hand tonight."

Rick starts to leave but pauses in the doorway. "Keep your schedule free next Monday night. We're setting up a fundraiser downtown. Inviting all the players."

I spin in my swivel chair to stare at him. "What kind of fundraiser would the bureau possibly be sponsoring?"

Rick frowns before he laughs to himself. "Maddox got out there and found me some leads. Because one of Dark Fox's men has a soft spot for local musicians, we've organized a trap he can't resist. We're hoping to draw him out, curiosity and the cat and all that."

"That sounds like a disaster waiting to happen." I turn back to the computer. "I'm sure you and Maddox have it covered."

Rick lingers, not willing to let go. "You act like you're here to be an accountant, Palermo, but I've seen your aptitude scores, I've seen you in hand to hand. You're a good shot. Don't you think it's time to step up to your full potential?"

I don't see the difference. If I catch them in the paperwork, I still catch them. I put the bad guys away, but I don't have to slap on the cuffs myself.

Rick shoves my chair, but only to tease me. "Besides, you could bring a date. Maybe a little romance could snap you out of this funk you've been in."

"What kind of girl wants to go on a date and get shot?"

He tilts his head as if he has to think about my question. "I wouldn't lead with that. Tell her it's cocktails and good music." He spins his keys on his finger once before he backs out. "Let me know."

What kind of girl? There's only one girl I'm thinking of, but it would be stupid to ask her into a dangerous situation, especially without apprising her of the risks.

From the corner, my phone rattles against the table. I flip it over, hopeful Kennedy found some excuse to call me, but instead it's my mother.

I swipe the call on and brace myself for whatever follows. "Hi, mom."

"Roman, sweetheart, are you coming by tonight?"

"I don't know. It's getting late. Isn't dad in bed by now?"

"He's headed that way. But we haven't seen you in a bit, so I figured you might find some space in your busy schedule for your ailing parents."

She's always loved guilt. They're old friends. They hang out on the weekend and make plans with shame to visit me and stay for the month.

"I was planning on coming by tomorrow for lunch."

"Lunch? No, how about dinner? We have the sweetest nurse coming by to cook for us. She's single, you know."

Ah yes, along with guilt and shame, her other best friend, matchmaking.

"Is she? What a pleasant coincidence."

"I took the liberty to tell her about you. She's extremely interested. And if she's not your type, your father's occupational therapist is also looking for love."

I clench my jaw to try to keep from saying what I shouldn't, but it doesn't work.

"Mom, you don't need to set me up. I can find someone on my own."

"Your track record says otherwise, Roman. Pardon me for wanting a grandchild before I end up in the grave. Between you and your sister, you'd think I'd have someone to bounce on my knee. But she's off living the high life with her new husband, no babies in sight, and you're stuck with your nose in books. It's a good thing Sebastian is around. He restores my hope for some type of future."

My brother, Sebastian, the world class liar. He's been feeding my parents stories about his girlfriend, the supermodel. Last I talked with him he had supplied them some line about planning to marry her next year, "if she'll have me". It's the least of what he's done over the years. Sebastian was blessed with the Italian looks and charm, but none of my parent's integrity. Usually I'm left having to cover his tracks or pull him out of the mess.

"Mom, I've got to go. I'll see you for lunch tomorrow."

I hang up before she can protest, all the while knowing I'll pay for it later. The numbers on the spreadsheet tangle into a ball of confusion. My brain isn't worth much at this point. Better to start again tomorrow. There's a missing piece, I just don't know what it is yet. When I find it, everything will make sense.

I click off the desk light and snatch my cell phone from the desk. For a second, I consider calling Kennedy, but for what purpose? At this point I'll only create trouble in her life.

Still, I need to keep my cover intact. The Cartwright name keeps coming up in Dale's files. If I get close to her, I'll be able to get a better look. At least, that's my justification for dialing her number.

❊ ❊ ❊

Kennedy

I'm debating between "Kiss Me Crimson" and "Tease Him Teal" nail polish when my cell phone buzzes. At ten p.m. I'm not the type of girl to pick up a number I don't know. I click it to silent and go back to my internal polling panel.

A knock on my door brings my attention around. Hudson ducks through, looking every bit as guilty as he does every time he steals cookies from the jar.

"What's going on?" I ask before he skirts the issue.

"Nothing."

"Doesn't look like nothing."

"I did a thing."

"Was it a bad thing?"

His cheeks glow brighter than my nail polish. "I don't think it was *that* bad."

"Hudson," I can't help the mom tone in my voice, "what'd you do?"

"I went out with Jill Larsen."

"*The* Jill Larsen?"

Hudson has had his eyes on one girl, and one girl only, since grade school. We live in a tiny town, I've always told him it was just a matter of time before Jill finally noticed him for more than a school buddy, but by the look of his face, she more than noticed him.

"Yeah." He shakes his head like he can't believe it himself. "I asked her out yesterday. Dad said I could use the 'Vette, and I just got back in."

Hot on the heels of juicy gossip, I ask, "Did you kiss her?"

"I thought you said a gentleman doesn't talk about it."

"There's an unwritten exclusion for older sisters."

I expect him to come inside and spill the details like Vic would, but he hovers in the doorway instead. "Yeah I kissed her, and she kissed me back."

"How many times?" I cock an eyebrow to let him know that my motherly side will only accept one answer in this case.

"Just once, creeper."

"And you're going out again?"

"Tomorrow, after school, and then this weekend to the movies."

"Sounds like you're going to be picking up a shift on Friday to pay for it. The McKlintock wedding needs an extra hand or two."

He rolls his eyes and turns to leave. "Yeah fine. It's not like dad will just give me the cash."

The kid has a point. Dad's never been one to spoil us, even though he could.

"Hey, Hudsie," I call after him as he's leaving. I wait for him to duck his head back in before I ask, "What gave you the guts to finally ask her?"

His grin goes crooked with mischief. "You."

"Me?"

The true intent of that grin becomes clear in an instant. "I figured if Roman could get you to notice him, I probably had a better shot than I thought. I mean, we all know I'm prettier than both of you."

I chuck a pillow from my bed at his head, but he's gone, leaving only laughter where the pillow falls flat. I can't stay mad long. He's too precocious. Always has been.

Bouncing my pencil against my notepad, I consider the long list of chores for the wedding on Friday. Besides being the music scout, I am the event coordinator for the ranch. Every wedding, birthday party, prom, and yes summer concert series, goes through me. The wedding Friday doesn't have me worried. Music is booked, but the barn still needs to be cleared. The bride is bringing in flowers, Victoria is coming home to cater, and I'll put Hudsie in charge of set up. He'll probably grab a few guys from school to help out. Everyone knows dad pays well. I'll get the décor up tomorrow and Friday morning. Everything should go off without a hitch, at least, that's my plan. I live by the standard that if I write it down in my planner, then it's law.

My phone chirps beside me. It's only then that I realize I have a voicemail. Setting my notebook aside, I press play on the message.

"Hi, Kennedy. It's Roman. I know it's late. I'm sure you're asleep. I was curious if you'd found any leads on new talent, or if you'd followed up with anyone from the club. To make this place viable, I need to sign some contracts around here, and I thought…I don't know what I was thinking. Could you call me back? I'll be up for a while or you could call tomo—"

The automated robot lady cuts him off and asks if I'd like to keep the message or delete it. I didn't think I'd hear from Roman, at least not this soon. He could be calling strictly for what he said—business, for our purely professional relationship. Or he could be calling for other reasons, the kind of reasons that made him linger on that goodbye the other night.

I press his number on my phone before I can think about the repercussions or conclusions one might draw from a girl who's willing to call a guy she barely knows late at night.

He picks up on the second ring, because he's been waiting for me.

I manage to keep my squeal inside.

But only just barely.

"Kennedy?" His voice isn't sleepy. It's eager, as if he's been hoping I'd call. My number must be in his phone. I need to slow down, stop jumping to conclusions before I go over the edge, but I fear it's already too late.

"Hi, Roman," I say, pleased with myself that I've hidden every trace of anxiety away so I sound like a demure woman, not the giddy girl I feel like.

"Thanks for calling me back. I know it's late. I hope I didn't wake you."

"No, not at all. I was finalizing details for a wedding this weekend."

"At the ranch? Will you have a live band?"

"Booker Jennings. We saw him at the club. He plays with a couple other guys when they do receptions." Bravery takes the wheel for a second. "You should come. It'll give you a second chance to hear him, and in a different environment."

"I should," Roman says. "Are you sure it's okay? I don't want an angry bride on my hands."

"I'll keep you with me all night," I say, only half teasing. "Vic always makes too much food anyway. It'll be fine."

"Okay. That sounds great."

"I'll see you then?"

"Absolutely."

When I hang up the phone, I can't help but notice my smile in the mirror against the wall. It's rather reminiscent of Hudson's.

I don't think I did a bad thing either. At least not *that* bad.

CHAPTER 5

Kennedy

"That string is blinking, Hudson. You've got to sort that out," I yell up at my younger brother from where he's perched in the rafters. It takes all my self-control to call him by his real name, not his nickname. With half the football team helping out with set up, Hudsie would kill me if I gave them ammunition to tease him.

I glance around the barn. The bride, Trina, wants every surface covered in twinkle lights. I called an audible and added some glowing spheres to the count, knowing there aren't enough lights in all of the North Pole to illuminate the whole barn without some help. Thus far, she hasn't complained, but like most of the brides I work with, that hasn't stopped her from bossing around every person within the sound of her raised voice.

They're an interesting sort, brides, I mean. Enough rage to be a dictator in a small war-torn country. Overabounding in entitlement, at levels rivaling even the most rotten toddlers. Yet, strangely more emotionally fragile than a five- foot house of cards. I once saw one of the brides crumble over the shade of her roses, bubble gum pink instead of blush toned.

Trina is no different. I've watched her scream at Vic for using too much salt in the appetizers, cry when she heard the sound test from Booker and his band, and then nearly pass out from sheer starvation, because, heaven forbid, she might not fit into her size two wedding dress.

After working with brides for years, not much can rattle me anymore. They're a bit like a thunderstorm, brewing in the distance, threatening destruction, but even the most ferocious typically blow out in an hour or two. Bouquets are forgotten. The flavor of the cake is a distant memory, and all that is left is a stack of pictures and a hefty bill.

If I ever get married, it won't be like this, a circus of people and lights and chaos. It'll be about me and him. Maybe our families if they're playing nice. I think our trellis in the south pasture would be a nice backdrop, maybe a few sunflowers in a bouquet, and a white sundress with bare feet. Some quiet to balance out the cacophony of weddings I've endured over the years.

"I didn't even use salt this time!"

Victoria drops the plate on the barn floor, sending her shrimp wonton cups flying in four different directions.

"I can taste it!" Trina yells back at her. "You're covering the shrimp in salt and mark my words, if you kill my dear aunt Trudy, I will sue you for everything you have!"

If I had a nickel for every lawsuit, or dear aunt Trudy for that matter...

I move to intercept Victoria before she unleashes on the bride. My sister is tough, even more so because of her rebellious years, but these days she's typically a kitten. Until it comes to her food. She'll take a head off for insulting her food or cooking ability.

"Hey Vic, what about that crostini you showed me. Has Trina tried it?"

Her rage turns on me, made more severe by her tight bun pulling back her auburn hair that usually softens her face. "You expect me to feed her something else?"

"That is your job," I say, hoping to remind her.

"Fine." She whirls on her boot and stalks away.

"She's a nuisance," Trina mumbles once Vic is gone. "I don't know how you're related."

"Yin and Yang," I tell her, but it's only to appease her. To a point, it's true, but not entirely. While I look like Mom, Vic looks like Dad, but we both have the same auburn hair. We're both focused, determined, driven and single-minded, though centered on different goals. My temper is every bit as strong as Victoria's. The only difference is that I've learned to control it.

I spend the next twenty minutes finalizing the rest of the details and timeline for the following day. I stick around when the appetizer plate, complete with pomegranate and goat cheese crostini, slams down in front of her. Approval is given and with great joy in my heart I escort Trina back to her car.

Watching the car vanish down the driveway, Victoria stops next to me. "She's the worst one yet."

"You can stand a little less salt, Vic." I smirk. "Think of dear Aunt Trudy."

It breaks her resolve for anger, and she melts into a wicked snicker. I follow her back to the kitchen, more than happy to play taste tester for her while she finishes her prep work. She's living in town these days, her own apartment away from the ranch, not that any of us have ever seen it. Vic loves her secrets.

I miss when she was only one door down. Dad even built a cottage out back, hoping one of us would take it. I'm too much of a homebody, and she's too much of a gypsy.

"I heard you've got a guest coming tomorrow night." Victoria acts as though her focus is on the piped frosting for the cake, but I know a fishing expedition when I hear one.

"Who told? Hudsie?"

"Dad."

How'd he know?"

She rolls her eyes. "The man knows everything. It shouldn't surprise you." She pauses to examine her work and pipe a bit of frosting onto her finger. "But Hudsie did tell me he's a bit of a nerd, decent looking, but a nerd."

"Roman doesn't look like a nerd. He's gorge—" I stop myself. "He's fine, I guess."

"Look, it's cool if you're into nerds. They're not my type, but if he makes your heart flutter..." She bats her eyes like a smitten schoolgirl until she can't keep her snarky giggle to herself. "Come on, tell me about him."

"There's nothing to tell. It's all work related."

Her left eyebrow twitches. "Fine. I'll figure it out myself."

Conversation moves on to other topics, but Roman has a way of weaseling beneath my skin. No, there isn't much about a wedding or a bride that can get to me anymore, but Roman, Roman is trouble.

❊ ❊ ❊

Roman

I can wait five minutes for mom to make it to the door, or I can walk right in and she can scold me for giving her a heart attack. It's the same dilemma I face every time I'm at her door. I jiggle the handle. It gives way, and I take my chances.

"Ma? It's me, Roman. Don't shoot me or anything."

It's best to make her laugh. The idea that the five-foot nothing would ever handle a gun is beyond a joke. I still enjoy teasing her about her Italian mobster heritage.

"In the kitchen, sweetheart."

Her cheerful mood sets me on edge. She's up to something.

I take the twelve steps through the small house to the arched entry of the kitchen. But it's not dad at the table with her.

It's her trap.

Blonde hair stretches the length of her back, slinky like spun silk. She shifts and her hair moves with her, swashing like an ocean wave. Crisp blue eyes catch mine from the instant I step into the room. She not only looks at me, but peers into my heart as if looking for flaws.

Mom knows how to pick them. Too bad it never ends well for me. Last week, it was the swim instructor. A few days before that, Dad's nutritionist. Both were attractive women. Both appeared interested at first, but I find I lack the wow factor to keep their attention. Both interactions ended after no more than four minutes. I'd like to say it's the first time it's happened, but I can't. I count three sandwiches on the counter, properly plated, each with their own bag of chips and a drink to match. Mom has been busy getting ready for this little setup.

"Roman," the triumph in my mom's voice is like a gladiator standing over his victim, "so glad you could make it for lunch. This is Charlotte, your father's occupational therapist. I've been telling her all about you."

My nerves pull tight. Number one issue, my mom doesn't know me, not really. She thinks I work as an accountant at a tech firm. She doesn't know I went to Quantico, the training center for FBI agents, six years ago. She doesn't know I dread either of my parents finding out who I really am. Number two, what she does know about me is mostly embarrassing.

It takes all of ten seconds to see the photo album open on the window ledge behind her. It's open to the picture of me playing in the mud, naked.

I was three.

Perfect.

I cross the room and plant a kiss on my mother's forehead. With smooth hands, I slide the album shut and set it on the counter out of sight. Reminding myself that I've faced worse than this, I steel my nerves and face Charlotte.

"Don't believe everything she tells you. I've grown up a bit since those pictures were taken."

Charlotte glances my way. She gives a quick smile and gathers her keys from the table. "Well, you *are* taller," she says, leaving me wondering if that's the only redeeming quality she's found in me.

Once again, mom oversold me. If my younger brother were here, the whole situation would be reversed. She'd be steaming to get her claws in him, not rising to her feet to leave.

"You're my dad's therapist?" Small talk feels meaningless,

Like the others, I assume she's made her decision, but I also see no point in being rude and calling it for what it was—a thirteen second blind date that failed. At least, that's my impression. If she were interested, she'd stay and have the lunch mom obviously made for the three of us, but she's moving like she means to get on with her life.

"Occupational," she says. "Your father is a real teddy bear. I love working with him." It's all business now. She's perfectly polite, but not interested.

"Roman is just like his father," mom says, oblivious to the way Charlotte is edging her way out of the room. "He's always been my snuggle bunny, but then he's also as smart as they come. He's a bookkeeper."

"What a combination." Charlotte humors Mom, but I feel as though I'm back in high school trying to talk with one of the popular girls. Or maybe a bit like a zoo animal. I should do some tricks to keep her interested, but I'm not one to jump through hoops.

"I made you a sandwich, Roman. Grab a chair and eat with us."

"Actually, Sylvia, I have to go. I have another appointment." Charlotte shifts toward the doorway, twirling her keys in her hand. I know that trick well, a sign that she can't wait to leave. Most of my blind dates end this way. "Tell Gio to keep up on his exercises. I'll check in on Monday."

"Nice to meet you, Roman. I'll see you next week, Sylvia."

I close my eyes once she's around the corner, but don't exhale until the door shuts and she's gone.

"Isn't she great?"

Mom's voice brings me back to life. I rub my palm over my face to hide my embarrassment over mom's latest matchmaking failure. One deep breath in, and I compartmentalize the whole ordeal.

"She's something." I snag the plate with my Rueben from the counter and pull out the seat across from her. "I'm not sure she's my type."

"Maybe you shouldn't be so picky."

"Maybe you shouldn't be so nosey."

"The Lord gave us all talents, dear. I'm just perfecting mine."

I roll my eyes before I take a bite of my sandwich. "I don't think she was interested, mom."

"She's thirty-one, and looking for a successful, independent man. That sounds like my Roman to me." She's always seen more in me than anyone else. I guess that's what unconditional love will do for a person.

"Ma, you're meddling."

"I'm being your mother. Come over tomorrow. You can meet Kelley, she's the aerobics instructor at the senior center. Very fit, very slender."

"I told you. I can do this on my own."

Her mouth puckers into a frown. "Really? Then where are those grandchildren of mine? You don't even date, Roman. All you do is work, work, work."

"I have a date this weekend." The words fall out before I can stop them. The wedding with Kennedy isn't a date, it's part of my cover. It's work. It's trying to figure out who Dale was working with to launder the money. With most of his dealings coming from the Cartwright family, I'd be stupid not to check it out, talk with her father, and if I happen to catch a slow dance with Kennedy...

I stop myself. It's not a date. Maybe if I keep repeating it, I'll believe the lie.

"Who is she?" Mom drops her sandwich and leans forward. "How long has this been going on?"

"It's new," I tell her. "We just met. She's invited me to an event, and I'm meeting her there."

"You really like her, don't you?"

"I told you, we just met. Why would you think—"

"Because your cheeks glow red when you talk about her, just like they used to when you talked about Mallory Monroe."

"That was fifth grade, Ma."

"Still, I haven't seen you this excited about someone in a long time."

"So, you'll lay off the matchmaking for a bit?"

"I don't think I'd ever agree to that," she says with an infuriating twinkle in her eye.

I wish I could confide in her about Kennedy's age, about how uncomfortable it makes me to know she's still a child compared to me. But then I'd have to tell her about my brother, Sebastian, and the mess he made, and we don't have that kind of relationship. Secrets never stay secrets with her. By noon tomorrow, half the senior citizens would be gossiping about Roman Palermo, Sylvia's son, with the predilection for younger women.

"Do you have your grocery list ready for me?"

"Pinned to the fridge, just like every week." She pats my arm, love warming my heart at the simple gesture.

"Where's dad? Is he coming for lunch?"

"He's tired. I told him to rest. Maybe you can sit with him for a bit after lunch?"

"Yeah," I say, "I'd like that."

❈ ❈ ❈

Kennedy

"Grab the castor sugar too." Victoria gives me a gentle shove into the baking aisle. "The bride wants macaroons. You're charging her extra, right? Those aren't cupcakes, ya know? They take time."

I shake myself free of my daydream, the one where Roman happens to stop by the ranch, and I'm dressed to the nines and don't look so young anymore. In all truth, I'd rather go back to my imagination than help Vic with her supply list.

"Anything else?" I start down the aisle, walking backwards because if I know my sister, she has at least six other items on her mind.

"Look for some kind of coarse sugar too, and I think I'm low on baking powder. Thanks, you're a peach." She tosses the last bit at me as she moves for the meat aisle. The bride wants a mini-pizza bar. Of course, Vic can't go simple and has to take it to the next level.

Sometimes I wonder if it's all worth it. Sometimes I think about cutting her loose, letting her go her way and chase her dreams without the rest of us bogging her down. Sometimes I wonder if that's a little bit of transference on my part. What would I do if my family did the same for me, took away the responsibilities that have been mine since my teenage years and turn me out to find my own path? Where would I go? Would I stay? Would I finally make a few of my own plans happen?

I stuff two boxes of castor sugar in my arms and scour the shelves for baking powder. I spot it, but a sweet old woman is taking her time considering her options between brands. I smother my impatience the best I can, but my schedule is tight. Hudson is getting all the paper products we need, Victoria is getting the cheeses and meats, and I'm in charge of baking supplies. We still need to go by the banner shop, the butcher, and Hudson's dance class in less than an hour. I don't have time to wait for Granny to pick the best brand.

I'm not alone in my frustrations either. Apparently, baking powder is in high demand in our area because I feel other people backing up behind me. When the oblivious white-haired woman finally moves, I push forward, reaching for the baking powder, knowing Vic will be back any second. My hand bumps someone else's going for the same package. I retract, apologizing and scolding myself internally for my impatience.

"Kennedy?" Roman's voice catches me off guard.

I stare up at him, my eyes wide with surprise. "Roman? What are you doing here?"

He glances around, more confused than ever. "I'm not allowed to shop?"

"Of course, you are," I clear my throat, "I didn't expect you to be here, that's all. I didn't know you lived nearby."

"I don't." He moves out of the way to let someone else grab

their supplies. "My parents needed a few things. Their community isn't far from here."

"That's sweet of you to help out." I can't stop looking at him. Try as I may, I can't think of anything smart to say.

"That's a lot of sugar." He motions for the boxes in my arms. "And I believe you need one of these." Roman snags a canister of baking powder from the shelf for me but doesn't hand it over.

"Brides," I say. It sounded smarter before I said it. Wasn't I just obsessing about my schedule? Don't I have a million more things to do today? Why do I want to cancel all of it and hang out with Roman in the baking goods section for the rest of the day?

"Okay, Kenny. I think I've got everything." Victoria comes up behind me, nearly ramming me with her grocery cart. "Are you ready to go?"

I dump my boxes of castor sugar into the cart and turn back to introduce Roman, but Victoria has already started to leave.

"Vic." My sharp tone catches her attention and she whirls back, annoyed. Hoping to avoid a scene, I smile and say, "I wanted to introduce you to Roman Palermo. He's the new producer over at Santos Sound."

She glances at Roman as though she's seeing him for the first time. "Oh! You mean…" She smiles at me like she knows a secret. "Hi, Roman. I've heard so much about you."

Before I have a chance to smooth things over, Hudson bursts through us to drop a pile of napkins and energy drinks in the cart. "I'm ready. Let's get going. I don't want to be late."

While it's likely a ploy to keep me from throwing half his energy drinks out of the cart, I still feel the burn from my obnoxious siblings.

"Roman, do you remember Hudson?" I glare at my brother, so he'll mind his manners.

Hudson glances at Roman for the first time. "The music guy, right? Cool to see you again."

Roman extends the baking powder to me, looking like he's planning his escape. "You look like you're in a hurry. I'll let you go. Great to meet you all." To me he adds, "I'll see you around, Kennedy."

I want to stop him from leaving, but with him going one direction and my family leaving in the other, I feel torn.

"Rome, you forgot this." The nickname feels too familiar for our relationship, but when he turns back, he's smiling. I snag another canister of baking powder from the shelf and extend it toward him. "You're still coming Friday night, right?" I struggle for the right words. "Or have you changed your mind? Or made other plans?"

"No," he shakes his head like I'd have to be crazy to believe it, "I haven't changed my mind, not about anything."

"Kenny!" Hudson calls from the end of the aisle. Dance class might as well be a life and death situation. "Come on, we're gonna be late."

Roman takes the baking powder, familiar sparks igniting between us just from proximity. "I'll see you Friday?"

"Count on it."

I turn on my heel, only glancing back once before chasing after my siblings. I catch them at the checkout line, both whispering like the gossipy old ladies they are.

"Okay, let me have it." I brace myself for whatever faults they've found in him, not to mention the teasing I know I'll endure for at least the next hour.

Vic never misses her chance to come after me. "I've heard of cradle robbing, Kenny, but are you a grave robber?" She winks before she starts laughing at her own joke.

I shoot her my best death glare, but I have to admit it was clever. Hudson picks up her thread before I have a chance to come back at her.

"Maybe it was the lighting, but I swore I saw some gray at his temples."

"Oh, whatever." I cross my arms over my chest, trying to look tough, but my laughter gives me away. "He's handsome, and mature."

"Seriously, he's what? Forty?" Victoria shakes her head,

laughing.

"He's thirty-three," I fire back, but immediately regret it when it gets Hudson going again.

"Thirty-three, Kenny? He's thirty-three? That's older than Vic, and she's *old*."

"Hey!" Victoria shoves him, but not hard enough to do anything. She wraps an arm around his neck yanking him back down to her height to mess up his hair. "You're just a baby, that's the problem. Poor baby, Hudsie."

Hudson pouts, but it's the fake one he's always used to get his way. As his sisters, I think we're both immune to it after all these years. Victoria pays the cashier and starts for the car.

"Anything else?" I raise my eyebrows, daring Hudson's worst. It's like taking awful medicine. Better to get it over with. "Get it out of your system."

His fake pout fades as quickly as it came, replaced by a devilish glint. "When you were in the fourth grade," he has a hard time speaking around his laughter, "Roman was graduating high school." He runs ahead of the cart, so he can see my expression. "When you got your braces off, Roman was graduating college."

"Hey," Victoria sets a hand to his arm, "cool it, kid. That's enough. No one bought tickets to your standup show."

"One more." He pretends to beg us both. "It's a good one."

It's a laugh or cry kinda moment. I might as well laugh. Mom taught me that. "Let me have it."

His grin spreads wide as the sunrise and twice as bright. "When you entered preschool, Roman's voice started changing."

Victoria starts laughing so hard she snorts. I wish I could stay mad at him, but I have to admit he hit it out of the ballpark on that one. Home run.

"Are you good now?" I poke at his stomach like I used to when he was little. The same string of infectious giggles burst out, until he's begging me to stop. "All out of your system, both of you?"

"I promise, I'm done. Do whatever you want." Hudson scurries away for the backseat to escape my tickle torture, leaving me alone with my older sister. I raise my eyebrows to ask the question again without words.

Victoria puts her hands up like she was never involved. "Who am I to tell you what to do?"

Still I can't help asking her opinion.

"What do you think of him?" I scrunch my nose, bracing for the worst. "He's cute, right?"

Victoria shrugs. "He seems nice. He looks reliable. Like a number two pencil or something."

I pull a face at her analogy. "Seriously? A pencil?"

My sister shrugs. "He's kinda nerdy, but I can see how you'd like it. He's just not my type."

It's my turn to tease for once. "Yeah, not a single tattoo in sight."

"Oh, come on, I've grown up." She makes her way for the driver's side. "All I'm saying is be careful. We love you and don't want you to get hurt."

I'm not that young. They act like I am. Laughable because I've been the grown up one since mom died. I've held the family together since I was fifteen. At some point, shouldn't I be able to make my own decisions? Haven't I proved over and over that I know what I'm doing? It might be time to start putting myself first at least a little bit.

CHAPTER 6

Kennedy

Weddings should always be romantic, a thoroughly heart stopping, love drenched affair. I swear there's not a dry eye left on this hillside. Even stone-cold Victoria is teary, and she hates the bride. The setting is perfect. Timed with absolute mastery, if I do say so myself. The sun is melting into the horizon, pinks, oranges and purples paint the sky behind the bride and groom, standing under an arch of white lilies and gerbera daisies that match the watercolor sunset to perfection.

"I now pronounce you husband and wife. You may kiss the bride."

Cheers erupt as Trevor takes his bride by the waist and kisses his wife for the first time. The sun vanishes completely. And I'm staring at my watch, starting the countdown for the next half of the event. I nudge Victoria with my elbow, hoping to pull her out of her lovesick trance. She glares at me like I've interrupted a great movie.

"Can't you enjoy this for one second?"

"Not when the appetizers are going to be late if you don't get a move on."

She rolls her eyes and sticks out her tongue before she leaves for her kitchen. With her back on track, I start in with the help, aka, Hudson and his team of friends all clad in their Sunday best to act as wait staff. I have every second planned. Every minute is accounted for.

From the barn, the early strains of Booker's band call to the guests. Without a word, they move across the grass, following the well-lit path I've marked for them. Can't leave anything to chance. My only wild card is the bride and groom. They haven't moved, still surrounded by stragglers and well-wishers. Does no one have respect for a tight schedule?

I used to carry a clipboard with a list of the night's events attached and any notes I might need throughout the evening. But dad said it made me look like a wedding tyrant. Now, I memorize it. I glance at my watch again. The bride needs to get moving if she's going to make her entry by seven-thirty.

Instead of berating the bride, something I've been scolded for in the past, I quick step my way to the barn to check on the progress there. Every light is gleaming and thank goodness I added the extras. Happy chatter fills the space, along with Booker's band.

Ten minutes until the bride and groom make their entry.

Fifteen until appetizers are delivered.

Dinner served in twenty-five minutes.

First dance in fifty minutes.

Nothing can derail me now. I've made weddings a perfectly scheduled train on the tracks with no room for error or distraction.

I glance toward the entrance and my heart drops to my stomach.

An old warning from my mother pops into my head, *"Never underestimate the power of a man in a well-tailored suit."*

She wasn't wrong. If I'm a train, then Roman Palermo just sent me screeching from the tracks, barreling through the woods, until I landed in the neighbor's pond. He waves and I smile, but I fear only half my mouth tipped up. He's going to think I had a stroke again.

❋ ❋ ❋

Roman

I should have asked her what I should wear to this. A quick glance around the barn tells me I'm overdressed. The only other suits I can see are in the wedding party. Last thing I need is someone asking me how I know the bride or groom. The best answer I've got is that I'm scouting local musical talent, and even that's a lie. I certainly can't tell them I'm an undercover FBI agent.

But lying is what I'll have to do tonight if I plan to reach my objective. I need to get in the main house and sneak a peek at Ace Cartwright's financial records, if possible. Kennedy spots me and every thought in my head evaporates. Like a bunny staring down a semi-truck, I'm transfixed by my own doom. Her dainty hands slip over the length of her black lace dress, as if to smooth the fabric, but how can it wrinkle when it's molded to her like a second skin? Where the body of the dress is lined with black fabric, the arms are sheer. A delicate weave of roses and vines twist and curl where the lace covers her arms. The neckline cuts wide on her shoulders, displaying two perfectly formed collarbones that are begging me to grace them with affection. How can one woman be this perfect? Charlotte was beautiful, age-appropriate, and obviously accomplished. But Kennedy, Kennedy is a different level of distraction. I can't take my eyes off her. I haven't thought of Charlotte for hours, but I doubt I'll ever forget staring at Kennedy across this crowded barn.

I manage a wave, kick myself for being informal, but revel in the smirk she shoots me. Every covert thought blows away in the breeze as it dances from one side of the barn to the other. Night is coming on, the chill is sneaking in, but she's got me all kinds of warm.

"I'm happy to announce, for the first time ever, Mr. and Mrs. Trevor Ramsey!"

The young man's voice tears me away from Kennedy. Applause rises up around me as the bride and groom make their entrance. I join in before someone sees that I don't belong here.

The bride takes her spot at the front table, and I swear within seconds teenage boys appear in suits carrying trays of food. The timing is such that I wouldn't be surprised to see them all break out in song and dance like my mother's musicals she likes to watch. The entire event is choreographed to perfection.

"What do you think?"

Her voice catches me off guard, but her presence nearly knocks me to my knees. Kennedy impressed me on our business outing, and then again at the club, but this, tonight, she's under my skin. Her eyes are dark, not the shade, but the makeup she wears. Her pouty lips, pale and pink the last time I saw her, pucker a deep crimson. The sultry appearance makes her seem older than I know she is, and it weakens my resolve by the second. I'm not my brother. We're nothing alike. Maybe I'm making something out of nothing.

Not that it matters. I'm here to investigate Ace Cartwright, not date his youngest daughter.

"It's a beautiful wedding. I'm impressed by the organization."

Pride rises up in her expression. She must be the one calling the shots. If so, she's talented beyond her years.

"Are you hungry?" she asks.

Every seat is accounted for. If she's inviting me to sit, I have to admit I'm at a loss. Kennedy takes my silence for an answer and tilts her head to the open barn doors. I follow on her heel, like a puppy seeking an owner.

She follows an unmarked path, unlike the others streaming with white ribbon and colorful flowers, until she stops at a cottage and pushes the door open. I trail after her, surprised by the bustle and noise emanating from within.

"Hey! Make sure that plate is sparkling!" A woman yells from behind the kitchen island. "Jeremy, if you wipe your nose one more time and then touch one of these plates, I might cut off your hand, understand me?"

I catch Kennedy's eye to see if she's alarmed, but her bemused expression doesn't betray any fear. Apparently, threats are commonplace.

"How's it going, Vic?" she asks the violent chef behind the counter.

"One day, can we hire competent workers instead of Hudson's sports buddies? Someone with a resume? Someone who can *spell* resume?"

Leaning close to me, Kennedy says, "Vic gets tense when she's cooking. You get used to it."

"Last plate!" Victoria yells at a cowering teenager. "Drop it and die, you got it?"

Kennedy may know she's kidding, but by the look on the kid's face I'd wager he's not so sure. I hold the door open for him and pull it closed when he's gone.

"Okay, ten minutes before we start serving dinner, are you ready?"

"I have the soccer team plating in the dining room. I'll go check their progress. I'm sure it's a disaster."

I hold my breath in anticipation for her reaction once she's left the room, but either they've managed to hold it together, or she's too far away for her yelling to carry. I doubt the second option is possible.

"She's intense." Kennedy moves into the kitchen, but I don't dare follow her. Sure, I'm tough, a decent shot, and I've been in my fair share of fights, but something about that five-ten ball of fury has me nervous. Kennedy is unphased, cool and collected as she picks through the food, loading a plate. She extends it to me over the island. I take it, but I'm nervous to eat any of it.

"Go ahead. Once a course is over, she's forgotten it. Everything is fair game in here." Kennedy checks her watch for the fifth time and calm and collected fades away.

"Vic, get a move on. Three minutes until service."

I set my plate on the counter, admiring the power packed into her petite body. The back door opens, and a flood of teenage boys crowd the space. I back up until I'm against the wall. Undaunted, Kennedy begins shouting orders at the staff she's assembled. She's young, in age at least, but she's got maturity beyond her years. I doubt half the older women I've dated in the last year could pull off an event like this. Within five minutes, she and her sister have sent out every entrée. When I glance back at the counter, my plate of food is empty.

An infectious giggle sneaks from behind Kennedy's lips. "You have to eat fast around here, or you'll end up hungry." She pinches a spear of antipasto, salami, cheese, olive, basil and a cherry tomato and extends it to me. "I've seen Hudson snag food right off another person's plate. No remorse."

Despite my best efforts, I'm lost in her. Every time she speaks, every move her graceful arms make, every quirk of her mouth when she smiles. I have a mountain of responsibilities on my shoulders, and yet she has me transfixed to the point that I can't look away, let alone speak in coherent sentences.

I'm still searching for something witty when my phone buzzes from my pocket. Setting the spear on the counter, I apologize, but check my cell, worried it might be mom. Rick's name lights up the screen. I look up to Kennedy, but she's already motioning for the door.

"Go, it's fine. I really don't mind."

"It's my boss," I start to try to explain why I'm ducking out, but she smiles again, no animosity in sight.

"Then you better answer it," she says. "Tell him I distracted you before you could listen to Booker's band. I promise it won't happen again."

With every fiber of my being, I hope that's not true. I click the call through and say, "Hello?" just as I'm stepping out the doors.

"Can you talk?"

"Go ahead." I move away from the party to the far side of the cottage, away from prying ears. My rational mind takes over, reminding me I have a job to do and staring at an attractive woman ten years my junior is not that job.

"A couple analysts were going through the rest of your paperwork. Looks like Dark Fox's lead guy, Dante Alvero, has done some work with Ace Cartwright in the past. These are old connections, at least a decade ago. Have you seen anything more recent?"

"No, can't say I have, but I can tell by the way the money moves that Dale works with a bigger fish. Could be Dale was keeping Ace Cartwright off the books. Could be your guy." I glance over my shoulder. Kennedy is headed back for the barn; the party is well underway. She stops by the barn doors and plants a kiss on the cheek of the older gentleman leaning against the frame. I recognize Ace Cartwright from my files. An idea tilts my heart into full tailspin.

"Where are you?" Rick asks. "I hear music. Don't tell me you have a social life. I didn't think it was possible."

"No, never." I shake the nerves from my free hand. "I'm checking something out, a hunch I have about Ace Cartwright."

"You think he's in on this?"

"Unclear. Dale has been friends with the Cartwright family for years. I feel like Ace had to know something, but there could be deeper connections."

"Good work. I'll expect a report in the morning."

I don't need to answer. I end the call and draw in a breath, hoping my plan will work.

Pacing in front of the cottage, I groan as loud as I can without sounding forced. Out of the corner of my eye, I spot Victoria through the window. I hold my phone above my head, spinning in a slow circle as if searching for a signal. As I hoped, Victoria pops open the door.

"Drop the call?"

"Yeah, and it was my boss. He's gonna be ticked."

"Coverage is spotty out here."

"Do you happen to have a landline in your place?" I ask, confident that she doesn't.

"Not out here," Victoria says, "but you're welcome to use the phone in the main house. The back door is open. Take the first right and you'll be in the living room. Phone is by the lamp."

"Thank you," I breathe the word out with my relieved sigh as if she's saved my life. She nods and pulls the door shut.

Kennedy is still at her father's side. I don't know how long the patriarch sticks it out at his events, but I wager from his shifting stance that I've got ten minutes at best. I quicken my pace and stay in the blind spot for most of the guests at the barn. No one follows me or seems to have noticed my absence by the time I have my hand on the back door. I slip inside and click it shut behind me.

Instead of turning right like Victoria told me, I turn left and follow the hallway, barely managing my distraction when I pass childhood pictures of Kennedy on the wall. A picture from her teenage years, complete with a thick set of braces, catches my attention, but I have to keep moving.

The office, two doors down, is a shrine to his family. A massive portrait of Ace and his three children adorns the right wall, directly in his eye line from the mahogany desk. I slide around the corner and shake the mouse, hopeful it's not hibernating. The screen flickers on, no password needed. Ace must have left not long ago. I set my hand to his chair, still warm. My keys jangle as I fish them from my pocket. I carry a mobile flash drive between my car and house keys for such an occasion. Moving to his financial records, I copy the entirety of his files. A board creaks in the hall. I hold my breath, waiting, but it's nothing. Old houses creak.

While the blue bar shows the progress, I click in and out of other folders, searching for any indication that he might be involved in illegal activities. For the first time in my career, I'm hopeful that he's not. I don't want to be the guy that busts Kennedy's dad.

There's a second spreadsheet under the files for the ranch detailing the musical talent they keep on retainer. I add that to my flash drive, and glance at my watch. My time is up, I know it is, but the missing piece might be in this computer. I need more time.

"Roman?"

Her sweet voice stops my heart.

❋ ❋ ❋

Kennedy

"Roman? What are you doing in here?"

He's bent over dad's computer, staring at the screen. Vic said he went to use the house phone, but he's nowhere near the living room. I'm sure there's an explanation, a rational reason, but for the life of me I can't think of one.

"I, uh, I got lost. I think I turned left when I should have turned right, but I saw the phone in here and figured I might as well use the one I found. I hope that's okay."

"But why are you on the computer?" I sound like I'm accusing him of something. I don't mean to be. If he'd explain what he's doing, I'd be glad to give him the benefit of the doubt.

"Oh, that?" His sheepish smile melts my heart to goo. "He has a screensaver with family pictures. I guess I got distracted."

Dad and his dumb screen saver.

"Please tell me you didn't see the one of me and Hudson in the mud."

His eyebrows arch with mischief. "And here I thought your teenage braces were the best shot."

I groan and motion him toward me. "That's enough of embarrassing dirt on me."

As I turn to leave, his keys grate against the desk. I frown and turn back. "Are you leaving?"

Roman stops mid-step as if I've caught him off guard. "I thought I had to, work stuff, but it looks like I can stay."

Like a kid, a goofy grin creeps over my cheeks.

"Good."

I'd feel embarrassed, but I notice he's got a matching grin.

CHAPTER 7

Kennedy

"Have I told you how beautiful you look tonight?"

His question catches me off guard. We're standing at the door of the barn, counting down the seconds until dinner ends and the first dance begins. I glance at him, but he's staring out over the gathering, pretending that statement was innocent.

"I thought we were keeping it professional, Roman." I'm not upset about his compliment. On the contrary, I hope he hears my teasing tone.

"Consider it a professional courtesy then."

I want to press him more, ask him why he cares so much about my age, but my schedule won't relent. "I'll be right back," I tell him. On impulse, I squeeze his hand. Butterflies erupt in my chest because he squeezes it back.

I'm still running my teeth over my bottom lip when I reach the stage where Booker is waiting for me. Hudson catches my eye and takes his spot behind the microphone. It's his first wedding getting to take on a few emcee duties. After begging me for a year, I gave in. He has four lines total, and I made him practice until he had them memorized.

"Ladies and Gentlemen, would you please join me in welcoming Trina and Trevor to the dance floor for their first dance as a married couple."

Per Trina's request, I help her to her feet and check her dress before she travels to the floor. In our initial meeting, Trina told me she had a friend from college do half her first dance before someone told her she'd gotten barbeque sauce on the skirt. I told her I'd never let one of my brides suffer that kind of embarrassment.

As the bride and groom move to the center of the dance floor, Hudson fills the groom's only request, and says line two of four.

"After the first verse, the bride and groom ask that you join them in their dance."

Poor Trevor is petrified of being the center of attention. It took every bit of problem solving on my part to make his bride's dream of a first dance happen.

"You're busy," Roman says as I stop at his side once more. "I think I clocked you circling this whole place in less than ninety seconds."

"Life of an event planner. I'm the grease that keeps it going."

Music builds and Booker's voice croons the notes to their song with perfect cadence. He was a good choice for them. Trina's normally unhappy face beams with her delight.

"She looks happy," Roman says.

"Then I've done my job."

"And you've done it well."

I like this side of him, relaxed, open, not worrying about what people will think of us standing close enough that our arms are brushing.

"We all do our parts. Victoria handles the food. Hudson does a lot of set up and works with the sound guy for concerts. I manage our little circus, working with the brides and musicians, and running the events."

"And what about your dad? What's he in charge of?"

"The money." The man keeps a tight grip on the cash flow, despite the fact that we've been in the black for years now. "He prefers it behind the scenes."

"How'd this start anyway? How does one break into the wedding and event business?" It's like he's looking around for the first time, appreciating the work that goes into one of my events.

"My mom always wanted a farm, a ton of animals, a huge garden, you know, the whole nine yards. Dad set his sights on this place and didn't stop until he had it. They were poor back then, nothing to their names, and she recognized the beauty of it, started letting folks rent out the back for events. It grew from there. Dad's only regret is that she didn't get to enjoy it longer, never saw what she started fully blossom."

Something I've said has caught his attention. He hesitates a second before he asks, "If they were poor, how did they afford a place like this?"

"Well, that's the funny part of it all, I guess. He won it in a poker game."

"A poker game?"

"Yeah," I search for dad, but he's likely gone back to the house with a plate of Victoria's leftover food. "He used to be a real card shark, hung out with some seedy folks. Even now he's got connections to everyone in the area, I swear. He needs something done; it gets done."

Roman has more questions for me, but Trevor is starting to look pale from all the eyes watching him. No one is standing up. No one is listening to the instructions Hudson gave.

Eager to make good on my promise to the nervous groom, I look up at Roman. "Dance with me?"

❉ ❉ ❉

Roman

If she'd punched me in the stomach, I don't think I'd be more surprised than this. One second, I'm listening to her spill all the details about her father's possibly underhanded dealings, and the next she's expecting me to hold her close on the dance floor. But when her slender fingers catch mine, I can't help but follow.

For a second, we're the only couple on the floor with the bride and groom. If I hadn't heard the announcement, I'd be dying of shame, but as if they only needed permission, other couples follow suit.

She pulls my arm around her waist, forward to say the least, but since it's where I've been dying to be all night, I'll allow it. My palm rests on her lower back. She catches my opposite hand in hers and the arc beneath my grip begins to sway with the music. She's grace and elegance. Once more I'm lost to her spell, ignorant of the rest of the party watching us, oblivious to my responsibilities beyond this moment.

I need to memorize her face. Every dip, every curve, the way her lips twist and pull at her cheeks, carving deep lines in her perfect skin. I'm urging her closer with every second, but she's not resisting. She's giving in as if it's part of the dance. In my heart, I worry where my steps might lead but can't deny the feeling growing between us.

"What did your boss need?" Kennedy tilts her face up to mine. Green eyes captivate me. It's always been my favorite color, but her shade of deep jade is reaching the top of the list.

"Work stuff," I tell her. "It's pretty boring."

"Not really. Not if it's about the music."

But it's not, and I've got a flash drive with files I've stolen from her father's computer in my pocket.

"It's more about the books and business aspects." Needing to see her smile again, I add, "Trust me, I prefer the music."

"Of course, because with music comes dancing."

I'm not sure you can call what we're doing dancing. More like cuddling to the beat of a song, but if it gives me an excuse to hold her close a little while longer, I'll take it. For at least the length of the song, I plan to ignore every negative voice in my head that says it won't work.

"Where do you put the animals when you have these events?" I ask, hoping she'll keep looking up at me to answer. When she looks at me, it feels like I'm the center of her universe, like I can do no wrong. She doesn't stare through me like other people.

I'm not another face in the crowd. Kennedy sees me.

"The animals?"

"You said your mom wanted a farm, are they gone now or..." I let it trail off because I don't want to upset her with memories of her mother's death.

"Oh, no this is the event barn. There's another side of our property with the animals, far away from all this. It's older, and smelly. You can't clean up animals this fast. Though in truth, only a few chickens are left, and Victoria's horse. We don't have mom's passion for a menagerie. Plus, the storage for all this equipment is over there, a whole warehouse full of decorations and farm equipment. We built this event barn and the new auditorium to replace the older models."

It pricks my ears. There are a number of ways to launder money but purchasing large machinery would do the trick. If Ace needs to funnel large amounts of cash for Dale, a tractor purchase wouldn't raise any red flags. I need to see that warehouse.

Those two perfect lips curve into a gentle smile and blood rushes to my cheeks. "Every now and then," Kennedy says, "you disappear, as if you've gone to a whole different dimension. And then poof! You're back. I keep wondering where you go."

Guilt grates on my heart. Telling her I'm equally attracted to her as well as suspicious of her family won't gain me any rewards.

"My mind wanders," where our hands are linked, I rub my thumb over hers, "but you always seem to bring me back."

"And what do you think of Booker and his band?"

She's changing the subject. She does it every time I compliment her. Hard to believe a girl like her isn't drowning in adoration from every man she meets.

"I think, I need to stick around and keep listening," I say, but it's far too close to a whisper because she's stealing my breath away again.

She's about to speak when the music drops out. Instead of more words, she squeezes my hand and pulls away. "Thanks for the dance."

With a quick slip of her hands down her skirt to straighten the wrinkles, she's gone again, back in charge, back to the world she knows. She can turn it off, the attraction we're feeling, but me, there's no hope for me.

* * *

Kennedy

I suppose it would be unprofessional to demand he get it over with and kiss me already. All this romantic tension and heavy chemistry is distracting. I nearly missed starting the Best Man's toast on time.

The night is smooth, but everywhere I go Roman watches me. Not a creeper, mind you, but interested as if I'm a good book, and he can't put me down. The floor opens to dancing, and, of course, Hudson is the first one out there, running any girl through whatever steps he can. He's a slave to the music in a way I'll never be. My place is behind the mic, not counting the beats.

Near the end of the night, after the bride and groom have gone and the guests are filtering out, my baby brother grabs my hand and drags me to the floor. "Come on, Kenny. One dance," he says even though I'm shaking my head no. But the kid is smart and makes a point I can't ignore. "You know you look good when you dance. There's no way Roman will ignore you."

Like a teenager, I roll my eyes but give in and let him lead me through a lindy hop piece. I remember his first classes, the way dance lit him up and chased away the grief of growing up motherless. His true joy is dancing, and it gratifies my heart to help him live his dreams. I only wish I had the power to do the same with my own life.

Even if I could shake the stage fright, find some bravery, what would they do without me? Like I told Roman, I'm part of a team, my family needs me. We're already down Mom, we can't afford to lose me too.

* * *

Kennedy

"Did you starve him?" Victoria whispers to me as we're washing dishes. "He's on his third plate of food."

"Maybe your food is just that good," I say. But behind us, at the counter, Roman chuckles, and I know we haven't been stealthy enough.

"More like I couldn't keep food on a plate long enough. Every time I turned around some kid snatched it." Likely sensing he might anger the chef who fed him, he adds, "but it's good food too. Really addictive."

It's enough to keep him in my sister's good graces. "I'm going to take these pots back to the house." She winks at me before she adds, "Y'all behave while I'm gone."

Laughable coming from her, but I smile and wait for her to leave before I turn back to the dishes. Hudson left the radio on in the next room. Faint melodies twist through the silence hovering between us.

It starts with a hum. It always does. The vibration quickly turns to a soft voice, a gentle song, a memory of the melody. I sing along with the songs as they come. The stack of dishes lessens with time. Victoria will be back any second, I'm sure of it. My volume escapes me, and for a second, I forget I'm not alone. When I turn, Roman's plate is pushed away. He's listening with the same interest I saw in him at the club.

"Sorry," my bashful nature takes hold of my nerves, "I get carried away."

"Did you hear me complaining?"

"Of course not. You're too polite."

"I enjoy your voice."

I turn back to the stack of dishes and grab a towel from the drawer, eager to justify away his compliment. "Sure, I mean, I can carry a tune. But I'm suited for back up singing, or choir singing. One voice in many, not the star of the show."

"I could listen to you all night."

"But you wouldn't expect my name up in lights." There's a difference in my mind, an important difference, especially in the eyes of a music producer like Roman.

For a split second, I figure I stumped him. He looks down, shifting his jaw side to side as if debating whether he should voice his response. Finally, he looks up, hazel eyes locked on mine.

"The marquee lights aren't good enough for you." His eyes drop to my lips for a second before he finishes his thought. "If I could, I'd write your name in the stars."

The air thickens between us, charged, heat rushing my heart and my cheeks all at once. I'm breathless at the compliment. Before I can ask him more, he makes like he needs to leave.

"I should probably get going." Roman pushes to his feet but remains on the opposite side of the island.

"Already? You haven't talked to Booker yet."

Roman exhales through his nose, lips in a tight line. "I'm trying to keep things professional between us."

I'm not young enough that I don't recognize what I see smoldering in his eyes. It grants me bravery to push him on the issue.

"Keep it professional? That's your story? Even if you're thinking of the four best ways to get around this island to get to me?"

Roman presses his lips together before he says, "Five best ways, but who's counting?"

"I am."

He looks away, but it's only two seconds before he's drawn back to me. Whatever archaic tradition he's holding on to, I bet he's losing the battle in his mind. I swear I can taste the desperation to pull closer, even while he says, "I'm trying to be the good guy here."

My mother was a red-head, and a streak of stubborn runs through us all. Sometimes I refuse to let it go. Sometimes the argument is worth the battle.

"Why? Why can't you let this go?" I ask.

Roman takes a second to think about it before he says, "I've seen it before, an older man with a younger woman. Small town, and a lot of gossip. It didn't end well. I don't want that for you."

"You're not that much older than me."

"I'm not young either."

"What if I don't care?"

I've been told I'm frustrating. I can see it in the way he rubs his palm over his mouth but refuses to look away from me. I'm wearing him down, and it elates me. I don't back down from arguments. I always have a counterpoint. Roman steps away from the bar and moves around the island until he's in front of me. Setting his hands to my shoulders, he tries again.

"Trust me, you want this to stay professional. It's the safest option."

"How do you know what I want? You've never asked. We're bound to spend time together, what's your solution for that, Roman?"

His jaw hinges with unspoken words, but his palms slide the length of my arms, lace rippling as they move. Maybe he meant for it to be innocent, but the way he touches me, it's never plutonic. The very act brings us closer, wears on his control, and lights a fire in my gut. I've broken through, changed his mind at least for the time being, at least for now I know he can see how well we fit and he's not willing to deny it much longer.

"We'll have to do professional activities, that's all."

"Going to the club was professional."

His hands twist until our fingers are linked. My breathing quickens and his deepens. Roman takes a step toward me.

"Listening to music is part of our jobs," he says. I feel like these justifications are exactly that, little reasons that help him rationalize our time together, and more importantly, excuse these stolen moments. If it's all normal, then we're not doing anything wrong.

"Maybe we should go to a concert."

He nods, but his right arm drops my hand and slips around my waist.

"Maybe we should go to ten concerts. One every night."

His palm presses against me, urging me into a gentle sway to the faint music. I've never been one to seek dancing, not like Hudson, but this is different. This is connecting. This is a tinderbox set to ignite.

"What about this?" Roman asks. "Is dancing okay?"

"Dancing is always fine. All sorts of people dance. It's not always romantic. I was dancing with my brother, for instance."

"And dancing well," Roman says, inching closer.

"Friends dance."

"Coworkers dance, if the occasion is right." His eyes flit to my lips and linger.

"I could see that happening." Without thinking, my head tilts up toward him, an invitation if he's willing. "Even strangers have been known to dance."

Roman's grip wraps my other arm around his neck before he releases it there and whispers, "But lovers dance best."

I could break in half, right down the center, with the way he's torturing me. I'm burning for more, for some indication that he means what he's saying. His free palm catches my waist, still in time with the music, still maintaining our lie that this is about a dance.

"When can I see you again?" Roman asks.

"Professionally?"

"You might have convinced me not to care anymore."

The thought brings a smile to my lips. "We have an appreciation party for the staff Sunday afternoon. You should come. Booker and a few other acts will be there."

The swaying stops, and his phone vibrates from his pocket, dragging him back to thoughts of work and responsibility. But his hands slip from my waist and slide over my cheeks until he's captured my face in his palms. With a quick glance over my expression, he dips closer, bending until our lips almost brush.

"Count on it," he whispers. Roman pulls away and I follow, heart linked to him as if by the synchronized beats. "I need to go. I'll see you Sunday."

"Yeah," I say, but it's weak, confused, and hurt that he won't stay a little longer. "I'll watch for you."

Roman pulls his suit jacket from the chair and slips it over his arm. He starts for the door but pauses before he can leave. Without turning, he says, "I'll be the one who can't take his eyes off you. Even if I know better."

CHAPTER 8

Roman

A cold shower didn't do it.

Staring at files for hours didn't do it.

I spent an hour at the gym trying to get her off my mind, but nothing's working. I can't deny it any longer. No matter of logical thought will undo the fact that I'm undeniably attracted to her. More than that, I could fall for someone like her.

It's not just her looks, or her personality. It's more than anything I've ever felt. For the first time in a long time, if ever, someone sees me. Not just that, she can't look away. She can't let go. She'll fight for me. Is this really something I want to let go of? Maybe that's why I can't. Maybe that's why I can't forget her.

Rick snaps his fingers between my eyes. "Hey, you in there?"

"Yeah," I say, shaking off this haze I've been in, "distracted for a minute."

I open another one of Ace's files and start cross referencing the data against Dale's. Part of me is disappointed I haven't found anything, but most of me is relieved. Kennedy loves her dad. I don't want to be the one to haul him away. That would strangle out any chance for a rela—I stop myself. There can't be a relationship. My job deals with hardened criminals, and I don't want to put her in danger.

"Who is she?" Rick asks.

"What?"

He slaps a picture on the desk in front of me. "This girl, who is she?"

I can't escape her, not even at work. She's coming out of a building in the photo, black skirt, tiny heels to hide her petite frame. From the angle of the camera, I'm guessing Rick's having her followed.

"Kennedy Cartwright. She's one of Ace's daughters."

"She was in pretty tight with our buddy Dale, but you're not listing her with your suspects. You clear her already?"

"She's the one I went out with for my cover this week. She doesn't have it in her."

"People surprise me, what they're capable of at least." When he draws in a deep breath, I realize I'm holding mine. "I want to meet her. Bring her to the event. We'll see who she interacts with. That'll give us an idea of her innocence."

"Sir, I don't think that's a great idea. She's a local event planner and talent scout. I don't want to put her in danger."

"Then she'll fit right in. We're having some locals do sets. It'll give you a good reason for taking her." He pinches her photo between two fingers to examine it. "She's cute, young, but cute. I don't think this is the worst thing the agency has asked of you."

Why did he have to say young?

"No sir, it's not."

"I saw your plans for Sunday. You're hoping to get a look at the Cartwright warehouse next? Checking inventory? You think Ace is linked to Dark Fox?"

I shake my head. "Just the opposite. I don't think he is, but I need to confirm that he hasn't been on the payroll or helped to launder cash. Buying equipment would be the easiest way to move large sums of cash. I have a list of his machinery that should be there, and I'll compare it to what's actually present."

Rick sucks on my words for a second or two. "I like seeing this side of you. We're bare bones for now, can't afford to have an agent hiding behind a screen. Field work looks good on you, Palermo. Keep it up."

He leaves before I have a chance to respond, not that it would matter. Easily forgettable, that's why the bureau loves to keep me around. The best undercover agents aren't overly ugly, or good-looking. We're the ones who look like everyone else, one more drone in a long line of drones. Unremarkable. Not out of place.

I've never felt comfortable with the other agents like Maddox, and my choice was clear from the start. Let the alpha types take the glory and the risk. I've stayed behind the scenes, working the paperwork, finding leads, and occasionally pulling undercover work when the risk was low. I spend more time with the techs than other agents, but I get it done. Rick's right, I scored well in training, I'm good at it, but I've never had a reason to stand at the front of the pack. I've never had a reason to fight for leader of the pack.

Still, it's different this time. Cartwright Ranch is tied up in this case, and I can't leave Kennedy to fend for herself, not when I have the training to keep her safe. She gives me a reason to fight, to protect, and take a few risks. She wakes up my training and my need to excel. I could let the others take point like I always have, but could I live with myself if something happened to her? Especially if I could have prevented it?

❋ ❋ ❋

Kennedy

The wedding went off without a hitch. Even the dreaded macaroons were perfect. But at the end of every party at the ranch, the next morning there's always the dreaded clean up. I pull the final strand of lights from the trellis, and start walking toward Hudson, wrapping the strand as I move.

"Hudsie," I ask when he's close enough to hear me, "what's an acceptable age gap?"

He smirks, knowing instantly why I'm asking. "You want me

to say nine years? Because I will, if it'll make you happy."

It's the truth. When it comes down to it, the kid would do just about anything to keep me happy.

"What do you think of Roman, really?" I hand him the last of the lights to wrap and store in the container.

"I don't know the guy." He jams them inside and snaps the lid. "I can't really have an opinion."

"Do you think he's cute?"

Hudson laughs. "I'm exclusively into Jill, so no, I don't think Roman's cute."

"Objectively. I'm not asking you to date him." I start through the high grass for the trail. "I'm hung up on what Victoria said, that he's average."

"Ah, the number two pencil theory."

It irks me all over again. "I think he's gorgeous, but I'm starting to feel like I'm the only one. Is that crazy?"

Hudson bumps into me with his shoulder like he's gonna start teasing me. Instead, he turns introspective. "Remember how dad used to say he didn't know what mom saw in him. He talks about how he never thought he could get a girl like her?"

I smile at the story. I used to have mom tell it to me all the time growing up. Once she died, I told it to Hudson as least twice as many times. My little brother smiles like he wants me to tell it all over again.

"But mom always saw him for everything inside, not just the physical. She said she fell in love with his heart long before she fell in love with his looks. She said he was made just for her."

"Maybe that's what's happening with you. You see more than the way he looks. Maybe you found someone made just for you." He pulls a face. "I mean, *I* don't see it. But if you see it, then maybe that's enough."

In my heart, I hope he's right.

❊ ❊ ❊

Roman

My cell rings. A quick glance tells me it's Rick. I draw in a breath and answer it. "Palermo."

"I'm sending an address to your phone. I need you to get over here."

"I was headed back to Santos Sound. I wanted to compare—"

"You're headed here. That's an order."

Orders. It's the lifeblood of a good agent, but I find myself wondering if it's the path I want to follow. With most of my time spent behind a computer, maybe I'd do better as an analyst or forensic accountant.

"What about Maddox? He wanted to take point on this anyway."

The line falls silent for six seconds. "Maddox was found in an alley this morning, beaten and left for dead. Some garbage man happened to find him in time. He's in critical condition. Get down here. We need to check out the scene and then his apartment."

The world skitters to a dead stop. Maddox wasn't a friend, but an attack on one of our own is never easy. I know I can't let it get to me. Compartmentalize, and move forward. Splitting focus gets good agents killed.

"What are you thinking? Dark Fox knows we're onto him?"

"Or Maddox was on their payroll, and it went south. Either way, I don't like it."

I stare at my phone after the call ends. More and more I feel like I'm standing at a crossroads, two career paths stretching out in front of me. I've flown below the radar for years. I've never felt the pull to take the lead, but this case is different. I don't have the luxury of staying back at base anymore, not with Maddox out.

No more hiding behind a screen. At this point, I'm either all in, or I'm out.

CHAPTER 9

Kennedy

By my count we have thirty-eight guests so far. I expect sixty, but four more cars pulled in a few minutes ago. A quick glance at the refreshments tells me ice water could use a refill, and the lemonade isn't moving. I hustle across the back patio, careful not to look alarmed. It's hardly an emergency.

I pour a small amount of lemonade into a cup and take a sip. My mouth waters like I've bit into a lemon. I try to hide my reaction, hoping no one noticed. Vic forgot sugar again. She's been distracted, always slipping off to her secret life. Where I'm drowning in family loyalty, my sister can't wait to cut free. Guilt is all that keeps her grounded to us at this point.

I heft the clear dispenser, smiling when a few guests shoot me a questioning look for stealing the lemonade. Vic rushes to my side, throwing daggers with her eyes.

"What are you doing?"

I shove the dispenser at her, happy to unload the weight. "Taste it. You'll see. Fix it and bring it back."

Her jaw clenches hard, storms igniting in her eyes, but she doesn't say a word before she spins on a heel and starts for the house.

"Should have hired a caterer," I say under my breath. From the way her feet stall for a second, I wager she heard me. I shouldn't have said it. Vic does good work. Maybe I'm just jealous. She has a life outside the Cartwright name. I live and breathe this place. I have since mom died. Is it awful to want a few dreams of my own? It's not a path I need to travel, not when we are supposed to be simultaneously thanking our vendors and employees, as well as encouraging them to stick it out another year.

The appreciation party was mom's idea to begin with. Back then we had a handful of folks helping us out. Granted, we weren't fully booked like we are now. She suggested dad throw a party for his employees. He agreed and set a date for October, after the season calmed down. Mom changed it to June, the peak of our season. When he pushed her about it, she explained she'd rather thank them early and keep them happy, than thank the ones we had left at the end. From then on, the tradition stuck. Because of that mentality, thanking them early, we had very little turnover and a steady stream of people wanting to help out Cartwright Ranch. Mom would be so proud.

*　*　*

Roman

Normally, I'd enter the party and find an excuse to slip away. No one misses me. I've got it down to an art. I talk to a couple people, make an excuse to leave, slip off, do my work, and keep to the fringe when I return. By the time I ease back into the swing of it, they assume I never left.

I know it's not possible with Kennedy. When I disappeared at the reception, she not only asked around, but she sought me out. If I show up and disappear, even if I make it fast, she'll notice. Because of her, my reconnaissance strategy has to shift.

Zipping my leather jacket to hide away my white dress shirt, I duck under the fence line at the back of the property. I can't help feeling like this should be Maddox's role. That's not an option right now. After visiting the crime scene, I stopped by the hospital. Rick didn't oversell it. Maddox's face was swollen almost to the point that I couldn't recognize him. Sedation kept him from telling us anything. Doctors are worried about brain damage. Moments like these remind me that the dangers are real in my line of work, and even hiding behind a computer won't always help.

Sounds from the party hum on the wind. I swear I hear Kennedy's sweet voice on the microphone, speaking, not singing. I might have stopped to listen if she was singing. There's a buzz of laughter, and I yank open the barn door in the lapse of silence. Slipping into darkness, I roll the door shut again. A deep rumbling sound catches my attention. Fumbling for my phone, I flip on the light, swing it around and blind a startled horse in his stall. Apologizing, I drop the light from the poor creature's eyes. A gold nameplate displays his name, "Harley".

It must be Victoria's horse. I can't imagine Kennedy mucking stalls or tossing hay. No precision in it. Too many variables. As if it senses my ill feelings, it lets out a high-pitched whinny. The sound bounced off the walls, almost splitting my eardrums it seems.

"I'm going. I'm going."

I'm trying to reason with a horse. What's wrong with me? I shove open a door at the back, hoping for better luck. Thankfully, I'm rewarded with the warehouse full of barn equipment. I shut out the horse, bent on my discovery, and pull out the notepad with the ranch's supposed inventory.

"Okay, Ace. Let's see how good you really are."

※ ※ ※

Kennedy

A quick glance at the clock tells me I'm an hour in and every guest is accounted for but one.

Roman.

He said he would come, and yet, I'm alone.

This hot and cold dance he does is enough to drive a girl batty. I swear back in the cottage he was into me. There was even a moment in the grocery aisle where, I swear, he was interested, but not showing up after making a promise to be here, not even a call after a night like that… I don't know what to think. Maybe it's all been in my head.

"He's not here yet, huh?"

I turn to find Dad, a knowing twinkle in his eye.

"Who?" I might as well play dumb for as long as possible.

"Roman, Dale's replacement. Your brother told me you invited him. I was looking forward to meeting the guy who had divided your attention for the first time in your life."

I pin a frown on my face. "I'm not divided." A thought occurs to me. "Wait, you haven't met him? I assumed from that message you sent me that you'd met."

"Not yet. I heard through the grapevine that someone young had taken over Dale's work. Still not sure where Dale's gone. You haven't heard anything, have you?"

I smile and shake my head. "It's anyone's guess, I think."

His eyes narrow a bit, as if he knows that I know something more. "Tell me about this Roman fellow."

The first thing that pops into my head is Roman's age. Knowing my traditional and overprotective father, that can't be my starting point.

❋ ❋ ❋

Roman

The warehouse checks out. Right down to the three augers against the wall, complete with labels and maintenance records taped to the wall above it. I suspect Kennedy's work.

Close as I can tell, Ace Cartwright is clean. Great for Kennedy, not for me. And if he's not involved with Dark Fox and Dale's activities, then the family is unaware of the danger surrounding them. That's somehow worse. Naivety gets people killed.

I start for the party, trying to think of an excuse if Kennedy asks me why I'm entering from the wrong direction. I let my eyes sweep over the acreage that makes up the ranch. In the distance, I spot the event barn where the reception was held, and the cottage not far behind it. I've seen aerial shots of the property, so I know the expansive building to the south is the new auditorium they put in two years ago. That's where they hold the Summer Concert Series Kennedy's been working on.

I spin, looking off toward the east end of the property. Another gray building sits at the base of a valley. It looks abandoned, dilapidated, wrong in a place as new and well-kept as the Cartwright Ranch.

The party calls me, but I can't help my curiosity. I steal down a side path, keeping to the trees and out of sight. If they have secrets to keep, that building would be the best option. No foot traffic, off the beaten trail, no one would ever think to look.

I push back the door. It groans, but not loud enough to give up my position. I slip inside. Between the heat and the musty smell, the air chokes me. Voices catch my ear, overpowering my growing desire to escape the place. Staying low, I move down the entry hallway, sticking to the shadows. A bulky lighting apparatus blocks my way, but it's easy enough to get around it. If I had to put a name to the building, I would wager it's an old auditorium. My hands grate the walls. Cinderblocks, from what I can tell. The voices start up again. I cling to the wall, pushing to the edge to peer around the corner.

The main hallway curls around the center room. Only one way in or out. It's an agent's worst nightmare. Seats rise up from the stage, a sound room sits off to the side, and a single spotlight glows center stage. If I was hoping for criminal activity, I'm out of luck.

Kennedy's brother stands center spotlight, a teenage girl

tight in his arms. Music swells over the speakers as he leads her through steps, I have to assume they've practiced. No one dances that well without rehearsal. I couldn't dance that well *with* rehearsal. For a second, I watch, transfixed by the way they move. A simple waltz, easy rise and fall, a few lifts that he executes with ease. The kid has more game in his right pinky than I've had in my entire life. Maybe I should ask for a few pointers when it comes to his sister. He can't be much more than eighteen. No, my mind corrects me, he's seventeen. That' s what she told me.

I instantly go back three years ago, Sebastian and Brinley. My brother, his younger girlfriend, and the disaster he created. There's something to be said for equally matched partners. The two teenagers on the stage show it, not only in their dancing, but the way they look together. I can't help but wonder if I'm crazy to even consider trying with Kennedy. Or maybe she's right. Maybe our age isn't a problem. Intellectually, we're a great match. Conversation never stalls. She challenges me in ways I've never experienced. Maybe being equally matched is about more than age.

But what about my career? Once I close this case, I'll be moving on to the next one. In another city, with new threats. It's not fair to her to start something I can't finish. Worse, what if I hang on, but she doesn't. She sees me now, but absence makes the heart grow forgetful, isn't that the saying? Can I stand a world where I'm not even a memory in her life? I know that feeling too well. Add long distance to our relationship, and could we last? Is our bond strong enough to make it through all the trials we're facing?

I back away from the performance on the stage, away from their simple love and easy choices. I shouldn't stay, shouldn't make an appearance at the party, but I gave my word, and despite everything, I can't go back on that. With her father in the clear, and her family not complicit, seeing her one last time can be a reward for a job well done. One last time.

✽ ✽ ✽

Kennedy

"Kennedy, great party. I can't wait for the season to really get in full swing."

I smile at Booker, happy he made it. I do wish Roman were here so he could talk shop with him, but that's starting to feel like a pipe dream.

"I know. The concert series is going to be amazing. It's the perfect way to kick off the summer."

"With you running it, that's true." Booker grins and snags two glasses of punch off a passing tray. He extends one to me. "I bet you have no idea how much we all feel the impact with you taking over the management around here."

I shrug because it's not me, it's the team. "I keep things going behind the scenes."

"Yeah, I know, greasing the wheels, same story you sell us every time, but not a single one of us would be where we are without Kennedy Cartwright. You're the hidden gem in this family, and I really think you should start taking center stage with us more often."

"I don't know, Hudson is doing a great job learning to emcee. I think I'm ready to pull back a little." The kid lives for attention, like I'd ever take it away. "You know I belong in the wings."

Booker motions to Carly and Marco, the lead singers from *Mega Compass.* "We were talking a bit ago, and you came up. Not a single one of us has missed you singing under your breath, or backstage when you think you're alone. Carly said she went looking for you two weeks ago and found you in the old auditorium, sweeping the stage, belting out Broadway tunes."

My throat tightens like the spotlight is shining on me, excited at the news but nervous for the attention. "I didn't think anyone ever heard me."

"Heard you?" Booker laughs. "Kennedy, we're dying to hear *more* from you. You've put us all top billing and helped us in ways we can't ever repay. You can't expect us to let you hide forever with that voice, can you? Why don't you ever save a set for yourself? Two songs, three if they ask for it. Heck, I'll play for you if you want. I doubt anyone knows what they're missing with you backstage instead of dead center."

Blood rushes to my cheeks at the sound of his flattery. "I couldn't ever do it if people were listening. My stage fright is—"

"It'll go away with practice." Booker sets his hand to my shoulder, trying to catch my eyeline. "Your voice needs to be shared."

I stuff my feelings down because what he's suggesting isn't practical. "And if I'm center stage, who is backstage running it? Who would remember to have your key lime seltzer water waiting for you at the optimum temperature?" I give him a warm smile to let him know it's okay, I accepted this a long time ago. "But as for stars, I'm hoping you'll be getting some good news soon enough."

His hand slides from my shoulder to my forearm, evidence of our comfortable friendship. "Oh, really? About what?"

I give the crowd a once over, wishing Roman would materialize. "Well, I shouldn't say anything, but that guy you saw me with at the wedding you played? He's a producer from Santos Sound, and he's taken a real interest in you. I was hoping he'd be here today, and you'd get a chance to network, but I haven't seen him."

"I kinda remember him. Dark hair, average build. Your everyday business type guy, right?"

"You'd remember him if you saw him."

"Maybe." Booker looks over my shoulder, squinting. "Wait. That guy? In the leather jacket?"

I spin to search him out. Coming up the trail from the old barn where Victoria keeps her horse, Harley, Roman strides with quick steps, slowly unzipping his jacket. I'm elated to see him, but at the same time, confused. Why would he be coming up from the old barn?

*　*　*

Roman

Not only am I caught in the first ten seconds, but she's also standing way too close to some Rockstar wannabe. It's all but impossible to smother my jealousy.

The questions about my absence and sudden appearance are written all over her face. My mind reels through every lie that might work in this sort of situation, but I'm having a hard time ignoring that guy's hand on her arm, whispering in her ear while she laughs softly at something. That something might be me. Whatever spell I had her in, it's likely fading.

"Roman," her face still holds the traces of the laughter as I approach, "I'm so glad you made it."

I can't help but wonder if that's something she says to everyone.

"Yes, sorry I was late." I should explain why, but I'm hoping she'll let it go. I should know better.

"You're coming up the wrong path," her companion says to me. I recognize Booker from the times I've seen him play. I had no idea they were such great friends. Possibly more than friends by the looks of it. "Did you walk here from Santos Sound?"

"Car trouble. I left it with a mechanic and walked the rest of the way." The ease with which I lie used to alarm me, but my jealousy makes it easier. It's not hard to see that Booker is about her age, and clearly interested. His fingers tangle into Kennedy's, grabbing her attention. I look away while he whispers something in her ear, then bids me a quick goodbye.

She watches him leave, a dazed look on her face like he's given her a reason to keep on living in this dreary world. When she looks back at me, I can't help searching her expression to see if any of her attention has waned. Last I saw her, we sparked.

She takes a step toward me, eyes bright and glittering in the evening glow. "I really am glad you made it. You could have called; I would have picked you up."

"You can't leave an event. The whole place would come to a crashing halt." It feels good to tease her, to seek out that slight intimacy we had from before.

But my words do the opposite of what I planned. Instead of helping her see how important she is, how great she is at her job, they seem to upset her.

"Yes, I guess it would." She smiles, but it has none of her usual shine. "Excuse me, I need to check on the food."

"Kennedy." I don't know what makes me call after her, let alone follow on her heel, but I can't help myself. If I said something wrong, I can't leave it alone. I catch her arm, halting her footsteps. "I'm sorry if that was wrong, or if I interrupted your date."

"My date?" Her eyes widen at the thought. "Booker? We're not dating."

Air rushes from my lungs, dragging all rational thought alongside it. "I just thought, I don't know what I thought." I swallow hard, trying to remember that I'm a federal agent, and I shouldn't get this flustered. "I know I didn't like what I thought."

A smirk teases at her lips. "Are you saying you were jealous?"

Words won't form. I've still got both her arms in my grip, hoping she won't leave. I'm sure my eyes are pleading with her to rescue me. I don't know what I'm doing. I don't talk to beautiful women. I hide behind a computer screen and let other guys go save the world. This isn't like me to fight for someone, but I can't stop myself. She's different than the rest.

"Kenny," the booming voice isn't familiar to me, "introduce us."

Like a cop on a back road, Ace Cartwright materialized out of nowhere. From the way he's looking at me, I gather he's not happy about how I'm holding his daughter.

I release my grip on her, taking a half step back. Kennedy flashes me a smile, but it's tight and hurried.

"Dad, this is Roman, the new music producer over at Santos." She motions to her father. "Roman, this is my dad, Ace Cartwright."

I take his extended hand, trying to match the intense grip of the man I've been investigating for the past week. He oozes intimidation from every pore. Raising two beautiful daughters mostly on his own, he plays the role of protector like a professional.

"Pleasure to meet you, sir. You have an impressive set up here. It's been a pleasure getting to watch Kennedy work."

"A pleasure, huh?" I don't miss the twitch in the patriarch's brow. "Don't worry about calling me sir, leave that to the young men."

I pull my hand free, as if his grip turned electric. He may not be saying much, but his disapproval over our age gap is apparent.

"I can't get a clear answer through the grapevine," Ace nods his head to Kennedy, "or even from my own daughter. Where did Dale run off to? Surely his replacement knows."

"Family trouble." I shrug. "You know how it is."

"His parents are dead. He has no wife and no children. What family is in trouble exactly?" His voice turns sharp on the last word. Ace might as well demand my real identity.

"Sister, on the East Coast." I shake my head slowly. "She had a bad fall." I've spent enough time at Dale's desk to know his sister is alive and well. Thank goodness for keeping my nose in the paperwork.

"Good for you for stepping in. I'm sure Kennedy is learning a lot from an old pro like you."

"Daddy, that's enough." Kennedy tries to keep her voice low, but it's not hard to hear her reproach.

"What? Guys our age have to teach you young bucks how it's done." He kisses the top of her head but doesn't take his eyes off me. "Isn't that right, Roman?"

"Something like that, sir."

Kennedy grits her teeth so hard I fear she might crack something. "Daddy cut it out. He's only thirty-three. Hardly *your* age."

"Hardly your age either," Ace whispers back.

Apparently, I'm not the only one worried about the age gap.

* * *

Kennedy

I hate feeling out of control, and whatever game my dad is playing is definitely out of my control. I knew he wouldn't like the idea of an older guy on my arm, but I didn't think he'd have this much of an issue with it. He's acting like Roman is decades older than me and out to do me wrong. Nothing could be farther from the truth. Because of Roman's hot and cold act, nothing has even happened. Despite my best efforts.

Movement on the trail from the barn catches my eye. Hudson and Jill, sneaking back in from wherever they ran off to. He catches my eye and I shoot him a look, hoping our innate ability to speak telepathically will kick in, or at least he'll see my desperation. He kisses Jill's cheek, then rushes to my side.

"Hey, Dad. There's an issue with the cars out front. I was hoping you'd come take a look."

Dad gives my hand a squeeze, as if to tell me this discussion isn't over yet and bids a quick goodbye to Roman. I must have been holding my breath through the whole exchange because the second he's outside my immediate presence, I exhale my relief.

"Sorry about that." I don't want to talk about it. I don't want to acknowledge the fact that, at least on some level, Roman is right. Some people will have an issue about our age gap.

"I expected it." Roman keeps the distance between us, but I wish he'd take my hands, pull me close, and use dancing as an excuse again. Anything to go back to where we were in the cottage not too many nights ago. He's about to say something else, but his phone rings from his jacket pocket. He checks it quickly, disappointment written all over his face.

"Bad news about your car?"

His brow caves in for half a second as if my words make no sense, but he recovers quickly. "Yeah, I need to go. I'm sorry."

He finally takes my hand, but only to hold it for a second before he lets it go. I watch him make his quick exit, standing alone, music swirling around me, wondering if I'll ever have the guts to chase what I want, in music, and in my heart.

CHAPTER 10

Roman

"What do you have?" I ask Rick as I climb into the surveillance van.

"Suspicious figures," he points to the monitor with two men standing outside a restaurant. "This is Dante Alvero. From what Maddox was able to piece together, he's Dark Fox's right-hand man. This is his restaurant. I want you to look at these numbers, tell me what you see."

He hands me copies of spreadsheets. I bounce from one line to the next, working the numbers in my head. "Yeah, these don't add up. Food cost is through the roof. They've bought two new walk-ins this year. And I don't think anyone needs two thousand dollars' worth of pepper shakers."

"You're going in," Rick says.

"I'm what?"

"You're going in, right now. Health department surprise inspection." He snaps his fingers and the analyst at the computer hands me a clipboard and ID badge. "Put on my suit coat and tie. Do we have any glasses in here?"

I tilt the ID Badge for Forest Addimer, health inspector, in my hands. "Are you sure about this? It feels rash without more intelligence."

"You've seen Maddox. Does it look like we have time to waste? I know you're more comfortable with the computers, but I need you. All I want is confirmation whether these items are in that building. I need a thread to chase."

"Do I get hazard pay for this?" I'm joking, but not really.

"It's hardly a hazard. Nobody shoots the health inspector."

"Yet," I say, slipping on the sports coat. "You have a thermometer for me?"

"What for?"

"My cover. I have to check temperatures."

Within seconds the agent tucks a red digital thermometer in my hand. My last excuse is expended. I step out of the van and hope I'm not risking my life for no reason.

❋ ❋ ❋

Roman

The bell over the door of *Mama Cocino's* jangles, alerting all criminals inside that I'm fair game. I blow out a deep breath through tight lips and remind myself that I'm Forest Addimer, uptight, joyless, health inspector.

"I'm sorry, we're closed," a deep voice says from the darkness.

"Not here for food," I try to keep my words clipped like I'm already late for my next appointment, "surprise inspection. I'm sure you understand."

"We had two this month already." The voice still hasn't revealed himself. I have no idea if a gun is trained on my head or not.

"Yes, well," I adjust the thick glasses Rick gave me and twirl the thermometer in my hand, "with all the violations you've had in the past, that's not surprising. You can expect us to be climbing up your tailpipe for quite some time, mister."

The shadows shift. A body slips over the vinyl. Air releases from the cushion as he stands. I recognize Dante Alvero from the surveillance Rick showed me.

"And you are?"

I keep my smile as tight as possible. "Forest Addimer."

"You're not the normal guy."

"He's sick."

"It's Sunday."

"Nothing says surprise like a Sunday." I told Rick he was being rash. Oversights like this get agents killed. Fear creeps into my chest, but I can't let it infiltrate my voice. "Are you going to show me into the back, or should I write that you refused to comply?"

Two black eyes narrow to slits before he says, "Let's get this over with."

I follow him through the back, senses alert and waiting. If I have to be out in the field, I'd feel better with a gun, but I guess health inspectors don't carry guns. Once in the kitchen, Alvero waves his arm wide as if to give me full reach. The place is empty, not a single pot on a stove. A quick glance at the clock on the wall confirms what I suspected, four thirty. "Shouldn't prep be underway by now? What time do you open?"

"Closed tonight."

My mind races with worry. If he suspects me, if there's a chance he knows I'm not who I say I am—I'm dead. I pull out my thermometer, committed to my cover. "I'll check the fridges then."

"Do what you gotta do." Alvero stands at the end of the row, arms crossed, glaring, possibly trying to see through my cover.

I pass the cooktop, at least ten years old. I count two walk-in fridges, not the four I would expect, and neither one of them have been replaced in the last fifteen years. I know enough now but leaving early will only put me in danger. I jerk open the door and step into the chilled air. Fearing for my own safety, I jam a slip of cardboard into the corner of the door to keep it slightly ajar. Last thing I want is to be locked inside.

I check the temperature of most everything in the fridge, careful to write the information on my fake paperwork. Dates are written on the outside of the plastic serveware, everything is in order. Other than money laundering, the restaurant is on the up and up.

A new voice outside the walk-in catches my attention. "Hey, there's a van out back. You want me to check it out?"

I move to the cracked door to try to listen in on the conversation happening on the other side of the steel.

"It's those feds. Leave 'em alone. Think they're gonna find something. Like I'm gonna put it under their noses." Alvero makes some off-color jokes about Rick and his team. I hold my peace, hoping to make my exit at the right moment.

"You want me to take care of them like I did that other guy?" The second voice makes a few "pew, pew" sounds like murder is something out of a video game.

"Hey, keep your voice down, Pedro. We've got company."

"You want me to do him too?"

I don't want to hear Alvero's answer. Instead, I make a show of shoving back the freezer door and rubbing my feet on the mat.

"I don't know why they gotta waste my time like this." I press the door shut and flip the handle to a locked position. "You're clearly running a clean kitchen here. I'll tell you what. I'm writing you up a clear report, and if someone asks, I did every test on the list."

Alvero's right eyebrow twitches. "And why would you do that for me?"

"Sick of working these surprise shifts on a Sunday, man. If I stop finding things, they'll stop sending me."

I'm banking on him wanting me out of here just as bad as I want to leave. Alvero watches me with scrutiny, weighing my lies for truth. He extends a hand, and I take it, careful to keep my fear from my grip.

"You have a good day now, okay?" I say over my shoulder on the way for the door. I'm sure he's suspicious. I don't head back for the van. Instead, turn and leave toward my jeep. Checking the rearview mirror, though I'm quick, it's not hard to spot my tail. Alvero sent a subordinate to be sure I didn't climb in that van.

I fire up the engine, shake out my nerves and head for home, just like any good old boy would do.

※ ※ ※

Roman

"You're positive he knew we were there?"

"Rick," I wish he could have heard it himself, "he not only knows you were there; they were debating whether shooting you would raise too many red flags."

"Well Anita has you covered. She made up some fake profiles for your cover. If they go hunting, they'll find a guy obsessed with fishing and collecting garden gnomes."

"Why gnomes?"

"It's just crazy enough to be believable."

"Fine. Look, nothing in there has been replaced. He's using the restaurant like he used Santos Sound." I switch my cell to the other ear. "They know we're here. They know we're onto them. I don't know what your plan is, but—"

"We flipped one of his guys. That's what this fundraiser is. Flipped the guy, set up the sting, let him feed it back to his bosses. Dante won't be able to resist. The guy has some weird obsession with musicians. We'll snag him tomorrow night, red-handed. He'll give us Dark Fox. It'll be over and you can go back to your gnomes."

"I don't like gnomes."

"Fine, whatever it is that guys like you are into." Rick's exhale fuzzes up the phone. "You got that girl yet?"

"What?"

"The one from the picture, did you ask her out yet?"

"Maybe someone else should." Even the idea of it tangles my insides to knots. I don't want anyone else with her. The honest truth is I don't want her anywhere near the event.

"Did you not hear me this morning? There isn't anyone else. It's you or me at this point. And my wife isn't going to let something like that slide."

"Don't you think I'm a little old for her? It would hurt the cover."

"Yeah, you're old for her. Too ugly too." He thinks he's teasing in good-natured fun, but it cuts a little too close to my insecurities. "But you're the best I've got, so you're gonna do it."

"I don't know why you pretend like I'm something special. I'm only here because Maddox wanted to shine, and he thought I'd stay out of the way. You only picked me because my file says I excel at undercover jobs, but there are at least a hundred other agents who can do what I do."

I know better than to talk to my superior like that, no amount of exhaustion or frustration changes that. Rick's side of the call remains silent for a minute. I brace myself for the worst.

"Palermo, you're a good agent. I didn't choose you because you blend in. I picked you because I saw your record. You've been under the radar for years, but your name pops up on almost every major bust in the last six years. Never mind your scores, your shot record, your undercover work, you're with the FBI for the right reason, not to feed your own ego. We need leadership like yours. The rest of these agents could learn a lot from you. Call the girl. Set it up."

The line cuts out. Rick's not one for goodbye. Give a command, confirm the command, and walk away. The order was clear. Five seconds later, I have my phone to my ear, waiting on Kennedy Cartwright.

※ ※ ※

Kennedy

I stare up the ceiling, running over the party in my mind. It's a habit I've had since I took over. Like I'm watching a movie, I roll through the event, looking for flaws and follies. What usually helps me improve, only leaves me unsettled. I'd planned to push things further with Roman. But after the afternoon we spent together, all seven minutes of it, I feel more distant than ever.

It doesn't matter what they all say, attraction is attraction. Roman is different. He's not all bravado and steal your thunder machoism. He's strong without ever having to showboat. He's tender in every touch. When he's around, I gravitate toward him. My phone buzzes beside me on the bed. I thump my palm over the bedspread without lifting my head. I have every intention of ignoring the call, content to be alone with my thoughts instead of dealing with some insecure bride calling after hours, but I check the display.

Roman Palermo.

I added his name to my address book after the last call. I press my lips together. It buzzes again. My finger swipes the call through.

"Hello?"

"Kennedy?"

"Hi, Roman. What's going on?"

"I was checking on you. Things ended," he hesitates, likely searching for a word to describe my awkward family, "weird. I wanted to apologize."

"It's me who should apologize. Everything with my dad..." I let my voice trail off. None of it needs to be repeated or relived. "How's your jeep?"

"Fine now. Running great." He clears his throat. "I was actually calling to ask you something."

He pricks the hope in my heart that I wasn't wrong at all. "What's that?"

"Are you busy tomorrow night?"

"No. Why? Is someone playing?"

"I have this event I need to attend. It's a fundraiser for my company. I have to rub elbows and mingle, in a tux no less." There's another heavy pause before he says, "I need a date."

"And I'm the only girl you know around here."

He laughs, but not because what I said was funny. "You're the only one I'd like to go out with."

I catch my bottom lip and pull it back into my mouth. "What time?"

"I can pick you up at seven."

"I'll be ready."

CHAPTER 11

Roman

I should have told her to wear something fancy. I'm kicking myself not only for that, but because I didn't show up with flowers either. I shift my jacket, hoping to adjust the shoulder holster I haven't worn in longer than I want to admit. Out of practice doesn't even begin to cut it. Wearing a Glock under my jacket should feel natural, but I've been hiding in an office long enough that I feel every ounce of it. I knock on the front door anyway.

This isn't about not wanting to see her. It has more to do with not wanting to involve her. I spent the day helping Rick clear the venue. Something must have changed since we last talked. Our barebones crew grew overnight. I counted at least ten other agents at the event center. When I asked him about it, he simply said, "But they aren't you."

If it was some attempt at flattery, it doesn't sit well with me. I'm sure one of the others could step in and take my place in an instant. Rick seems intent to teach me something, and I follow orders. I wanted to ask him more, ask him to explain what he meant, but timing didn't permit it. After a full day searching for bombs, listening devices, and any other illegal contraband, I barely had the time to put on my tux and drive to the Cartwright Ranch.

The front door rips open, but it's certainly not Kennedy.

"Hey Hudson," I say to her younger brother, "is Kennedy

ready?"

"Not yet." He pulls the door back and motions inside. "But lucky for you, Dad's off with Vic, so no one's gonna chase you off with a rifle."

She's got interesting siblings, that's for sure.

"Great. I guess that's good news. You're not planning a third degree or anything?"

"Nah," Hudson crosses his arms over his chest, "she doesn't get out much. It's nice when someone can take her off my hands." He takes a step closer and *sniffs* my shirt. "No cologne?"

I can't say another guy has ever sniffed me before. Caught off guard doesn't begin to cover my shock.

"No, I was in a hurry."

Hudson frowns, but puts up a finger. "Come on, I can't let you screw this up. You've got enough working against you."

I glance up the stairway because that's where Kennedy ran down before, but there's no sign of her. Wanting to make a good impression on at least one member of her family, I follow Hudson through a door.

His bedroom is bigger than half my apartment. I doubt he has any idea how spoiled he is. On the back wall he's mounted, what I'd guess is, a sixty-inch flat screen. I know his bed is bigger than my single. Jealous feelings creep into my chest, but I'm quick to stomp them out. Chances are, he'd trade it all to grow up with a mom like I have.

"Okay, I've got musky, woodsy, oriental, clean, and spicy. Pretty much anything you could want. What's your poison?"

He's not kidding. His dresser is lined with more cologne bottles than I've owned in my life.

"I have no idea." I throw myself at his mercy. "Do you know what she likes?"

"You've really got a thing for her, don't you?"

I hate admitting it to him before I say anything to her, but it's the truth. "She's amazing."

Hudson grins and reaches in the back. "She always wants me to wear this one, and I never do."

Like a crop duster over a field, he attacks me with a cloud of cologne until my lungs seize, and I feel like I might puke.

"Okay, okay," I throw up my hands, "I surrender."

"Where are you taking her?" Hudson asks as I cough and struggle for air. "Little overdressed for dinner and a movie, aren't you?"

I clear my throat one last time. "It's a fundraiser being thrown by my company." I unbutton my jacket and flap the sides forward and back to air out the fabric. Last thing I want is to drown her in this scent.

"It'll fade fast," Hudson says, "I mean, this one time I—"

He stops mid-sentence. I pause to look at him. His eyes are round and wide, staring at me as if I'm his worst nightmare. It's only then that I realize my mistake.

"You're packing heat?" His voice tips up on the end like he's about to become hysterical.

"You can never be too careful," I say, buttoning my jacket once more. "I have a conceal and carry license."

"But why are you taking a gun on a date with my sister?"

"I'm not some psychopathic murderer."

"You know who says that?" Hudson asks. "Psychopathic murderers."

He's got me on the ropes. How did a seventeen-year-old take me down with a bottle of cologne? Normally, I have a plan, an excuse, something, but I'm coming up empty.

"I'm deep in this music business, right?" I wait for him to nod. I spin the lies as they come. "That means, I know who the players are. Tonight, there are some unsavory characters coming to this event. The last thing I want is for your sister to get hurt. I'm *packing*, as you put it, to be ready for the worst."

His jaw shifts side to side as he thinks about it. I don't blame him. That was terrible.

"Sure you aren't a spy or an undercover cop or something? That's a lot more believable at this point."

"I'm a good guy," I say, hoping it's enough.

"Hudsie!" Kennedy calls from the top of the stairs. "Have you seen any sign of Roman yet?"

Hudson presses his lips together until they turn white. He could destroy my chances with her if he wanted, blow my whole cover in an instant. I hold my breath waiting on his verdict. Finally, he yells, "I think he just pulled up."

I exhale my relief, but Hudson takes a step closer and narrows his eyes. "I may be a kid, but if anything happens to her, I swear no one will find your body."

Kid or not, he could have a future in the FBI with stones like that.

"Got it."

I follow him out. He pulls open the door and shuts it again. "Kennedy, your date's here!"

"Coming!" Her voice nears, and I turn to watch her descent.

Black heels come into view first, spiked, tall, to the point that I wonder if she's self-conscious about her height. Her sister is at least five inches taller than her, Hudson, even more so, but the heels give her an even playing field. She kicks the skirt to her dress out as she walks down. The slinky material clings to her frame in a way that makes my mouth water. The black glittering fabric sets off her eyes, deepens the tan of her skin, and enhances the red tint to her dark hair that trails over her shoulders.

"Wow, wow, wow, wow," I can't stop myself from repeating it under my breath, "wow, wow, wow."

"I think you already said that," Hudson tells me.

"Not enough," I say, because if I repeated it the rest of my life, it'd never be enough. I reach for her hand, and she gives it easily. "You're, I don't even have words, Kennedy."

"Don't wait up," she says to Hudson. "And make dad eat something healthy and go to sleep early."

"Yes ma'am." He salutes but gives me one last hard glare before I escort Kennedy from the house. I get the feeling he knows something is up. I'm on thin ice with that one.

* * *

Kennedy

The hour drive should have tested our conversational skills, but we talked easily like old friends. I'm almost disappointed when he pulls into the parking garage and hurries to my side to open my door. I'd be happy to spend the rest of the evening in his car shooting the breeze, but I suppose I agreed to be his arm candy for the night instead.

He takes my hand to help me out of the car, for which I'm grateful because moving in a mermaid style dress is no easy feat. But the way he won't look away has me happy with my choice. I don't suppose I look young in this dress. For once, the looming age gap doesn't appear to bother him. Once I'm on my feet, Roman offers his arm, and mine loops through as if a perfect fit.

Other happy couples enter the building with us. Cheerful conversation filters from the open ballroom doors. To my surprise, I know quite a few people. Not well, not the type where I'd wave and make small talk, but the kind I've crossed paths with in my work. Roman pauses at the door to hand in our invitations before we step inside.

The ballroom is barely lit, basically relying on the lighting on the stage where musicians are setting up. Neon green and white glow from a bar set up on the far side. Cocktail tables dot the room, perfect for Roman's dreaded mingling. We move through the groups of people. I smile at the ones I know, acts I had at the ranch, singers from *The Nightingale*. It's good to see Santos Sound might actually make good on a few deals and at least promote a few talented people.

"Stay close to me, okay?" Roman asks in a tone low enough that it's meant for me.

"You have something to prove? No one thought you could get a date?" I tease, but he's not willing to play along. If I had to label the expression on his face, I'd say it's fear, or at least tension.

"Shall we get a drink?" Without waiting, Roman starts to lead me toward the bar on the far side of the room. Before we arrive, a hand catches my arm.

"Kennedy?"

I spin, breaking my grip with Roman. I recognize him in an instant. Pedro Marquez, the manager at *The Nightingale.*

"Pedro! Fancy meeting you here." I turn back to Roman, but he's moved on to the bar, his rule of staying together quickly forgotten. Annoyance flashes inside me. I'd hoped we would avoid his hot and cold game tonight, but it feels like that might be unavoidable.

"Are you here alone?" Pedro asks. He leans and peers into the space around me. "I thought I saw someone—"

"My date is around here somewhere," I say, frustrated that I have to cover for his rude behavior.

"Are you singing tonight?"

My eyes widen. "No, not at all. Why would you think that?"

"Figured it was about time. We know you have it in you. Everyone talks about you at the club. You're the hidden gem of our area. What's that old saying? Always the bridesmaid, never the bride?" Pedro nudges me with his elbow. "One of these days I'll have to drag you up on stage at Nightingale."

I roll my eyes. "Oh really? What will you do when I don't cut it?"

"Tell the haters how foolish they are." Pedro leans forward and kisses my cheek, breath faintly stained by alcohol. "I'll let you get back to it, enjoy your night, gorgeous."

"You too." I watch him walk away, curious if he brought a date as well, but he vanishes into the crowd too quickly.

I search for Roman, but he's nowhere in sight. A bit defeated, I take a seat at the bar and wait like a good lap dog.

"Sorry, I slipped off," Roman whispers from behind me. "Work matters called me away."

I spin on my stool, determined to let him have it, but between the apology in his eyes, and the careful cut of his tux, I forget to be angry.

"Roman!" I search in the dim light and spot a man headed toward us, calling to my date. He stands just an inch shorter than

Roman, hair cut short to disguise his balding head, wrinkles around his eyes. His wife looks to be similar in age, but her dress is cut for someone far younger. I have to look away to avoid feeling embarrassed on her behalf.

Roman squeezes my hand as if to tell me to brace myself. "Rick," he says, "I'd like you to meet Kennedy Cartwright. Kennedy, this is my boss, Rick Henderson."

His boss reaches out for my hands and gives them a squeeze. "Pleasure to meet you, Kennedy. Your family is a bit of a legend in this area, aren't they?"

"I don't know about a legend, but yes, we've been afforded some success from our hard work." I don't like the way he said that, as if we were handed the ranch on a silver platter. We've worked hard to get where we are, and certainly there have been hard times.

"This is my wife, Inga." Rick motions to the woman beside him. "Am I mistaken, or were you talking to Pedro Marquez a moment ago?"

"Yes, I was. He's an acquaintance of mine." I wouldn't call Pedro a friend. We've only spoken for the most part at the club, then last year at the Summer Concert Series. While he's a perfectly decent soul to deal with, we've never crossed paths socially, let alone romantically. My instincts tell me that's what Rick is getting after. Is he worried I'm stepping out on Roman?

"How do you know him?" Rick asks. I can't help but feel like he's interrogating me, waiting for me to wither and confess a torrid love affair Roman doesn't know about.

Patience waning, I answer, "He manages *The Nightingale*. It's a local club with open mic nights. I scout talent there for our events at the ranch."

"What a fun job," Rick says, but it doesn't feel entirely genuine.

"It is a fun job." I feel the need to defend myself and glance at Roman to ask why he's not stopping this brute from rolling over the top of me. But Rick takes Roman's arm before I can catch his attention.

"Roman, do you mind if I borrow you a moment, leave the ladies to chat perhaps?"

My date shoots me a worried look, but I relent. His boss is a bit of a beast, and I'm not looking forward to speaking with his wife, but if it'll get him out of our hair for the night, I'm all for it.

❊ ❊ ❊

Roman

I wait until we're out of earshot before I lay into my superior.

"Has no one ever taught you covert tactics? Or even general manners? That was an interrogation," I tack on "sir" at the end like an afterthought.

"Pedro Marquez is high in the ranks of the Dark Fox organization." Rick looks away. "Did you see her talking with him like old friends?"

"Of course, I did. I had to duck out like a jerk so he wouldn't recognize me. Forrest the Health Inspector has no reason to be here dating a friend of his."

"And this friendship she has with a ranking member of Dark Fox, that didn't have you the least bit curious about this girl you're dating?"

"She's clean," I say without removing the razors from my voice.

He waits, staring me down, measuring my worth, before he finally says, "I agree. We have intel that Dante isn't coming. The new plan is to pull in Pedro, try to flip him instead."

"You don't have anything on him, do you?"

"Petty crimes for now. I'm hopeful that something will turn up in the twenty-four hours we have to hold him."

Rick glances over his shoulder to where the women are standing. I can't bear to look. My behavior thus far has been less than chivalrous. Hudson would have my head if he knew.

"Get your date away from here. It might get ugly, and I don't want her to get hurt."

I could take what he's saying at face value, but I see through the lines. "You don't want me to blow my cover." If I stay, she'll see me for who I am, and Rick isn't done using her yet.

Rick's head tilts to the affirmative. "That's a concern. You're in a good position. I still need you."

"I told her this was a work function. What's she going to think when I cut out early?"

Rick's smile turns wry. "Hasn't anyone ever taught *you* about covert tactics? Or romance for that matter? It's a huge building. Get a little lost for an hour while we make the arrest."

With a clap to my shoulder, and a gesture to his wife to follow, Rick melts back into the mingling crowd. I sigh and scramble for a plan, some sort of brilliance to cover yet another lie.

"He's interesting," Kennedy says as she slips in beside me. "I'm not sure I'd enjoy working for him though. Feels like it would have its share of ups and downs."

"You have no idea. It's a real rollercoaster."

CHAPTER 12

Kennedy

The longer I know him, the more I realize I know nothing. Roman changes from moment to moment. Conversation flowed easily on our way here, but now he's a bundle of nerves, eyes darting as he searches the dim ballroom for who knows what. A threat? What kind of threat is there at an event like this? Close as I can tell, it's wall to wall musicians and talent. Hardly the type to make trouble.

"When do the performances start?" I'm hoping to jar him loose from whatever funk he's fallen into, but he shakes his head as if he's barely registered my words.

"Not for a little while." His hand takes mine, tighter than I expect from him. "Do you want to get some air?"

Is he claustrophobic? Is that what's happening? He doesn't wait for my answer before he pulls me for the door that leads to the bathrooms. Maybe he's got social anxiety issues. I can be patient, but a heads up would be nice. He's acting like we're on the run.

He exhales once we're in the hallway, as if he's been holding his breath. He closes his eyes, counting under his breath, watching the exit door to the ballroom.

"Roman," I squeeze his hand to gain his attention, "do you have problems with crowds?" His brow folds in, obviously confused by the question. I scramble to explain myself. "It's okay if you do, I'm not judging you. I'd rather hang out on our own anyway. Maybe we can find somewhere quiet to talk, and we'll hear the bands like background music."

It takes him a minute to process my words, slowly nodding as he agrees. "Yeah, crowds. Social anxiety." Roman steals a quick glance back at the ballroom, but the door remains shut. "I know just the place."

He leads me through empty corridors, a veritable maze I'll never find my way out of. Each hallway is dimmer than the last. I doubt we'll hear any music this far from the ballroom, but the tension is leaving his hand, so I stay on his heel.

"Have you been here before?" I ask as we turn another corner.

"Earlier today." He points with his other hand. "I want to show you something."

It sounds sweet, but if I'm wrong, then this is how more than one true crime story has started. About the time I consider asking if we can go back, Roman shoves a metal handle, and the door grates as it swings open. It's nothing but pitch-black darkness. I raise my eyebrows, waiting for his special surprise, but he only smiles.

"Wait here. I'll be right back."

Maybe he senses my reluctance to follow him any further in the dark. Maybe he can tell my faith is waning. For all I know, he's got a gun under that jacket, and I'm about to be murdered.

"You're safe," his whisper catches my ear, closer than I thought he was. His hand slips over my bare arm. "I won't let anything happen to you."

His warmth pulls back. His footsteps grow softer and farther away from me.

Maybe I should be scared, but even though I don't know him as well as I could, I trust him. If he says I'll be safe, then I will. A hinge groans in the darkness. A couple clicks. Two deep thumps bounce from the walls in surround sound. A blinking red-light signals from the black ether stretching out before me. I take a half-step back. Then, like a deer on the highway, light explodes in front of me.

A strangled cry erupts from my throat until I realize what it is, a spotlight. I step into the auditorium, taking in the stage, the red velvet curtain, the rows upon rows of stadium seats, and Roman, dead center working the control board.

"What is this, Roman?"

"I want to hear you sing," he says, all the tension from before absent from his voice.

"Are you kidding? We can't use this place. We'll get in trouble." My heart starts to hammer in my chest. Excitement? Nerves? Fear of being scolded? I'm not sure, but I can't stop it. Dead center on the stage, a microphone rests in a stand, waiting for a voice.

"This is silly. You don't really want me to sing, do you?"

"More than anything," he says. "Mic is hot. It's just you and me. Not that different from the car or your sister's place. I've only had a taste up until now. Dazzle me, Kennedy."

I want to shrink back into the shadows where I belong, but what he's offering me, it's more than most artists get. Roman's a music producer. This is a personal audition with a major producer. I'd be crazy not to at least give it a shot.

No one's here," Roman says, as if it'll change my mind.

"You're here."

I watch his mouth screw up tight.

"I don't have music." It's a lame excuse. Lack of music has never stopped me in the past.

"You don't need music, but I can play for you." Without waiting for an answer, Roman stands and heads for the piano set to my far right. The stage is calling for me. A halo of light I've never been brave enough to step inside pulls like a magnet. One foot in front of the other I close the distance between me and that spotlight halo.

He's right. We're alone. It's not that different from all the other times he's heard me. The piano bench creaks. Roman has his place and the first notes of music lilt through the air. My next step will land me in the spotlight. Hasn't that been my secret wish all these years? Who cares if I never end up in lights or top billing? For one night, I can forget every obligation that's held me back. For one night, I can be the star.

I take a breath.

I take a step.

* * *

Roman

I've never been as grateful for those piano lessons my mother forced on me as a teenager as I am in this moment. My fingers glide over the keys, an old song I memorized years before, and one I'd love to hear her sing. Though soft at first, her voice is velvet and cream, curling and twisting. The song suits her voice to perfection. Her body comes alive, swaying, reaching for the invisible crowd, volume and tone increasing until she's holding very little back.

Kennedy glances over her shoulder to catch my eye, singing a line or two and singing only to me. The lyrics talk about her unforgettable love, the one she'll remember long after he's gone. Her focus moves back to her adoring, invisible fans, but I'm left breathless, barely hanging on to playing the notes long ago memorized.

I've been mediocre since I can remember. Always the last kid on the block invited to play, a good kid but never the teacher's favorite, and now everything with dad, I'm the forgettable son. It's been one of my greatest strengths in the work I do, something the FBI covets—my ability to move without anyone remembering I was there in the first place.

But Kennedy, Kennedy not only remembers me, she's memorized me. She won't forget me, another quick look from her assures me it's true. I don't know whether to be grateful, or afraid of the consequences.

* * *

Kennedy

Singing like this, it's like wearing a tailor-made dress. I've never felt something fit as perfectly as this song, this microphone in my hand, let alone this flawless moment. I roll through the bridge of the song, having fun with the melody and timing while Roman plays without fault. This is nothing like singing in the old auditorium. This feels real. This is sublime. My eyes adjust to the darkness. I try to imagine every seat full, every person leaning forward and hanging off my notes.

What a dream this is, to be able to perform without fear because Roman believes in me. Because he does, for some reason unbeknownst to me, a big-time music producer actually believes in me. It's enough to unshackle the chains holding me back, if only for a moment.

Unclipping the microphone, I stride the length of the stage, making eyes at people who don't exist. I'm lost in a world of pretend, where dreams come true, where I'm more than a talent scout, more than a stand-in mother for my brother, more than Kennedy Cartwright, the middle child. For a second, when Roman's eyes meet mine, I'm Kennedy Cartwright, the star.

The spotlight warms my skin. I close my eyes, stretching not only for the light as the music crescendos around me, but stretching my arms up toward the object of my innermost desires.

The spotlight.
The star.
The music.

The moment is drawing to a close. By my count I have maybe eight measures left to revel in this feeling. I open my eyes and stare into the darkness as I sing the last words.

Movement catches my eye near the doorway, two men hover in the doorway. I recognize Pedro. The other man mimes applause on my behalf. Pedro nods and says something to his companion. Roman rolls through the last of the notes. Pedro claps a hand to his companion's shoulder and disappears into the outer hallway.

"That was beautiful." Roman's voice catches my attention. I whirl to face him. "Do you want to do another one?"

My concern is for the men intruding on our moment and my fear of using the auditorium without permission. If Pedro's companion is somehow in charge of the building, I don't want Roman to get in trouble. But when I glance back, they're gone. I strain to be sure, squinting into the darkness.

"Are you okay?" Roman rises from the bench. "Did you see someone?"

"I don't know." I'm not sure now. I swear they were there, but my mind could have been playing tricks on me. I saw Pedro in the ballroom before, it's believable that I'd imagine him, I suppose.

Roman follows my stare into the darkness. The last thing I want is to go back to how he acted in the ballroom. I cut the distance but keep the piano between us while I set a hand on his arm. It steals his focus entirely.

"It's fine. I'm sure it was nothing."

The air stills. His hand captures mine. The piano bench grates against the floor as he stands because he needs to be closer. Roman's arm curves around my waist, as if we're dancing again, but there's no music, no reason to stand this close.

"Just when I thought you couldn't get any more perfect, you exceed expectations." Roman stares down at me as if trying to memorize this moment.

"I sincerely doubt that. I'm lucky to reach expectations."

He's not willing to let me brush it away, not this time.

"Why do you do that?" Roman takes another step until I feel his warmth against my bare arm. "You never let me compliment you."

"You wanted this to be professional."

"You're doing it again."

"I'm following your rules, Mr. Palermo."

"I think we're past my rules, Miss Cartwright." As if pulled by magnets, he's edging closer. "Answer me."

His breathy whisper sends chills down my spine. I don't want to answer him. There are a dozen things I'd rather do, and none of them have to do with talking. But he's not going to give me what I want until I answer his question.

"I'm not the star," I tell him. "I fade into the background. I'm the glue, but Hudson, Victoria, they've always shone brighter than I do. Compliments come when people *notice* me," I laugh without mirth, "like they feel bad I was there all along, and now they need to make up for it with some gallant gesture. It makes me doubt the sincerity of it all."

"You think I'm lying when I tell you you're beautiful?"

"I think you're a nice guy." My wandering fingers curl around the back of his neck where his hair is cut short and prickly. His eyes fall closed for a second before they reawaken with desire. "Maybe you just feel bad for me, forgotten daughter, running the ranch, playing at mom, needing a compliment or two."

"You're wrong. I feel a lot for you, Kennedy, but none of it is bad." His lips part, before he draws in a quick breath. With renewed conviction, he stares into my eyes. "Believe me, I'm not lying when I tell you how incredibly talented you are, but even that pales in comparison to your beauty."

I look away, but his palm catches my chin to bring me back. A sneaky grin creeps up his cheeks.

"This is the part where you say, 'Thank you, Roman'."

He has no idea how hard it is to repeat it, but hoping to appease him I say, "Thank you, Roman."

"Good." The playful smile sinks too fast, a hint that he's likely going to put the brakes on everything again. "Kennedy, I need to tell you something about me."

"What is it?"

I wonder if he's struggling as hard as I am to keep from kissing. With only nine inches between us, I wager it'd take less than two seconds before I make it zero. His gaze drops to my lips, his shoulders slump, and he leans closer still.

A scream splits the air. Roman's grip changes, whirling me back to stand behind him. Two shots cut through the building.

"Back here," Roman urges me through the velvet curtains, "keep your head down. There's a room on the right."

More shots ring out. My head swims with adrenaline and questions.

"Straight ahead." Roman pushes me again. I fumble with the knob. Screaming wails like sirens, more voices than I can count. More gunshots echo and respond.

"Is this a terrorist attack?"

Roman doesn't grant me an answer. Not because he doesn't have one, but because he isn't there. He left me. I spin in the room, searching the empty space, hopeful that he's hiding somewhere, or I've missed him. I start for the light of the auditorium, but the spotlight dies an instant later. Six rapid shots in the distance shatter my psyche. I reverse, slamming into the back wall of the room, sinking to my knees. Tears fall over my palms where I've smashed them against my face.

Pounding feet charge the halls, like cattle in a stampede. Voices shout and call to each other.

"You got him?"

"No! Clear this hall."

With no way to know whether they're friend or foe, I tuck my knees into my chest and cling to sanity. A cry of alarm catches my ears, closer this time. Someone is outside the room, and it's not Roman.

✳ ✳ ✳

Roman

I took too long cutting the power to the spotlight. I'm kicking myself for keeping her in the building. Should have known the bust would go south. They probably went to apprehend Pedro and he fought back. I had to desert her in that room to cut the light. Leaving it on would have attracted attention like bugs to a candle.

Never should have brought her.

Let alone wrapped my arms around her.

Or considered telling her who I really am, or how desperately I need her.

The auditorium's new darkness veils my movements. My hearing sharpens without my sight. I'm careful not to add to the silence with my own sounds. Four feet to my left, on the stage, I sense movement, too heavy to be Kennedy shuffling around. Breaking into a dead run, I plow into the second figure. Pain lights up my head as his gun cracks against my temple. I drive my fist into his gut, rewarded by the soft cushion of his exhale. I draw back an elbow and slam it against his jaw. A deep groan eases from his body.

My eyes adjust to the darkness, but I'm sure I'm not the only one. His fist is a shadowy blur, catching my cheek, knocking me back a step. I block a kick to my stomach and twist his leg until he falls. Sweat drips between my eyes, or maybe blood, I can't be sure. I swipe at the annoyance and wait for the next attack. The drive to protect Kennedy at all costs awakens the agent within me.

A bar swings faster than I can block, catching me hard between the shoulder blades. I fall forward, but reach back, wrapping my arm around the length of the microphone stand. I jerk it free and swing the base like a bat, connecting with a sick crack. My attacker falls with a grunt, but he's not getting up for a second round.

I stumble forward a step, clutching my knees to keep my head from spinning out of control. Metallic tang of blood in my mouth lights up my senses. It's been a while since I had to fight like this. I steel my whirling stomach, trying to shake the pain from my hands at the same time.

Her whimper catches my ear like a plea for help. Regret yanks on my conscience for what I've exposed her to. It's my fault she's here, my fault she's afraid and my fault she's in danger. I catch my hand on the doorway for support. From the dark, her gasp cuts the silence in half.

"It's me." I try to regulate my voice to hide the pain I'm feeling because it'll only frighten her more. "I turned off the light so no one would look for us here."

"Roman, I'm scared," she whispers.

Rick's crazy to have ever suspected she could be involved in criminal activities. I doubt she likes saying the word criminal, for fear of what bad mojo she might call upon herself.

I pull the door shut until it clicks in place. Using the light of my phone, I scan the room. Balled up in the corner, arms locked around her legs, Kennedy cowers. I cut the light and slide in next to her, arms capturing her body against mine.

"Are you hurt?"

"No," her breath brushes over my collarbone. "Frightened. What's going on?"

"I don't know," I lie. "But I won't let anyone hurt you. I promise."

She tightens her grip on my shirt, tugging until we're nearly melded into one. I doubt she can hear the gunshots like I can through the closed door. My trained ear knows the difference between government issue and otherwise. But it doesn't matter. None of that tells me the score. It doesn't change the fact that I've put her in danger with no way of knowing when it will end.

For five minutes, the air is still. No gunshots. No screaming. My phone buzzes from the floor. I snatch it up.

"Where are you? Did you make it out?"

"It's Rick," I tell her, hoping a familiar name might soothe her. "He's making sure we're okay."

She twists to see the screen, but I keep it out of sight for her safety as I type. *"Locked in a room off the auditorium. I left a body out there. Take care of it."*

"Is he okay?" Kennedy asks. "Is it over?"

"I think so, but let's stay a little longer to be sure."

I don't have to ask her twice. She's not made for this kind of living. Her heart races against my chest. I press my hand between her shoulder blades, pulling her closer, wishing I could take away the fear I've caused. Kennedy melts against me, accepting my comfort and taking what she needs. Her body conforms to mine, wrapping tight, her face tucked into the crook of my neck, lips against my skin.

Heat rises in my chest. I turn into her, unable to stop myself. I press my lips to her forehead, once, then once more. She peels back. The light from my phone catches the contours of her face. I don't think I could have worse timing if I tried. But my self-control failed ten minutes ago, and every trap door to my good sense has latched shut.

My lips touch hers, exquisite beyond my imagination. Eager for more, I kiss her again, lifting her up to where I can chase her worries away with affection. My worst fear would be Kennedy pulling away, telling me no, or giving me a reason to stop, but she's miles from that. She meets my kiss as if she's been waiting on me, desperate like I am to explore what we've been denying. Her fingers wrap around the back of my neck once more, and I bow to her wishes.

✽ ✽ ✽

Kennedy

I could blame it on the thrill of our escape, or on the relief of surviving, but this is more than that. Maybe it's one of those times people talk about, a brush with death forcing them to take inventory and do everything they might regret. I shift and steal his bottom lip between mine, knowing I'd regret dying without it. Maybe it's enough, maybe a terrorist attack like this will help him see that age is a stupid reason to keep us apart. I might not get the record deal I want; conflict of interest has to be drawn when you've crossed these lines, but that's not what I was looking for anyway.

This, this fire churning in my chest, exploding through my fingertips. This is better than singing, and I didn't think that was possible. Roman pulls back, but only far enough for our lips to break. His chest rises and falls against me. I push my hands over his chest, relishing the firm build and chiseled muscles. I mean to pull his jacket from his shoulders, but before I can explore the breadth of his chest, Roman's hands catch mine to stop me.

"Kennedy, I'm sorry. I started this and you shouldn't—"

"Shut up." I press my lips to his, expecting resistance, but find only acceptance. "You can't tell me what to do. I'm an adult."

"Barely." I feel his teasing smile against my cheek before he kisses me again. "Your dad hates this."

"He'll get over it."

"You don't know me. You don't know what you're taking on. I don't want to make your life difficult."

"Then stop arguing with me."

I'm about to kiss him again but sounds outside our door still my breath. Voices, muffled words, but clear male voices, shout commands. Roman's leg bends, taking the weight into his heel, as if he might stand. I curl my legs behind me. Roman pulls away from me, easing into a crouched position. My frame cowers in his shadow. The door rattles again. My heart thumps in my ears. Roman reaches beneath his jacket. The door rips open and light floods the small room.

"Stand down!" A familiar voice yells. "The area is secure. All clear."

Roman rises to his feet, arms falling to his sides. The men pull him outside the room. I want to follow him, but my legs won't respond. Voices fuzz in and out in my mind, hushed, secretive, and disconnected from their bodies.

"The target?"

"In the wind, and aware of our threat."

"Did we gain anything?"

"Not a thing."

I keep my head down, too shocked to fully register what's happening. I have to be imagining things. The voices continue, but I brace my fingers against the floor to stop the spinning. What have I stepped into? Did I hear them right? I could be hallucinating.

Roman's hand stretches down to me, pulling me to my unsteady feet. He grips my elbow to grant me balance. I can't look at him, not while I'm feeling this way.

"Rick needs me to stay and help clean up, deal with the authorities. He's calling you a cab."

His voice fuzzes and fades as if he's talking from underwater. I can't trust my ears. That's all this is. Adrenaline induced hysteria. I'm not hearing anything right. I nod because he won't look away, and I need him to look away right now.

Air.

I need air. I stumble forward toward the door, but on the third step my leg goes out from beneath me. Roman's arms catch me before I hit the floor. I look away, hoping to keep a grasp on my sanity, but in my search for a safe house for my sight, I spot it.

A gun tucked into a holster beneath Roman's jacket.

CHAPTER 13

Kennedy

My dress cuts the bedspread in half. It hasn't stopped whispering secrets since the cab dropped me off twenty minutes ago. The dress knows what happened tonight. The dress was there when I saw his gun, and it won't shut up. The secrets are in my head, more like anxieties and questions with no answers.

Why did he have a gun?
Why isn't anyone talking about a terrorist attack?
Do I tell anyone, or keep it to myself?

I don't have any answers, just more questions. All I want to do is forget it ever happened. But the dress was there, it saw everything, and I stripped it from my body the second I walked through my bedroom door.

Flannel. Flannel doesn't get involved in gunfights, or people screaming. Flannel pajamas are soft and cozy and stay home where it's safe.

I can't unsee it, the gun beneath his jacket. Every time I close my eyes, that's all I see, as if my mind is demanding an answer for the inconsistency. I roll the memory like an old school VHS in my mind.

It's hard not to get swept away in the thrill, the excitement of our passionate moment. I ran my hands over his chest. I must have been inches from feeling the hilt of his weapon when he snatched my hand away.

Three knocks at my door slam my heart into overdrive. My eyes snap open, searching out the threat, but Hudson has never been dangerous.

"How was your date?" He leans against the doorframe, eyebrows elevated, but I swear there's more there than a nosey younger brother.

"Fine, I guess."

"Cab took you home?"

Nosey is right, but his room faces the driveway, so I shouldn't be surprised.

"Something happened." I hesitate because if I say it, it might be real. "Roman had to stay and help with the cleanup."

"Someone get drunk and fall in the punchbowl?" Hudson enters, knowing he doesn't need permission, and sits square on the center of my dress. Serves it right for whispering things to me.

"Not exactly. I think it was a terrorist attack, or something."

Hudson mouth falls open. "Kenny, are you okay? Are you hurt?"

He should be more surprised, instead I swear he was expecting this, as if this were the reason he came to my room.

"I'm fine. Roman and I weren't there, we'd gone off to—" I stop when Hudson's left eyebrow cocks in surprise. "What?"

A grin quirks at his cheek, "You went off with Roman? Alone?"

I roll my eyes at his immaturity. "It wasn't like that."

"What was it like?"

I'm losing control of the situation. "We got to the party, and I don't know maybe ten minutes into it, Roman acted weird and said he needed air. We left and walked through the hallways." Hudson is hanging off every word like I'm going to admit some horrible sin. "It wasn't romantic. He wanted to show me something."

"That's the oldest line in the book, Kenny." Hudson mimes putting his arm around a girl. "Hey, come on, I want to show you something, in this dark closet, oh what was that? We need to make out? Okay." Like a beast, he rubs his hands all over his invisible date. I shove him off the bed and only smile after he lands with a thump on the floor.

"It wasn't like that. He took me to the auditorium." I catch my lip between my teeth for a moment as I think about standing on the stage in the spotlight. "He wanted me to sing for him."

I expect something snarky from my younger brother, but out of everyone, he understands what music means to me.

"About the time I finished the song," I edit out the bits about Roman telling how beautiful I am, not to mention talented, "shots were fired in the ballroom. People started screaming and running. Roman took me back into this room and locked the door. I was so scared, Hudsie."

He waits a moment, considering his words with more caution than he normally employs. "But he kept you safe?"

"Yeah, I was surprised by how calm he was." I rub my hands over my face. "It was weird though. Have you heard anything about this on TV? It seems like it would make the news, don't you think? And was it coincidence that he took me away from the ballroom? Or did he know something?"

My brother won't look at me. He shrugs and sighs. "I don't know. That's wild."

"Huds," I wait until he looks up, "what if he's a criminal? What if he knew about it because he was part of it? I mean, I hear about shady deals in the music world, what if he's mafia or something? He's Italian after all."

"Not every Italian guy has ties to the mob. Some guys carry guns. Our florist keeps one in the vase by the display case for heaven's sake." Maybe I don't look convinced because he presses it farther. "Do *you* think he's a criminal?"

The memory of Roman's touch lights up my senses. Soft, gentle, careful and cautious, it doesn't feel like he's a bad guy.

"I don't know. All I know is it doesn't add up. Maybe I shouldn't see him again."

Hudson gathers his legs underneath him and moves to stand. "Do you like him?"

I hate to admit it, but the evidence is stacking against me.

"Yeah, I really do."

He's never been one to give me advice, and he's not starting now.

"You'll figure it out." He pauses in the doorway. "But be careful, Kenny."

He's about to leave when I call his name. "Hey, how'd your date with Jill go?"

There's no willpower strong enough to keep the smile from his face. "Really well. We went to the movie, and then I drove her out to the pond by Fletcher's place."

"Hudson! What would possess you to do something like that?"

He smirks. "Well you know, I just wanted to show her something."

I grip the pillow in my hand, but he's gone before I can launch it. It falls to the floor with a thump. I draw in a breath, happy for a moment of distraction. But the dress calls my attention again, and the only recourse is to turn out the light and try to put an end to a long, confusing day.

❊ ❊ ❊

Roman

I've been staring at her name in my phone for over an hour.

Kennedy Cartwright-Cartwright Ranch-Talent Scout

That's everything they gave me in her file. That and a small thumbnail of her driver's license picture. She needs a new one. It's too old. It doesn't capture the woman I know now. And certainly not the woman that took my breath away the first day she knocked on Santos Sound's door.

"Palermo," Rick shouts my name from the other side of the room, "Come look at this."

I rub my face with both palms, trying to shake off my exhaustion. Three am, still combing the building for any evidence and coming up empty. I stop by Rick's side where he's leaning over a laptop watching a surveillance.

"There." He taps the screen. "That's Dante. He was in the building tonight. Took the back entrance, I guess."

The scene shifts, and I note Pedro walking down a hallway. "Looks like Pedro was going to grab him. Maybe bring him in the back way."

"Did they meet up?"

The tech with the computer shrugs at Rick. "This security system has rotating shots. I get ten seconds from each camera, but no continual feed. The best we can do is watch it in the entirety and extrapolate what they did by the end."

Rick's jaw tightens with frustration. "Do it. Get a report within the hour. I need to know what went wrong." He nods his head toward the back wall, a signal that I should follow him. "We were careful. We backtracked and cleared everything. I don't understand what happened here."

"Sometimes things don't pan out, sir. You plan for everything and still come up short."

"Not me. Not this op." He's exhausted as well, maybe more so. No one knows who fired first. Rick said they were moving to take Pedro in for questioning, and gun shots fired around the ballroom. Dark Fox operatives had infiltrated the event. They worked as a distraction and Pedro snuck out in the firefight. Two agents were shot. Both in critical condition the last I heard. Keeping everything under wraps feels impossible at this point, but Rick has a tight grip on the story. No media. No response. I don't know what I'll say to Kennedy. If I see her again, that is. More importantly, if she wants to see me again.

"The bigger question is what do we do now? It's obvious Dante knows we're chasing him." Rick's mind is whirling, and it's rare that I end up on the winning side of these rants. "We need someone on the inside."

I put up my hands. "I can't. Number one, I'm not cleared for deep undercover work, number two, they know my face."

His annoyance glows in his eyes. "Number one, I've seen your file, Palermo. You're more ready than half the men I've worked with. You're more than cleared in my opinion. I've been talking to folks. Everyone agrees, it's about time you stop hiding with the techs and become the agent you were meant to be."

"I'm not hiding, sir." It's too early in the morning to consider whether my tone is respectful. "I do my job fine, and I keep the people around me safe because I'm not out there putting my life on the line."

"You mean like tonight? Your life was on the line, and you performed admirably."

"I put a civilian at risk, and for what?"

"You think she isn't at risk, already? Your girl is running in dangerous circles and has no idea who she's up against. She talked with Pedro like they're in the same book club. I'll give you that she's innocent, but she's naïve as well, and you know it could get her killed."

Why does he have to be right? Kennedy is at the center of the case, and yet like the eye of the hurricane, she's unaware of the danger swirling around her.

"She's not my girl," I say. "But even if you're right about me, I can't do anything this time. They know my face now. Even I can't get by with a repeat this close together."

"Your file says otherwise. But no, I don't want you on the inside this time, at least not yet."

Relief floods my veins. Diving deeper into this hornet's nest is only going to endanger Kennedy more. "Then who? Are you bringing in new agents?"

"Why do that when we've already got someone in place?"

"Someone in place—" The horrible truth dawns on me at once. "No, not Kennedy. I'm not bringing her in on this."

"Why not? They won't suspect her. They'll bring her in and trust her implicitly."

"Because she's a civilian. She's not made for this work. You saw her tonight. You saw the way she—" I stop short. Was I really going to talk about the way she clung to me? "Find another way."

Rick watches me as if I'm keeping secrets from him. He's the type to rip your soul from your body, hold it up to the light and show you every mistake and bad decision you've ever made.

"For now, we'll keep looking at other options. But I'm not writing her off."

He turns on his heel and moves back to the tech with the laptop.

I look at my phone again. Her name is still there. I wish I could call and explain this mess to her. I wish I knew if she'll want to see me again, or if she finally realizes why I've been careful. She might want to walk away after something like this. I hang on to a shred of hope because I can't imagine walking away after a kiss like that.

✳ ✳ ✳

Kennedy

"I think it's going to be beautiful."

Tiffany smiles and gives her fiancé Ben a wink. After an hour and a half of drafting, her wedding is well on the way to being planned. I snap her binder shut and rise from my seat, relieved when they follow suit.

"I hate to rush you out, but I have another meeting in ten minutes."

It's mostly true. I have a phone call to make to the local florist because I have a bride with a specific rose she's looking for, not red, not burgundy, but scarlet. I spent an hour last week pouring over pictures trying to understand the difference between a red rose and a scarlet one. I still don't understand, but at least I have the rose's name. It's a start.

I close the glass doors on my office, sighing out my frustrations with my life. At least I've been busy, no time to think about Roman, or guns, or terrorists. I sink back into my chair, air wheezing out from the cushion. With a few seconds of downtime, that's precisely where my thoughts go. Back to his quick smile, careful hands and full lips. If only we could go reverse time, travel back to when our biggest stumbling block was our age gap.

My cell phone rings, jarring my senses back to the issues at hand. I wait through the second ring and pick it up in the pause.

"Cartwright Ranch, this is Kennedy."

"I was hoping I'd get you." The voice is familiar, but I don't place it at first. "This is Pedro Marquez from The Nightingale."

"Oh, hello Pedro. What can I do for you?"

"I was hoping you could help me out. I have a friend with a birthday coming up, and he wants live music."

"Of course, I'd love to help." I flip open my contact list binder. "What kind of music is he into? I know groups ranging everywhere from bluegrass to a funk band that plays in the city twice a week."

"That's the thing," Pedro's volume drops as if he's divulging a secret, "Dante isn't interested in any of that. He has his eye on one singer."

"Okay," my nerves pull tight. Pedro knows all the same players that I do, it's not like he couldn't call a singer up and ask them to perform. "Who is it?"

"You."

Involuntary laughter burbles out of my throat. "Me? That's a great joke, Pedro."

"Do I sound like I'm joking? He's only got eyes for you."

"That's silly. I don't sing in public. You know that."

"I told him too. He doesn't care. He heard you singing last night, and he's got a one-track mind. He told me whatever the cost, I had to make it happen."

"Wait last night? So that was you in the doorway. I thought I saw you."

"Drawn to beautiful music, I guess."

I bite my lip, considering my next words. "Were you there

when it all went down? The shooting and stuff? I didn't see any of it, but I heard everything."

"We left before it got hot." His tone turns stiff. I don't blame him. I don't want to talk about it either. "What do you say, Kennedy? It's a pretty intimate affair, and we're closing down Nightingale for the night. Will you come sing happy birthday and maybe a short set?"

My instincts tell me to turn him down, but if I close my eyes, I can still feel the spotlight on my skin. It's not a big deal. It sounds like an intimate affair. Booker told me I needed to practice to get over my nerves. I can't get the memory of singing in the spotlight from my mind. Isn't it time I chose my own path?

"Okay. I'll do it."

❋ ❋ ❋

Roman

"I hear you." I press the heels of my palms to my temples to stop the banging in my head, "I'm coming. I'm coming."

The knocks, more like bangs, at my apartment door are relentless. Each one echoes in my exhausted brain. Five more pounds before I jerk open the door. Sleep clouds my vision, but I strain, and he solidifies.

"Hudson?"

"Hey, Roman." Both his hands are curled into tight fists, safe to say he's talked with his sister.

"What are you doing here? How'd you know where I live?"

"Followed you last week, just in case. I had a couple questions to ask you, well, one really." His hand strikes, taking my shirt into his grip and retracting his opposite fist like he's planning to punch me. "Who are you?"

I shove him back. Easy enough since I outweigh him by a buck twenty. He stumbles, but never loses the fire in his eyes.

"She was shook last night, man. Straight shook. Tell me what's going on!"

Doors crack open down the hallway. I don't have the luxury of keeping the kid out in the open. I grab him by the back of his neck and yank him inside my apartment.

"Wanna keep your voice down? I don't need half the building knowing my business." I let my door fall shut before I lock it.

His stance changes once we're alone in a locked room. Much of the bravado is gone when he doesn't have witnesses.

"Who are you, really?" Hudson squares his shoulders like he's tough, but I remember being seventeen and thinking I could take on a guy twice my size. "Because you said you'd keep her safe and the story I got from her last night is totally different."

"She was safe. She wasn't hurt."

"That's a relative term, isn't it? Just to clarify, for any future adventures where you might feel like you should involve my sister, hiding in a closet from gunmen isn't safe."

"I didn't think it would go down like that."

"What did you think?" His eyes widen like I'm not hearing him. "Come on, man. I saw you packing heat."

"You realize no one talks like that, right?" I'm becoming sick of his learned-from-the-movies action talk.

"Well, educate me," Hudson says, "tell me how criminals like you actually speak."

"I'm not a criminal. I told you I was one of the good guys. You have to believe me."

"I don't have to believe anything. You tell me right now who you really are, or I'm going to tell Kennedy everything I know."

"You're blackmailing me?"

"I'm giving you a chance to explain yourself."

Once again, the little twerp has me up against the proverbial wall. Tell him and I compromise my cover. Don't tell him and Hudson will compromise my cover.

His steeled glare relaxes with a sigh. "I don't know what Kennedy told you about our family, but my mom died when I was a kid."

"Yeah, she mentioned it. That's a tough break."

"It really was," Hudson takes a few steps before he sinks onto my couch. "I don't remember much of her. A couple things here and there. But you know what I do remember?"

I take the chair diagonal from him, happy to be off my feet after a long night. Even happier that this kid is willing to talk, and I don't have to leave him a walking bruise.

"What's that?"

"I remember Kennedy reading me books at night when I couldn't fall asleep. I remember Kennedy taking me to little league try outs, and then when that didn't pan out, she took me to my first dance class and threatened to beat up any kid who made fun of me. I remember Kennedy folding my laundry and checking my homework. She helped me make my volcano in sixth grade. She skipped her junior prom to sit front row at my dance recital." Hudson catches my eye. "Kennedy has given up way too much for me to stand by and let some fool take advantage of her. Tell me who you are. Tell me why I shouldn't tell my sister to stay away from you."

I knew she was important, but I never would have guessed this level of attachment. I size him up, hopeful my instincts aren't leading me down a dangerous path.

"I work with the FBI. I'm a trained agent, but for the most part I stay with the computers."

If I was expecting a gasp or some sign of shock, it's not there.

"What was last night about? I know it wasn't really a fundraiser."

"Big bosses wanted to take some guys in. It didn't pan out."

"Why take Kennedy then? If you know there was going to be trouble, why involve her at all?"

"My boss wanted to meet her."

"Why?"

Kid has a future in interrogation.

"Your sister is mixed up with some dangerous people. She's clean. Close as we can tell, your dad is clean too."

"You're investigating my family?"

I'm too tired to deal with any of this. I sigh, rubbing my temples to keep the pending headache away.

"I'm investigating and your family keeps crossing my path." I lean forward, resting my elbows on my knees. "Hudson, you can't say anything to anyone. I'm undercover. We've got a big cat by the tail, and it's tenuous at best."

He nods, but I can tell he's thinking his way around it. Finally, he asks the hardest question.

"Do you like her? Are you actually interested, or is it just the investigation?"

I know what I should say. I should tell him it's all part of my cover. I had to get close to get the information I needed. But that would be a lie.

"I can't stop thinking about her. When I'm around her, everything else shuts off. She's all I see, and that's dangerous in my line of work. I don't know what to do." It's a relief to say it all out loud. I feel like my deep attraction for her is a bigger secret than my cover or my career. Telling someone, even if he's a teenage boy, makes it all real, solidifies my feelings in my mind. I can't escape her.

His shoulders lift as if he's shrugging a bit. "You want to be with her? Have a relationship?"

"That feels miles away right now. Our ages aren't ideal. I have to close this case before I can—"

"No, that's not what I asked. I asked if you want a relationship with Kennedy. That's a yes or no."

She's there in him. Traces of her personality have etched on her brother, evidence of what she's sacrificed to raise him.

"Yeah, but I don't know where to start."

Hudson draws in a breath and pushes to his feet. "She likes Mexican food. Eats the spicy stuff even though she has a terrible tolerance. I always order her milk when we go out because, without fail, she's fanning her mouth after the first bite of salsa." Hudson smiles at his next thought. "She hates chocolate, but thinks it's shameful, so she eats it anyway. She prefers strawberry. And she likes ice cream better than cake. She thinks frozen yogurt is an abomination, but she'd never admit it."

I stop him short, unsure of what's happening. "Why are you telling me this?"

"I'm giving you a hand up. These are her deepest secrets, stuff it takes people years to find out, and I'm handing it to you on a silver platter."

Without waiting for permission, he continues.

"She doesn't like roses because of all the weddings she does. She likes sunflowers. Brides never want those." He counts the next pieces off on his fingers. "She likes dogs, but not little ones. She likes cats, but not furry ones. She picks tomatoes out of salads but eats them on burgers. She blasts the AC until it's arctic temperatures, but if you turn it off, she won't say a word. Her favorite color is black, but she thinks it makes her evil, so she tells people she loves light pink. She spends all her time worrying about what people think of her, and whether she's doing enough. She'll never feel like she's enough, no matter how many times we assure her that she is."

I should have written it all down.

"It's all great information, Hudson, but—"

He starts for the door, our business finished. "Ask her out. Do something normal. Don't take your guns."

I rise to my feet, and the action stops him near the door.

"Knowing what you know, you're still okay with me taking her out?" I ask.

"Not really," Hudson says, turning the knob. "But she likes you, and that's hard to ignore."

CHAPTER 14

Roman

Sunflowers are impossible to find. After three florists, I consider myself struck out by the opposing team. Empty-handed, I walk the path to the cottage next to the barn, the one marked office, the place Hudson said I could find her. I stop outside the door, wondering for the thirtieth time if I should have called, but dad always said it's hard to turn a guy down face to face.

I twist the knob and step into the cottage. Cool air wraps around me, reminding me of what Hudson said earlier about his sister blasting the AC. She's sitting with a couple, leaning over a magazine, pointing to various arrangements of flowers. She's wearing a skirt again. I love that she wears them. I've always loved a girl who acts like a girl. It clings to her figure, dark blue and professional, hitting below her knee.

"Can I help you?"

Her voice brings my head around, completely unaware that I wasn't alone.

"I was hoping to meet with Kennedy."

Kennedy's sister, Victoria, dries her hands on a towel while sizing me up. "Do you have an appointment?"

"No," I rub the back of neck with an open palm, "I was hoping she could squeeze me in."

Victoria's eyebrows jut up in question. "Pretty presumptuous, don't you think?"

I let out a nervous laugh, unsure of how to deal with her. "I can come back if I need to."

She looks a lot like Kennedy, same auburn tone to her hair, same length to nearly her waist, but where Kennedy's face is soft, feminine and gentle, Victoria's is sharp, angular, and she resembles her father. Every second that passes, I feel her scrutiny sizing me up and forever finding me wanting. What is it with this family that they can reduce me to nothing, despite years of training?

"You here to ask her out?"

I grin, but it's all nerves. "Is it that obvious?"

"Oh, honey," she hefts a pan full of sloshing liquid into the oven, "it's written all over your face. Has been since day one."

"And you're cool with it?"

She laughs, but never turns around. "Talking to the wrong girl about that. Pretty sure Kenny's opinion is the only one that matters." She closes the oven with a hip. "But dad sure had an earful for me."

My stomach churns, and I might as well be fifteen waiting to pick up a date with her dad sitting on the couch cleaning a shotgun.

"Breathe," Victoria says, "he's up at the house. No one has to know you're here. In fact, I have to get over to the neighbor's house for some fruit, this couple is wrapping up, and I won't be back until that cake is done." With purpose, she enters the time on the oven. Like a bomb, the screen displays: 40:00.

"What about her next appointment?"

"Nothing on the books the rest of the day." As if the thought occurs to her, she pulls out her phone and taps the screen a few times. "There. Now you're her four o'clock appointment. Good luck." She winks once before she leaves.

If I'm calling favorites on her siblings, Victoria is certainly in the lead. She didn't even threaten to hit me. The knob jiggles and the doors swing open to Kennedy's office.

"I'll check into the food for you, but I don't see any problem with tarts for appetizers. We've done a dessert-based menu before." Kennedy looks to the kitchen, surely expecting her sister, but in her sweep of the room, all she finds is me. "I'll have to get back to you on them. Victoria has stepped out."

The bride-to-be says a few more words about her needs and dietary restrictions, but I'm not listening because I'm distracted by Kennedy Cartwright. The way she moves. The smile on her cheeks. The light in her eyes. Even the sound of her reassuring tone has me spellbound.

"Take care," catches my ears. Kennedy ushers them out the door and onto the path that leads back to the parking lot. She turns back to me, all smiles. "What did I do to deserve this surprise?"

She relegates me to an oafish teenager, scared to say the wrong thing to the most beautiful girl I've ever seen.

"I wanted to check on you, make sure you were okay."

There's weight behind that smile of hers, not nearly as carefree as it has been in the past. Mentioning everything from last night anchors it further.

"It was scary, and strange, and I can't find mention of it on any news. Not radio, not the internet, nothing. It's odd." When I don't respond to her unasked question, she pushes it further. "Isn't that odd?"

Knowing Rick, it's not odd. He has a way of shutting down the media.

"Maybe they don't want people to worry."

"But you know, don't you? Didn't they tell you something?"

I keep telling myself I'm lying to keep her safe. But is there a limit? Is there a point where I'm over the line? Unforgiveable?

"Authorities said it was rival gang fight. The event got caught up in a turf war. They're keeping it out of the news to discourage it from gaining attention and inciting more incidents."

I wait on her reaction. Whether she bought it or not, I can't tell, but I've done nothing to bring back her smile.

"I don't understand this world sometimes." Her mood falls to a flat line. "Why are you really here, Roman?"

I have nothing left but the truth.

"I wanted to ask you out, on a real date."

"Just the two of us?"

Gathering up my courage, I take a step toward her. "Just the two of us. I thought we'd try this Mexican place near my apartment, Miguel's."

"I love Miguel's. They have the best *sopapillas*." The tension between us starts to melt.

"Maybe some ice cream after. There's a shop near there with a homemade strawberry topping from a local farmer."

The brightness returns to her eyes, like watching a dying fire spark again. Hope surges in my heart that we have a chance despite everything working against us.

"Yeah, Scoopers. It's to die for. Have you had it?"

"Not yet. I've seen the sign."

She closes the space between us by taking my hand in hers. "Oh, I have to be there when you try it the first time. It's positively sinful."

Though forward, I switch my grip so I can run my thumb over her hand. "I can't wait."

Her eyes dart back to my lips for a second, and I choke on my heartbeat. Through dark lashes, she glances up at me. "Are we going to talk about it at all?"

Her words demand my focus, but her mouth is louder and distracting.

"Talk about what?"

"The kiss?"

"Which one?"

"All of them."

"Do you want to talk about them?"

"Actually, I'd kinda like to try it again."

Without waiting for a response, Kennedy closes the gap completely. Her lips wrap around mine and my brain goes to jelly. I drop her hand to take her waist, pulling until she's tight in my arms. She stretches on tip toe to deepen the kiss. Reason takes hold before I find myself lost in her affection. I break the kiss and draw in a breath to ease the burning in my lungs.

"Even better than last time." She's close enough that she bumps against me while speaking. "When do you want to go out?"

She expects coherent sentences after a moment like that? Laughable. I tuck the loose strands of her hair behind her ear, waiting for my breathing to normalize.

"Friday?"

Her teeth catch her lip. "I can't. I have something going on."

"Wedding?"

"No, that's Saturday."

My heart hits the bricks. I step back, willing it not to be true.

"Are you seeing someone else?"

She laughs and grabs my arm to pull me close. "Nothing like that."

I'm trying to take solace in the fact that she's dying to be close to me, but her secrecy grates on me.

"Then, what's going on?"

Her mouth opens but hardly a sound comes out at first. "I'm singing at a private party."

"Really?" My heart soars for her good fortune. In all my enthusiasm, I kiss her square on the lips. Her body bends and gives way to my touch like a reed in the river, perfectly happy to be mine. I break the kiss, smiling like a mirror to her excitement. "Where? How'd this happen?"

She wanders away from me, still lost in the thrill of it all. "I don't know. I'm freaking out about it, but he asked so nicely, and the birthday boy has already heard me sing, I guess." She whirls back. "He was there last night, Pedro. He was passing by the auditorium with his friend, Dante, and heard me singing to you. I guess he's got a bug in his bonnet wanting me to sing for his party."

If a rattlesnake popped out from behind the kitchen cabinet and struck me, I couldn't be any more stunned than I am right now.

"Pedro Marquez, from The Nightingale?"

"Yeah, you know him?"

"I know *of* him, not personally though." My worlds are colliding, and it's worse than a big bang. "Are you sure you want to do it?"

She draws her chin in. "You don't think I can?"

"I know you can, that's not the point."

"Why don't you want me to sing?"

"I want you to sing, I just don't know if that's the best venue."

Anger flashes in her beautiful eyes. "I know *The Nightingale*. I'm comfortable there. I think it's the best possible venue I can hope for in this instance."

I start to speak but swallow my words. There's no way to explain that it's not her, and it's not the venue, but it's the men hiring her causing my distress.

"I thought you'd be happy for me." Her smile sinks into a strained frown. "Out of everyone I figured you'd be happy—"

"I am happy," I say before she can jump off that cliff. "But, I guess, I'm jealous."

"Of Pedro?" Her voice tips up on the end to tell me how crazy I sound. "Trust me, there's nothing there. I barely know the guy."

Quick thinking is part of my job, like tap dancing across a swamp of crocodiles. "I'm jealous because they get to hear you, and if it's a private party, I'll have to miss out on your first live performance."

The last crocodile snaps behind me as her smile spreads. "Really? You want to come?"

"I wouldn't miss it for the world," I say, but my stomach flips.

"You could play for me. He wants the old feel like a twenties movie, gangsters and flappers and all that." Mischief creeps behind her eyes. "It means we'd have to practice all week to get ready." She walks her fingers up my chest, unaware of the torment wracking my psyche for what I'm planning. "That means a lot of time together."

"There's a piano at Santos Sound. Meet me there tomorrow?"

She leans up to my kiss, but my heart is burning with guilt for my duplicity. I make it quick, unable to lose myself like before.

"Until tomorrow," I whisper before I turn to leave.

I pass Victoria on the path, avoid her knowing glare, and wait until I'm sure she's inside the cottage before I call Rick.

"I've got our way back in," I tell him.

There's a special place full of fire and brimstone for people like me. I've told myself I've stayed close to her to keep her safe, but this proves otherwise. Not only am I unwilling to let her go, I'm dragging her into a lion's den without apprising her of the dangers. Yes, she's in trouble. Yes, she's too close to everything. Yes, she can make a difference in this case, but at what cost? Doing something wrong for the right reasons is still wrong. My fate is sealed. She'll never forgive me if she finds out what I've done. I only hope for another taste of heaven before I'm sent packing.

CHAPTER 15

Roman

"I'm serious, she'll be here any second. You have to get out." I shove the last analyst into the hallway and pull the door closed. With Kennedy set to arrive for our first rehearsal at Santos Sound, it's not like I can have an FBI presence around and still maintain my cover. It's bad enough the analysts are working in the back rooms.

I asked permission to tell her, let her in on what's really happening. Rick denied the request. He's afraid she'll give us away. While I understand, I'm sick of lying to her. I hate that I'm using her connections without her knowledge. It's another nail in the coffin trying to doom our relationship.

Who am I kidding? What relationship? I pull her close just to push her away. I'm sure she's beyond confused at this point. If only she knew why I acted the way I have.

Her light knock catches my ears. I give a hasty glance around the kitchen and dining room before I cross the living room to let her in. The plan is to stay within those three rooms. If she opens a closet, exits to the recording studio, or heaven forbid, opens the double doors to Dale's office, she'll know something is up. Clean up after a few agents, sure. Hide a full-fledged criminal investigation, not exactly possible.

I pull open the door, flashing back to that first morning she showed up. I can't help but stand in awe. She's left her hair down, added curl to the ends, done something to make her eyes bigger. Looking at her, I'd never guess her age, not because she disguises it, but because she carries herself far beyond her years. I'd never feel this level of attraction for her if not for her maturity. I've spent the last month dealing with my mother shoving women in my path, but Kennedy is the first one to catch my attention and hold it.

"Come on in." I swing the door wide, letting her enter. Her perfume snags me by the nose, almost yanking me along behind her. This is all for a cover. I need to remember that. If I forget, if I lose myself to the moment, if my attention wavers during the op, Kennedy could pay the price. Her life depends on me remembering that.

"I brought some music, a few songs I thought might fit the theme." There's a tremor in her voice when she talks about the party. Her nerves are getting the best of her, obviously I can't tell her what's really happening. She'd choke on stage.

"Let's run through them." Taking the sheet music, I cross the floor to the piano and prop open the top while Kennedy looks around Dale's living room.

"I've never been in here. Weird Dale's still gone. Have you heard anything?"

I clear my throat, hoping she can't hear my deception. "Not really." I pat the piano bench beside me. "Have a seat."

She comes my way, but ignores my invitation, instead standing by the open piano, drumming her fingers over the top. Kennedy makes no motion to tell me to start, but considering her nerves over singing, she might never give me the go ahead.

I set my fingers to the keys, sight reading the best I can. Five measures coast by, on the sixth she should join in. I draw the final notes out to cue her, but her lips clamp shut. Shaking her head, Kennedy backs away, headed for the door.

Quick on my feet, I take hold of her arm, stopping her before she makes her hasty exit. "Hey, it's okay. Let's take it slower." She won't look at me, so I catch her chin and lift until she looks into my eyes. I'm lost in a sea of emerald beauty before I remember I should speak. "What's going on in that head of yours when the stage fright takes over?"

She shrugs, shaking me off. "Too much. It's too much going on, and I can't fight through it. I don't know why I agreed to sing at this party, Rome."

"I do." I keep my hands to myself, allowing her space to wander and find her courage. "You love singing. You're good at it. You want this more than anything in the world. But something is holding you back."

I might as well be talking about how I feel about Kennedy. It's everything in me to keep from taking her in my arms and showing her how I really feel. These stolen moments we've had aren't enough. I want to be a part of her life. I want to be the one she relies on, the one she turns to. I want to be *hers.*

She wanders to the far side of the room, inching closer to the double doors that close off Dale's office. "It's fear of failure. It's an inability to imagine myself as anything more than Hudson's stand-in mom, or the event coordinator at the ranch, or the middle child who's been carrying everything for so long. I worry about making it. I worry about not making it."

She strides even closer to the doors as if they're calling to her. I trail behind, not sure if I'll be able to explain away what she might see if she pulls them open.

"As much as my family relies on me, sometimes I wonder if they even see me. The real me. I feel like they have no clue who I really am, or what I really want."

I'm tempted to let her in on the long list Hudson gave me, just to prove they see her, but that's not what she means. She means the parts of her she hides away. Those moments we've shared where she opens up. Even then, it wasn't me who helped her shine through, it was the music. Music is the key to her heart.

"I understand that." I close the space between us to only a few feet. Her hand rests on one of the knobs, but she isn't turning it. "Most of my life I've been unremarkable. Forgettable. Just another face in the crowd. I doubt my family knows me, not really. I don't open up to many people."

She hesitates, running her thumb over the smooth metal of the knob. "I can't believe that. I could pick your face out of any crowd. You're absolutely remarkable."

"To you." I slip my arm around her waist. I wish I could say it's about wanting to keep her from twisting the knob, but it's all about wanting her near me. "You see me, Kennedy, in a way no one ever has. You make me believe I can do anything, be anyone, as long as you believe in me."

She drops her grip on the knob, turning to look up at me. "You can. You're amazing, Roman. I've never met anyone like you."

Now it's my voice showing the nerves, betraying just how much she gets to me. "Let me do the same for you. Music opens you up. When you sing, your heart shines brighter than the music. Let me help you show who you really are. Because I believe in you."

I take her by the hand and lead her back to the piano. She takes the seat beside me, more relaxed, comfortable, and ready. I ease through the opening measures. She follows the music, a slight sway in her body. I slow for the final notes, and this time, she doesn't back down.

Her voice fills the room, blends with the music, and winds around my heart. The tempo, the timing, every time she sings, I swear the music belongs to her. Warmth rises in my chest, feeling the pride of knowing someone as perfect as Kennedy Cartwright. She follows my cues, plays with the notes, but respects the melody. The song wraps around us, pulling us closer. Every moment I spend with her, it becomes clearer. She's everything I've ever looked for. She's what I've always wanted. When her eyes meet mine at the end of the song, I know, I'll never find someone better.

❋ ❋ ❋

Kennedy

He talks about how I make him better, but the honest truth is I've never sounded as good as I do when I sing for him. Knowing how much he cares; it gives me the confidence to shake my fears aside and fight for what I want. A career under the spotlight has always called for me, but here, beside him, wrapped up in the music, I'm rethinking my goals. Why live in the spotlight when I could shine in his light? Why reach for the stars when I could reach for his arms? I've been fine on my own, not really missing the romantic side of life, until now. Now Roman has me wondering if it could be better, if life could be more, with him.

Not that it matters. He's obviously still keeping me at arm's length because of my age. He still hasn't opened up, not really. He's given me glimpses into his thoughts and feelings, but nothing that lasts. I feel like he's on the verge, just about to take the leap, but still something holds him back.

We run through five more songs, once or twice apiece until I'm comfortable. Every time my nerves start to get the better of me, Roman nudges me with his shoulder or shoots me a goofy face to throw me off. He's everything I never knew I wanted. The last song winds down, and I find myself wishing time would stop ticking for a few minutes.

The vibration of the music tingles through my bones, edging off to a soft hum. I close my eyes, relishing the way I feel. I could sink into this moment and stay, happy for the rest of my life.

"Can I keep you forever?"

Roman's head snaps to face me. "What?"

Color rises to my cheeks. I hide my face away in my hands, embarrassed that I blurted it out. "I'm sorry, I didn't mean anything by it. It's just," my voice echoes in my cupped hands, "this has been so perfect. It has to be because of you."

Roman peels my hands away from my face, watching me with an amused expression. "You can keep me as long as you want, Kennedy."

"I'm glad you're gonna be at the party with me." He keeps my hands in his, and I make no move to pull them away. "I don't think I could do it without you."

"I wouldn't miss it." Roman's thumb brushes over my hand, sending thrills through my gut. The sincerity in his eyes means more to me than any other compliment. But there's more there. Worry, concern, secrets he won't tell me. I still don't know what happened at the fundraiser but being close to him makes me think it doesn't matter. Before he can go cold on me, I brave the subject that's built a wall between us.

"Roman, why is our age gap so hard on you? It doesn't bother me. I don't understand why we can't—" I stop short, feeling his discomfort rise.

He drops my hands, turning back to the piano. His fingers find the keys, playing a melody that isn't on the sheet music. "I know. It probably looks old-fashioned, the way I feel. But I do have my reasons."

I ease my hand over his back, rubbing away the tension between his shoulder blades. "Will you tell me? Help me understand?"

Roman's fingers dance across the keys, more graceful than even Hudson in the studio. I close my eyes and sink into the notes. Music has always been my fondest friend. It makes sense that he has the same love.

"My younger brother, Sebastian, he's opposite of me. Great with women, everyone adores him. He's the star of the show. Always has someone on his arm." The song's tempo increases, then a key change, the soft notes are abandoned for heavy ones. "A couple years ago, he was back in our hometown. It's small, like yours, people talk. He started dating a girl, she was barely eighteen, and he was twenty-eight. She was nuts over him, and he was just looking for a good time. He got bored, like he always does, and broke it off. She took half a bottle of pills and ended up in the ER. People were already talking, but after that, her reputation was ruined. He called me, hoping I could help him get out of it. I came in, like I always do, and cleaned up his mess. I encouraged my parents to move out here before they heard the rumors. I got my brother a job overseas. I got the girl the help she needed, but the damage was done. Her life will never be the same."

He plays through the last couple notes, fingers on the keys until the piano is silent. I press my lips together, hurting for him, hurting for the girl, and even for his brother for making dumb choices. The quiet surrounds us, as if confirming he was right to keep us apart.

"That's really hard." My voice is the first to break the silence. He nods, but I'm not done. "But that's not what's happening here, Rome." I slip my hand into his. "You are not your brother. And I'm not some lovesick child who doesn't know how to live without you."

He shoots me a confused look. "That hurt a little."

I touch my fingers to his cheek. "That's just it, Rome. I want to be with you. I think we'd be good together, but if I can't have you, it's not the end of my world. I've seen too much, lived through too much, to let a relationship destroy me. I would cry over you. I might even binge eat some ice cream and live in my sweats for a few nights, but I won't try to end my life. And if you're worried about what people in this town will say about me? Trust me, my family has been the center of gossip for years. Dating an older man will hardly be news."

A grin peeks from his cheeks, timid at first, but growing. "Really? You've spent your time in the town gossip column?"

"If there was one." I take his hand in mine. "Dad probably started it all. Winning the ranch with an ace in the hole, no one called him Steven after that. And then add Victoria's shenanigans, every party, every weekend, and worse after we lost mom. The tongues never stopped wagging about Ace's little Queen of Hearts."

"Queen of hearts?" Roman's fingers slip between mine. "That's what they call her?"

"Years ago, yes, but it still stands. Everyone knows my family. I don't know half the stories from before my time, always too busy raising Hudson, or saving the ranch, but we are not unaccustomed to hearing gossip." I tilt my head, hair sliding to the opposite side to expose my neck. "All I'm saying is, don't hold back on my account. I can deal with some old ladies talking."

His eyes dart to my lips. Still, he doesn't take the chance. Instead, he says, "If Victoria is the Queen of Hearts, what does that make you?"

I frown. "No one ever thought to name me, I guess." The thought comes to me and I can't help a soft laugh. "I'm probably most like the instruction card that comes with the deck. Tells everyone what to do and then gets lost under the couch somewhere."

I expect him to laugh with me, but he's lost in thought. Using his free hand, he pushes the hair away from my face, tucking it behind my ear. "If she's the Queen of Hearts, then you're the Queen of Diamonds."

I meet his stare, curious about his reasoning. "How so?"

"Because I've never met anyone who sparkles and shines the way you do, without ever trying."

For a second, he has me. Heart, mind, soul, down to my little toes, I'm his. I think of mom's story, about being attracted to Dad for more than his appearance. Is it possible that it could happen again, that two people could connect in such a way that it wouldn't matter what anyone else ever thought? All we need is each other.

A quiet prayer fills my heart that mom was right all along.

CHAPTER 16

Roman

"Tell me what you've got?" The office door slams behind me. Rick whirls to check my identity but resumes his work at the computer with the analyst.

"It's still in production. We're designing the plan as we speak."

Knowing what's on the line, Kennedy, her trust, my life, I'm feeling less than friendly. It's been two days with no news on how we're going forward with the party. Two rehearsals, two nights of looking her in the eyes and lying through my teeth. I need to know this isn't for nothing. The second I said goodnight at the door, I set out looking for answers.

"I've handed you the whole lot of them on a silver platter, and you don't know what to do?"

"You've given us a birthday party."

"With an agent on the inside."

"Last I heard, he's hardly more than a glorified analyst. Isn't that the rumor?"

I knew it would come to this. I knew he'd put my back to the wall on this issue. He's not wrong. It's time. Pick a side. Pick a path. I've been straddling the line for too long.

"Yeah, well, things change. I'm in."

"Both feet?"

I clench my jaw and consider the implications, but not long

enough to think better.

"I'm all in."

Rick smiles as if he's won. I suppose he has.

"In that case, we have a plan."

He nods his head toward the computer, and I step in to take a closer look. The analyst has the floor plan to *The Nightingale* open, but also the neighboring pizza shack as well.

"We'll set up here," Rick circles the center kitchen of the pizza joint, "you'll have coms the whole time. You'll be armed, but assuming they're going to check you, we'll have to hide it on your person or—"

"I'll figure it out," I say before he can finish. "If things get hairy, I'll have something."

"You'll do your set, or whatever," Rick waves his hand through the air, "and after it's done, Dante will no doubt want to talk to your girl. That's when I need you to sneak off."

"You want me to leave her alone with him?"

"You think he's going to pull something in front of his guests? As long as they're in public, she's fine. I need you in the office. Download whatever you can. We'll try to get something set up between the buildings, a concealed drop box or something."

The analyst speaks for the first time, "We're working on it."

"When do we take them down?"

"It's gonna take a while."

"You have no guarantee that we'll ever have this many of their crew gathered in one place. We need to act that night." I glare at him, but he's shaking his head. "Rick, for all you know Dark Fox himself will be there. Come on."

My supervisor draws in a slow breath through his nose. "If we want it to stick, we do it slow."

I shake my head, but my voice is in line. "Yes, sir."

"Now, I'm gonna need your girlfriend to work on your costume."

I'm mid-sentence correcting him that she's not my girlfriend, but trip over the word *costume*.

"What are you talking about?"

Let it be known my supervising agent has a wicked sense of humor.

"We have to conceal your identity, and she said it's got a twenties vibe, right?" Rick nudges the analyst. "What do you think, zoot suit riot or something more classic, like Dick Tracy?"

* * *

Kennedy

Roman thought he could get away with a suit and tie to something like this? Considering my ensemble, not a chance. I can't go in looking like Ingrid Bergman and not have my Humphrey Bogart by my side.

"You have to show me," I say to him from outside the dressing rooms. "Come out and do a little twirl."

"I don't twirl, Kennedy."

"A sashay perhaps?"

The latch on the dressing room door pops open, and I shift to watch him exit the doors. At this point, I'm pretty sure there's nothing Roman Palermo can't pull off without looking gorgeous, at least in my eyes. Even a mustard yellow pinstriped zoot suit. The pants are about two sizes too big for his legs. I press my hands over my mouth to hide away my laughter, but his jaw stretches side to side with mild frustration.

"I look like a..." he struggles to find a word, "jar of mustard or something."

"Okay," I press my hands to his arm, only slightly distracted by them, "we'll find something that does. Try that double-breasted suit."

"It makes me look fat."

"Fine, how about the soldier's uniform?"

"That makes no sense with the piano. Why would a soldier be

playing for—" he stops short of the dressing room. "I don't even know what you're wearing."

"But I do, and that's enough."

Roman spins and catches my wrists. My breath hitches, my mind flooded with the memory of that gun beneath his jacket. I could be in danger. But the look in his eyes is a different kind of danger. He presses my hands against his chest and takes a step to collapse the distance between us.

"Tell me. I want to know."

For a second, I consider telling him about the silver dress with the slit up my leg, the cowl neckline and bare back. But I want to see his face the first time he sees it cling to my figure. I want his eyes to follow the bend in the waist and every highlighted curve. For once, age will be nothing more than a number, because I'm one hundred-fifty percent adult woman in that dress.

"Let's just say," I finger walk the front of his chest and trace from his ear to his neckline with one finger. "No one is going to be looking at you."

We haven't kissed, not since the cottage. Even with three practices at Santos Sound, he's been nothing but professional. But his eyes drop to my lips and nothing's changed.

"Even if I look like a bottle of mustard?"

His joke breaks the spell between us. I lean forward into his arms, laughing against his chest while he takes me close. For a moment, the professional Roman fades away. For a moment, he's content to hold me, breath rushing over my hair and neck. For a moment, it all works.

"I'll try on the last suit," he whispers. With a quick kiss to the top of my head, he reverses out of my reach into the dressing room. The latch slides into place, and once more I try to do the same to my heart. But that's the thing, I don't want to latch my heart closed. I want to invite him in, ask him to stay for tea and cookies. Maybe longer.

If not for that glimpse of the gun, nothing would hold me back. But I saw it. I saw the gun, and I can't erase that memory, no matter how hard I try. If it's not going anywhere, then I have to decide if it's a deal breaker. Hudson could be right. Maybe he's prepared like a boy scout, or a gun lover. He could have been carrying a weapon every time we went out; I don't know for sure. He could have a gun right now.

My heart quickens at the idea. I'm not a fan of firearms. I understand the purpose. I'm grateful to the people who protect us with them, but I never planned to have them be a part of my life. If Roman really is a gun lover, to the point that he can't leave the house without them, is our relationship doomed from the start?

"I think this is it. I think you might like this one." The latch slides back, metal grating hard. I whip around to see him, possibly to tell him we can never be, but the only part of me that's doomed is my self-control.

The cut of the vest highlights his build, lean shoulders tapering down to what I have to assume is at least a six-pack, if not a party pack, of ab muscles. He's rolling up the sleeves of the white shirt beneath, like the bartenders from old movies I've watched. The silver tie will match my dress to perfection, but I doubt my ability to sing without forgetting a few words with him around.

"You're right," I say, sounding star struck, "this is the one."

His grin rises with a rakish tilt. "Is that so? You think I might turn a few heads?"

I can't stop staring at his chest and wondering what's beneath that black vest. "You've got mine." I run my eyes over the shop, grateful I was able to call in some favors, so we'd have the place to ourselves. On the far side, I see what I'm looking for. I grab it from the rack and turn back to Roman, fedora in hand.

"It's all about the accessories," I say.

He crosses the space, each step deliberate, each one agonizing for my patience. I want his arms around me. I want to feel him take control and tell me there's nothing holding us back anymore. I want him to tell me he understood what I was trying to tell him about his brother and our situation is nothing like that. Most of all, I want *him*.

"Do you mind?" He nods to the hat, as if it's my job to determine the placement. "I'm hopeless when it comes to fashion."

The stiff bill runs between my fingers before I reach to set it on his head. Square is all wrong, so I tilt the angle to a roguish level, leaving my hands there to catch it in case it tumbles. Roman's hands take mine, wrapping them around his neck before he pulls me close.

"I can't stop thinking about you," he says as if admitting his worst sins. "I'm completely distracted at work."

"I feel the same way." I lick my lips once, dying for his touch. "Today Vic asked me what I was thinking about so hard, and I told her Roman. Before she could tease me, I had to cover by saying I wanted Roman blinds in my office."

He could tease me, laugh at the joke, brush this off, but I get the feeling he's aching as bad as I am to get past all this talking.

"If I talk about Kennedy in my line of work, everyone will assume I'm going into the secret service."

I barely hear him. My fingers trace the bend of his jaw, his face, study the way his eyes close and his lips press tight. But it registers like a light switch clicking on.

"What does the president have to do with the music business?"

Fear flickers once in his eye, but his mouth finds mine and every other thought falls blank. He tightens his grip, lifting me to my toes, then to my tip toes where I'm barely touching the ground. Combined with the spinning in my head, I might as well be flying. My heart races with excitement every time he's close, but this intensity is new, as if he's unlatched some part of him, something he's been holding back or guarding from me. His kiss deepens, lips insistent and eager. I match his pace, happy to show him that this is where I wanted to be all along.

Roman's head twists, shifting, but not breaking the rhythm of his affection. "Kennedy." My name flashes against my cheek, but there's nothing more, no direction, no request, nothing more than a gasp to remind himself who he has in his arms. We stumble back, colliding once with a clothes rack, then slamming against the counter. His strength takes my breath away. His grip on my hip, pulling me close, as if it takes every bit of his willpower not to lift me up on this counter like he did in his jeep. The jolt wakes up his common sense. Roman pushes back against my hips, shoving space between us, even though his head hangs low, forehead against mine, hot, rushed breath heating up my skin.

"Are you sure you want to do this show?" Roman's eyes remain closed, squeezed tight as if the sight of me might destroy him. "How well do you know these guys?"

Leave it to a music professional to want to talk shop at a moment like this.

"I don't know, okay, I guess. Why are you hung up on this?" I twist to set my lips to his jaw. Like aftershocks, his body quakes at the sensation. "What are you worried about?"

"I have to keep you safe." Chills flash across my skin where he's pulled back and left me exposed to the air. "I couldn't live with myself if you got hurt."

"It's a birthday party," I tell him, confused as always by his behavior. "I'm singing, and then we're eating cake. It'll be fine."

He nods, but I don't feel his confidence in it. "I should change back."

One by one his fingers slip from my hips. As always, he leaves me with more questions than answers. Hot and cold, like two people shoved into one body. One side of him that can't keep his hands off me, and the other determined to do exactly that. The problem is, there's only one version of me, and I want all of him.

❋ ❋ ❋

Roman

Safe to say, I lost control. I slipped up about Kennedy and protecting the president, tried to cover my tracks and fell off the cliff instead. Thankfully, I had enough sense to stop before I dragged her with me. This hot and cold act I'm doing with her has to be driving her away from me. That's not what I want. I don't know what I want, but I know that's not it.

I reach across the cab and take her hand. It's a simple gesture, but the tension exhales with her. Is there a future for us? She's probably right about our ages. We're nothing like Sabastian and Brinley. If only that was all that held me back. The bigger question looms in front of me. Is there a future for us while I work for the FBI? Can she forgive my lies? I don't work in the music industry. I can't sign her to a label. It's all stacking up around me, and I'm starting to fear I'm about to lose everything.

CHAPTER 17

Kennedy

I'll never get tired of walking down the staircase and watching Roman take me in for the first time. It's like watching someone open a present you know they want.

The excitement.

The wonder.

The absolute joy that it's better than they ever imagined.

The only part I could do without is my dad glowering from the kitchen, and Hudson watching Roman like he's gonna steal the fine china.

"Don't wait up," I call over my shoulder as I follow Roman out the door. Dad grumbles something, but I have to give him credit that at least he left his rifle in the gun safe.

"Be careful!" Hudson calls after us. I wave my hand, but he stays in the doorway, watching my date like he might murder me. I shouldn't have told him about the attack in the ballroom. I got him worried about nothing.

"Are you hungry?" Roman asks, pulling open my door.

"Starved, but I'm afraid I'll hurl if I eat before the show."

He smiles, but it's not as easy as it normally is. He's probably nervous for me. I have enough butterflies in my stomach to populate a botanical garden.

"Maybe we'll get pizza afterward or something?"

"I can look forward to that."

He shuts the door, and jogs to the other side. The fedora rests on the dashboard. It brings back memories of our last encounter, of the moment he actually let his guard down. I hope he's not back to keeping his distance. I don't know how much more I can take.

Roman slides into the driver seat and turns the key to start the engine. "I have to make a quick stop at Santos Sound. I forgot something. Is that okay?"

I glance at my watch, fastened around my matching silver gloves. "If you're quick."

"Promise."

It's fifteen minutes of uncomfortable silence before we arrive. I hate being late. He steals a kiss before he rushes from the car and slips inside. The blinds are drawn but cracked. Light slips through them. He's not alone inside. Through the slats I watch one shadowy figure hand something to another one.

The outline is unmistakable. Though smaller than most, I know the shape of a handgun. Roman turns, the light flips off and ten seconds later he jogs out the door. My heart hammers in my chest, nervous to be alone with the type of guy who has to stop by work to pick up a weapon.

Roman crosses the headlights with something in his hands, but the light reflects and blinds me. The door rips back. I face him with wide eyes, but it's not a barrel of a gun I'm looking at, it's a bouquet of sunflowers, my favorite.

"I left them here earlier. I'm sorry. I didn't want you to miss out."

The plastic crinkles beneath my grip. I cradle them close like a baby. One glance at Roman tells me I had to be wrong. With no jacket, he has no place to hide the gun. Shadows are funny that way, like clouds, they're open to imagination. I scold myself for thinking that Roman is anyone other than the guy I know.

✳ ✳ ✳

Roman

My nerves are tighter than piano wire. My only comfort is the .38 Ruger strapped to my ankle that I picked up from a tech at Santos Sound. Thankfully, he tracked down her flowers as well. That look she shot me when I pulled open the door has me wondering if she knows more than I think she does.

I stop at the curb, ten feet down from the pizza shop and, of course, The Nightingale. I smash the hat on my head, but Kennedy's soft touch pulls my face around to adjust it. It's impossible not to stare at her. The dress lights up my imagination with plans, none that I should share with her. The most innocent among them being the desire to shower her bare shoulders in my kisses.

But her face, her face brings me back to what I really want, and it's nowhere near those other thoughts. Spending the last couple days with her, listening to her sing, feeling her warmth beside me on the piano bench, it's what I've been searching for. Last night, after we finished our final song, her head flopped against my shoulder, as if she might fall asleep. I ached to let her stay the night in my arms.

I'm falling in love with her.

Despite my best efforts otherwise, I'm falling in love with her.

"There," she says with a wink, "I think that's perfect." I move to kiss her because I can't stand another second being apart, but her gloved fingers press over my mouth. "Don't you dare mess up my hair or make up. I might have to kill you. I'm at least seventy-two percent serious."

"Yes ma'am." I pop the door latch and hurry to her side to help her from the car in her towering heels. Her arm linked through mine, I lead the way to The Nightingale. Passing the pizza joint, I spot Rick in the back corner. He's pulled a baseball cap low over his eyes, and someone gave him a scraggly blonde wig that bushes out from beneath it.

"They have great breadsticks," Kennedy says, oblivious to what we're walking into. "You'll see."

Dinner later feels like another life, or rather a miracle if we make it through the next two hours without being shot or at least caught in a firefight. I grip the steel door handle and pull it back.

Immediately, two men pull Kennedy from my grasp, shoving me against a wall, gun to my temple. Kennedy screams, but the sound is cut short. Whether the thug hurt her, or simply covered her mouth, I'm not sure, but rage seeps through my veins.

"What are you doing here?" The guard's forearm cuts into my throat, limiting air supply. "Club ain't open tonight."

I grit my teeth, trying to gain composure while the muzzle of his gun burrows into my brain. "She's the talent. She's singing for the party."

My date's soft whimpers catch my ear. Afraid of what she's enduring, I jerk against the grip of my captor. The hammer on his gun clicks back.

"And who are you?"

"Hey, hey, hey, hey," a voice comes from across the bar, "boys, that's our lady of the night. Let them go."

Five seconds pass before the pressure pulls away from not only my head, but my throat where he had me pinned.

Pedro Marquez makes his way between the booths, acting like it's common business practice to attack patrons. "Boys, I said pat downs, not detainment." He shrugs at wide-eyed Kennedy. "I swear, you can't get good help anymore."

Pedro lets out a short whistle, and the goon presses his hands down my chest, between my legs, under my arms, but my concern is elsewhere. Kennedy's lip trembles as the bodyguard checking her rubs his hands down her frame, never lifting pressure once. I step away seconds before the bouncer finds the gun hidden under my pant leg.

"Hey," I growl the word out, "pat down, not a third date."

Pedro whistles again, and the goons take a step back. "Sorry, we've had some bad business in the past. We have to be careful."

Tears glisten in Kennedy's eyes, heightened by the low lighting of the club. "Even for old friends?"

Pedro reaches for her hand, and graciously she gives it to him. Fire lights in my chest as he presses his lips to the back of her gloved hand. "Especially with old friends. They think they've earned your trust. It's only moments later that they rob you blind."

She snatches her hand back, shifting to stand closer to me. Pedro laughs as if it was all a joke. "Come on, let's put this unpleasantness behind us. I'm sure you want to warm up, both of you."

Visibly shaken, Kennedy follows him, but not without linking her fingers between mine. She glances back at me, eyes full of fear and questions. Maybe now she understands why I've been dragging my feet.

※ ※ ※

Kennedy

The print his hands made are still glowing all over my body. Like trails of oil I can't see, another dress is ruined by memories. I can't sing, not when I feel like this. Not when I'm internally rattled.

They put a gun to Roman's head. I search him out at the piano again, wishing he'd show even the slightest crack in his armor. How'd he recover? He had it worse than me. I swear two more seconds and they would have shot him. I was two seconds from being covered in my date's brain matter.

Satin brushes my lips as I try to cover another sob with my hand. I spin away from the microphone, desperate for a little air. Too many eyes watch me. Even if they're nothing more than Pedro and his staff, they're all judging me. I'm sure Pedro told them stories about how his friend heard me sing one song and hired me on the spot. But I feel like a fraud with my shaking knees and trembling hands.

Roman's arms capture me. I sink into his embrace. Behind me Pedro yells, "What's wrong with her? She's gonna sing, right?"

"If your goon hadn't attacked us the second we set foot in this place, maybe she'd be doing better."

"It was security."

"He was feeling her up!" Roman's body tightens as if he might launch from the stage and take his revenge, but my weak body leaves him anchored. Weaving his fingers into my hair, he keeps me close. "Do you have somewhere she can warm up in private?"

I wait, hopeful, listening for a verdict that could give me enough time to find my feet again and shake off the stain of what happened. For whatever reason, Pedro is hesitating.

"Down the hall off stage. First door. Don't go any further, or she may never sing again."

I swallow the bile that erupts in my throat. I'm ready to quit. Something is wrong, incredibly wrong with this place. But Roman scoops me into his arms and carries me off stage.

The light dims as we enter the hallway. I nestle close to his neck, hiding my face, breathing in his scent. Five seconds pass before his shoe collides with a door and kicks it open. I pray it's the right one, and I'm not going to get shot. An overhead light flickers a couple times before it finds power. Roman sets my feet to the ground, but stays close, watching my face for any indication of my emotional status.

"I can't do this. You were right. This is way more cutthroat than I ever thought it would be." My whisper is still loud in the silence of the tiny supply closet.

Roman's mouth tightens as if he might say something, but he remains silent. None of this freaks him out. This is normal? He's used to this?

"Is this how it is? Is this what becoming a performer will be like?" I stare up at him, but Roman won't hold my gaze.

"This is extreme," he says. "Just like the rest of the world, you'll have good guys, and bad guys."

"And you knew these were bad guys? You knew I'd be treated like this?"

"No," he's quick to find my eyes, even faster to shut down the thought, "I never would have allowed this to happen if I thought they'd..." He can't finish. "I hated that, every second of it. I want to bash his face in."

His confession earns him a weak smile. "I'm sure it's standard security."

"Like you can hide anything under that dress. I've been staring at you all night, no way could you fit any—" Again he cuts himself off. "I'm just saying it's tight... or... that is... it fits well."

His awkward shifting and frustration have me lightening by the second. For being cool, calm and collected around the rest of this place, it sure seems like I unravel him in an instant.

"I'm saying, I care about you, Kennedy. I hated not being able to protect you."

"Me too."

I wish he understood what he's come to mean to me. I feel inadequate in explaining this bond between us. All I know is, I trust him, with my love, and if he'll take it, with my heart.

"I want to go home, Roman. Please take me home."

A war rises up in his features. Eyes narrow, brow furrows, his lips part with arguments and words unspoken.

"You need to stay." The words don't sound like his, as if he's rehearsing a line. "You need to finish this. You can do it. I know you can."

"I don't need the money. And if this is how the work will be, I don't need the job either."

Roman swallows hard. A tremble in his hand vibrates against my shoulder where he takes hold. "Please, do it for me. Sing for me."

I don't understand the desperation written on his face. It's a birthday party. It's not the end of the world if I walk away, but he's begging me to see this through.

"I don't belong here. This isn't who I am, Rome."

The musty air makes me nauseous. A knock at the door tells me my time has run out. But Roman captures my attention.

"You belong up there, Kennedy. Not a choir girl, not a backup singer. Front and center, star of the show. I meant it, you're the diamond. Show them." My heart jams into my throat because he doesn't understand, in my family I've never been the star. "Do one song, for me, if you can't stay any longer, I'll break down every door to get you out of here."

The second knock is no longer a knock, but a slamming fist. I cringe with every bang, but Roman pulls me close and whispers against my ear. "You can do this. I believe in you."

I draw in a breath, air mingled with the closet odors, but also Roman's cologne, my favorite scent, the one I always try to make Hudson wear. The sunflowers, the date to my favorite restaurant, the cologne, never has a man been this perfect for me.

If he believes in me, then I'll try.

CHAPTER 18

Roman

I prop up the top of the grand piano, as if I'm hoping for a bit more volume. Really, I'm looking for the gun Rick swore would be inside. It's hard to spot, and for a good reason, but there on the far left wedged beneath part of the piano's structural housing, I see it. Hoping to maintain my cover, I leave the top cracked.

Thus far, no one has recognized me. That forgettable face of mine strikes again. At least this time it's keeping Kennedy safe. That's all I can hope at this point, to keep her alive. I don't know if I'll ever pull myself out from under the guilt of talking her into staying so the mission will stay alive.

It's not fair.

It's not right.

She's behind the microphone, just outside the spotlight, as if she's not worthy to take that space. Kennedy looks over her shoulder for my reassurance.

I almost said it.

In that room, I almost whispered, "I love you".

And I don't think it'd be a lie.

I search the crowd for the man who calls himself Dark Fox. It's stupid to try. No has ever seen him. I wouldn't know him even if I stared him in the face. At least thirty, maybe more, people stare back at us, waiting, expecting something spectacular because I'm sure that's what they were promised.

I set my fingers to the ivory. Kennedy's nerves have a grip on her throat, but I play the first chord. Her eyes close. She steps into the spotlight and takes hold of the microphone. I play the second chord and her voice, her angelic, velveteen voice, curls around every heart in The Nightingale.

The first phrase of, *Can't Take My Eyes Off of You*, floats through the spell she's cast. How I wish she understood that she's singing exactly what's in my heart. She is too good to be true. Not once have I been able to take my eyes off of her. Those moments in her arms are pure heaven when she's touching me.

She's a vision up there, so much that I'm afraid I might drop a note, miss a key change, something, because she's got me hypnotized. Kennedy hangs on the notes and spreads the melody like honey.

The volume builds and with it her confidence. Kennedy's smile spreads over her cheeks, coming alive with her love of the music. I try to keep up, to balance her star quality with the music, but no way can I do talent like hers any justice. She opens her voice as she rounds the last set on the chorus. Whistles and clapping start early, egging on her performance. She's forgotten everything from before, only alive for this moment, this chance, and I love watching her take hold of her dreams and run with them. She belts out the last notes, stretching an arm over head as the notes climb and die out.

The lights cut to blackness. My heart leaps into my throat, but before I can retrieve my gun, the spotlight flashes back on. The crowd explodes to their feet. She turns, blows me a kiss and nods her head that she wants to go on.

"*We heard the song,*" Rick's voice chirps from the com in my ear, "*still working on the drop box. Here's hoping they want an encore.*"

Once more guilt grabs me by the lapels and tells me I don't deserve her. Not with the lies I'm feeding her. Not when I always come up short. But deserve her or not, I plan to give her my all.

* * *

Kennedy

I expected applause, but this is almost deafening. Each song it got louder, and after three encores, I have nothing left. I blow kisses to the crowd and say, "Well maybe now you can join me in a song. We're all here for one reason, to wish Dante an incredibly happy birthday."

I start the song, but I let the crowd carry it. Too much more and I'll be hoarse. I'm not used to this level of strain on my vocal cords. After the song and the fifth round of applause, I thank them, and turn to return to Roman's side. Pedro hops on stage, catching my arm in a vice grip.

"Dante wants to thank you personally. Please join him for cake."

Despite the word please, it doesn't sound like a request.

"I'm flattered, honestly I am, but I'm exhausted and sweaty. Let me get cleaned up and fetch a drink of water."

Pedro doesn't flinch. "We have water at the table."

"Let me grab Roman," I start to move, but Pedro's grip locks me in place.

"The invitation has been extended to only you, Kennedy."

The grand piano top smacks down. When I turn, Roman is tucking his shirt in at the back. I widen my eyes, hoping he'll rescue me.

"It's okay," he says, smiling. "I left something back in the supply closet. You tell the birthday boy hello, I'll grab our stuff, and we'll head out, okay?"

Oxygen rushes from my body but won't return.

He's leaving me with these men?

"I'll be right back, okay?"

There has to be a secret message in the look he's shooting me, but I have no clue what it is. Instead, Pedro leads me down the stairs by the hand, ushering me toward the birthday cake that's being wheeled to the center where Dante Alvero spreads his arms across the back of a booth filled with people. I look back, but Roman is already gone.

The closer I come to the table, the more I feel like I might puke. Dante, the birthday boy, is nowhere near a boy. He's got to be at least fifty, pushing sixty, with no indication of age on the cake. Clearly, he's not looking for a reminder. He extends a hand to me as if to shake mine. I grant him that social norm, but he twists my hand sharply and sets it to his lips.

"The only thing more beautiful than your face is your voice, my darling."

Seated in the booth, on either side of him, two women watch me. Each has a hand on his chest, touching skin where his silk shirt has popped open and a dark patch of hair looks more like shag carpet. I pinch my lips together to keep from frowning.

"Thank you for having me. I appreciate the opportunity."

I try to peel my hand from his grasp, but he's a python, drawing me closer with the pressure from his grip on my fingers.

"The pleasure is all mine. Come, sit, eat with us. We'd love to have you."

Looking at the other women on his arm, I have no interest in joining them. I don't even like cake.

"I'd hate to intrude," I say. One of his girls gathers his attention, and in that split second, I rip my hand free. The inertia makes me stumble back, landing square in Pedro's arms. He smooths my dress as he rights me to standing, but I fear even a hot shower will never cleanse me of this night.

Where did Roman go?

"Why have we never heard you sing before? I know I'd remember your voice."

"I'm here all the time, but not to sing."

Pedro steps in to spell it out for him. "Kennedy works at Cartwright Ranch, she's the talent scout for their events."

I smile with gratitude. "Yes, we have our summer concert

series coming up shortly. Should be an amazing line up."

None of that interests him. "Then you're Ace Cartwright's daughter."

It's not a question, but I feel the need to answer it.

"Yes, I am. Do you know him?"

"Everyone knows Ace." Dante waves my question away like a gnat. "We have a long history together, however, lately he refuses to work with me. It's been very disappointing. I wager you didn't mention where, or who you were singing for tonight."

"Well, no, it never came up, but I don't think you should worry, dad works with all sorts of—"

"Are you here with someone?" Dante asks, trying to draw my scattered attention back again.

"Roman." I toss his name out as if I'm looking for him to pop up.

"Who?"

"The piano player," Pedro says. "They came together."

Dante's laughter drips with animosity. "He's a bit old for you isn't he, Darling?"

I really wish he'd stop calling me that. I don't answer and Dante's eyes narrow. "If I'd known you were interested in older men, I would have thrown my hat in the ring. I could show you what a real man is capable of."

Bile churns in my stomach as anxiety turns to fear. I'm in a den of vipers, surrounded by hungry men with insatiable appetites, and my only hero is gone.

* * *

Roman

"Come on," I say to the computer again. The files aren't downloading like I want them to. Every second I leave her alone is another second Alvero might hurt her. She's a bunny in a pit of foxes, and I'm the only one on her side.

"Hit a snag with the drop box," Rick's voice comes over my coms. *"Can't get through the last layer. Wrong drill. Bring your girl over here. I'll organize a dead drop."*

The file pops up finished. I jerk the flash drive free. Footfalls in the hallways draw my attention. I'm closing the computer when I notice an icon in the corner.

The silhouette of a black fox.

I sink back into the office chair, jam my flash drive back in and try to copy the file. An error warning pops up on the screen.

Insufficient memory.

"Are you kidding me?"

The steps move closer, a countdown edging its way toward me. I jam my hand into my pocket and pull out the mess of my keys. I slip my personal flash drive into the slot. The floor in the hall groans. I click through, copying the file. The blue bar slides across as the files copy to my flash drive. A second later, the fox icon vanishes. I realize my mistake. In my rush, I must have pressed 'cut' instead.

"What are you doing in here?"

Backlit by the hallway, the guard who got handsy with my girl fills the breadth of the doorway. He reaches for his gun, but mine is level before he pulls the trigger. A dart catches his neck a second later, and another in his chest. Tranquilizer guns work best when dealing with a room full of criminals only thirty feet away.

The behemoth stumbles back, plucking the dart from his neck to stare at it in horror as he slides to the ground. Both flash drives in my pocket, I retrieve the darts, hoping to cover any sign of a government agency, and leave him with a bottle of cognac from the bottom desk drawer. Let his boss think he blacked out drunk.

Turning the corner, I search the crowd for Kennedy. She's there, terrified, tucked under Dante Alvero's arm. I shove the guy to my right in order to make room on my way toward her. A few cries go up, but as always with Kennedy, I have tunnel vision.

"Roman!" Her excitement to see me speaks more of the trauma I've left her in, not her feelings toward me. I'm sure I'm in the doghouse for abandoning her to the wolves.

"Ah, is this the Roman you were speaking of?" Dante says as I draw closer and extend my hand to Kennedy.

"Yeah, sorry we have to cut out. Miss Cartwright has another event. We can't be late."

Dante's eyes narrow, but not because of the lie. His next question chills my blood.

"Have we met? You're very familiar." He stretches his arm across Kennedy, working as a seatbelt to block her into the booth with him.

Kennedy jumps to my defense. "Roman works in the music business with Dale over at Santos Sound. I'm sure you've seen him around."

Dante won't look away. I will myself to look like anything but a health inspector.

"I'm sorry," Kennedy taps his arm like an impatient executive waiting on an elevator. "I really must be going. I hope you have a lovely party. It's been a blast."

Twelve seconds pass before he releases his arm. Kennedy grabs my hand, lacing our fingers for extra support. Without another word, she drags me to the door, eager to put distance between herself and Dante Alvero. I pull back the door. She drops my hand and runs into the night. I follow on her heel, cold air slapping my face as if Kennedy has asked it for a favor.

"Kennedy! Wait!"

She whirls, sparkling dress catching the light of the streetlamps. Her eyes flash with anger and tears, but mostly betrayal.

"Why did you leave me?" Every one of her syllables cut like a blade. "Why would you desert me to them?"

There aren't words to explain my behavior, not without the truth. Even then, it's hardly excusable.

"I'm sorry. I didn't mean to take so long." The flash drive burns from my pocket, screaming for attention because Alvero has to be putting together what's happened here. "Let me buy you dinner, make it up to you."

"No, take me home now, Rome."

Rick's voice catches my ear. *"We need that flash drive, Palermo."*

I make one last attempt. "You're absolutely right. I shouldn't have left you alone. Remember the breadsticks? I'll take you to ice cream after too. I'm really sorry."

Kennedy's shoulders slump in defeat. "I'm getting like eight scoops. I don't want to hear a word about it."

I raise my hands as if she's arresting me. "Not a single word."

She starts her walk back to my side. "And I'm not sharing."

"Not even a little?"

Kennedy doesn't stop once she reaches me. Instead, she pulls the door to the pizza place and inhales the smell of Italian cuisine.

"Not even a spoonful."

She walks in without me, more evidence of how far my stock has fallen.

I motion for a booth to the side, but being defiant, she picks a booth opposite and falls onto the cracked leather seats. Her arms cross around her stomach, cinching down like a child, but she's no child, certainly not in that dress.

"Hi, welcome." A server stops at our table, smiling ear to ear. "Our manager, Rick, has some great specials tonight, are you interested in those?"

She's one of our analysts, Anita Macroe. Obviously, the kitchen is closed, and this is my dead drop.

"No," Kennedy snaps the words out, "We want a full order of breadsticks and a large pepperoni pizza."

I dig a hand into my pocket to retrieve the flash drive. Palming it, I reach for Kennedy's menu. She won't look at me. I might as well be dirt at this point. Moving it to the front of her menu, I press my own menu over the flash drive and hand them to the agent.

"I'm sure Rick's specials are great, but no one knows more than Kennedy."

The analyst frowns and shoots a dubious look toward my date, who thankfully is too deep in her glowering to notice.

As soon as the analyst leaves, I try again with Kennedy.

"I really didn't think I'd be gone that long."

"So, why were you?"

"I couldn't find what I was looking for."

"What were you looking for?"

"My phone," I say, hoping it's good enough. "I must have set it down while we were in there."

She's not stupid, or easily mislead.

"I saw it in your pocket while you were playing the piano."

"I know," my lies are tangling around me, "I felt like an idiot when I realized it was there all along."

"Palermo," Rick's voice crackles in my ear, *"we need you to look at these. Come tell me if I'm seeing what I think I'm seeing."*

"I can't believe you didn't feel your phone in your pocket. Didn't you check before you went back there?"

"I must have missed it."

"I'm sending Macroe back to retrieve you. Go with it," Rick says.

I'm split in two, trying to calm Kennedy, while seeing Macroe walking toward me in her Pizza Palace uniform.

"Are you even listening to me, Roman?" Kennedy's volume rises with every word. "I swear, sometimes you're right here with me, and then in the next second you're fifty miles away, and I don't even know you."

"Kennedy, you know me. I'm sorry I'm—"

"Excuse me sir." Macroe stops at our table. "Are you Roman Palermo of Santos Sound?"

I don't want to answer her. I want to stay here and prove to Kennedy that she matters to me. But the analyst's eyes narrow with urgency. They must have found something.

"Yes, I am."

"There's a call for you in the kitchen, if you don't mind following me."

I swear Kennedy's eyes launch not only daggers but a full nuclear airstrike in my direction.

"I'll be right back," I say. "I'm sure food will be out in a minute."

"You have five minutes. If you're not back, I'm leaving."

"Got it." I swallow and square my shoulders, somehow more scared of the five-foot nothing across from me than the entire club full of criminals next door. Macroe motions with her arm for me to go first. I shoot one last look at Kennedy before I follow the order.

It's easier once I'm away from the table. Training takes over. I slam my palms against the kitchen door and swing wide. The kitchen is void of real staff, instead replaced by Rick, Macroe, myself and four agents I don't recognize.

"Nice evening?" Rick asks with his typical dry humor.

"It's been a delight." I lean over the laptop where they're searching the files I stole. "What'd you find?"

"Look here. I think we have our connections. You can follow the money back, watch the laundry happen so to speak. Comes in dirty," his finger moves from one spreadsheet to the next, "goes out clean."

"So, we have him?"

"We've got enough to build a case."

"When are we moving on it? Next week?"

"Tonight."

"Tonight?" I back up, trying to understand the implications. "You said it would be crazy to try something tonight. You said-"

"Yeah, and you said we'd be crazy not to. I called in for backup. I guess I've decided to trust your instincts. Tactical gear is in the back. Suit up."

The other agents are strapping on their gear, Macroe slams a clip into the bottom of an assault rifle and extends it to me. The world swirls with my fear.

Kennedy is stuck at the center of this mayhem.

❋ ❋ ❋

Kennedy

They better hurry up with those breadsticks. I'm starved and scared, straight shook at this point, and none of that is a good combination for me. I glance around the pizza joint. All the nights I've been to *The Nightingale*, I've only stopped in here a few times. Strange that the open sign isn't glowing. Someone forgot to turn it on, or maybe they're closing. That would explain why we're the only patrons inside. I can't remember if this is normal or not. Seems off on a weekend night to be empty.

I check my watch. It's only nine. Places like this would normally be hopping. Bass from the party next door vibrates through the wall. I hate being this close to everything that happened in there. While it's true, I sang and people loved me, I can't erase the feelings of violation that accompanied everything else. If this is any indication of where a career in music is headed, count me out. I'm not a girl who thrives on danger. Give me the simple life any day.

The leather groans as I turn to glance toward the kitchen. Voices shout, but I've lived with Victoria long enough to know shouting and cooking go hand in hand. Still, this doesn't sound like normal kitchen sounds. As usual, a night with Roman has gone totally off the rails.

Two minutes.

He has two minutes left.

*** * ***

Roman

"And what do I do about Kennedy? You want me to stuff her behind the oven over there? Hope the fight doesn't spread and I don't get a civilian shot?"

Rick's face darkens at my insubordinate tone. "Send her home. Get her a cab."

"I can't keep doing this. I tell her one thing, and then I do the exact opposite."

"I'm not here to be your wingman, Roman. I have a mission, and so do you. Do what it takes, get her gone, and get in your gear."

He shoves the assault rifle in my hands. "This is how you keep her safe. This is how we keep everyone we love safe. We lie, we tell them we're coming home, and we do what has to be done. You think we don't have people we care about? You think you're alone in loving someone? We all have someone. We all take risks. This is your job. This is how you keep her safe. Do you understand, Agent Palermo?"

I draw in a deep breath, struggling against my training, but knowing he's right.

"Yes, sir."

"Now get out there and do what has to be done."

"Yes, sir."

I turn on my heel, headed for the dining area, but stop short. Rick follows my gaze and lets out a soft curse under his breath.

She's not moving, only staring at me as the kitchen door still swings from her entry. Assault rifle in my hands, our waitress wearing tactical gear toting the title, FBI, all around her are signs that nothing was what she thought it was.

"Kennedy," I start, but she backs away, hands up, head shaking as if she can't trust me or her eyes. The kitchen door parts, and she's gone.

Rick takes the rifle from my hands and shoves me forward. "Contain her. And get back here, you have a job to do."

❦ ❦ ❦

Kennedy

"Kennedy, wait!"

I won't stop. I wave my hand above my head, hoping the oncoming cab will see me, but it flies by. I jog further, tilting once when my heel catches on the sidewalk. I wave my arm again, desperate to escape this nightmare. Warmth catches my opposite arm, halting my steps, and spins me all the way around.

"Let me explain."

Without another thought, I whip my open palm across his face. The sting of it brings tears to my eyes, but he drops my arm. I stumble back, determined to keep my distance from him.

"Are you kidding me right now, Roman? Are you—" Every word I can think of is a curse word, and my mother raised me to be a lady. I scream out my frustration from deep within my chest, reveling in the guttural sound. "How? How are you going to explain this?"

"Please, Kennedy, please calm down." He's inching toward me, but I haven't stopped trying to flag down a ride, any ride at this point.

"I don't even know who you are! You're not a music producer, that's for sure."

"I'm not but, that doesn't mean—"

"That's exactly what it means. I don't know you. I know your lies, that's it." Letting him weave more isn't an option.

An engine draws closer as a cab pulls to the curb. I back away from him, one finger up, watching his every move. "You stay away from me, Roman. I mean it."

"Please," Pain fills his voice to the brink, "please don't do this. I don't want to lose you, Kennedy."

He's as desperate to get to me, as I am to escape him. He looks the same as he always has, dark eyes, dark hair, thin layer of stubble at his jawline. It'd be easy to step toward him, test the air, see if he's telling the truth. But in the next second, my memory flashes to pushing open that kitchen door and seeing that enormous gun in his hands, as if it's perfectly normal to carry something like that. I shake my head to clear the memory and send him a final verdict.

"You can't lose something you've never had."

I pop open the door and fall inside, slamming it behind. But he's not moving any closer. He's stuck there where I left him, as if quicksand holds him steady and all hope has left his frame.

"Where to?" the cab driver asks.

"Cartwright Ranch please."

He glances in his review mirror as we pull away from the curb.

"You okay? That guy bothering you? I could call the cops."

"No." I don't have the heart to turn around. "He won't bother me anymore."

CHAPTER 19

Roman

If I don't move too fast, I can still breathe.

It's been a week since we raided The Nightingale.

For all my bravado, and all Rick's praise about how I'm made for this work, I took a beating. I squint into the bathroom mirror, pressing down the curling edges of the butterfly stitch over my eyebrow. Dante Alvero cracked the butt of his gun against my forehead before he escaped out the back. I run my hands over my bare skin, wincing with every bruised rib, and remembering the pain I endured. Rick keeps telling me it was worth it.

We got Pedro, and fifteen other members of the crew. Dante is on the run. Word is that he's in the wind, staying low, not even the Dark Fox himself will touch him. We have the records from their dealings. Five laundering points have been raided and shut down. It's only a matter of time before we have the lot of them.

I move back to my bedroom. The mattress gives way beneath my weight. I fall back, happy to feel something soft in a world that's turned hard and cruel. I cup my phone in my hand and pull up her number for the millionth time.

Stay away from me, Roman, I mean it.

I'm trying to do as she asked, but she has no idea how hard it is. I flip back to the home screen, then pull up my photos, shifting between the three I have. The three I took without her knowing. The first is a shot I snagged while she danced with her brother at the wedding. Her eyes flash even in a still picture. The second is seconds after she finished singing in the auditorium. Pure peace is written over her features. I meant what I said, music producer or not, Kennedy belongs behind a microphone and under a spotlight. The last is one Macroe grabbed on surveillance. My arms are tight around her. We're locked in a passionate kiss, seemingly alone in that costume shop she commandeered for me. The bend in her fingers clenched around the fabric of my top, tells me at one point she felt something, even if it's gone now. I ache to run my fingers through her hair, set my hand to the curve at her waist, anything at this point to alleviate this pain. Because that's the problem, I can't forget. She's a song, stuck in my head, playing on repeat, but when I reach out, the melody dissipates, and I'm alone.

* * *

Kennedy

When I was a kid, a girl on the bus wanted to cover my eyes with her hand. Being a trusting fool, I let her. I still remember how she held her hand there too long, how the darkness increased by the second until I became used to it. All at once, she ripped her hand away. Pain clouded my head. Pricks stung my eyes as they adjusted. She, and six others, stared at me, watching like I was a circus freak.

"That's so cool," she whispered. "Let's try it again."

I stood up at the next stop and put as much space between us as I could. It was harmless fun, I suppose. She'd learned about pupil dilation in school and wanted to test it on me. With my green eyes, the definition made the phenomenon easy to see. But I felt like a joke. Everyone knew what she was doing, except me. I followed along without concern for myself or whether I was safe or not. I've never done something like that again, not until Roman.

Without any regard for my own safety, I believed him. I trusted that every fluke was just that, a strange coincidence, some odd occurrence explained away by a few kind words, or passionate kisses. It's easy enough to forget those kind words, but the passionate moments seem to linger like a melody running repeat in my mind.

"Do you have *Mavis and The Spacemen* in a slot?"

Hudson's voice brings my attention back.

Summer concert series.

Normal life.

No more Roman.

"Yeah, Friday at ten after *Hot Service*, but before *Mega Compass*."

"Okay," his pencil moves over the paper on his clipboard, "how about *Backroad Brigade*?"

"Saturday at ten, before *Redneck Outlaws*."

"I think you're ready. That was everything left on my list."

I nod, but not because I'm listening. Why can't I forget Roman? Why can't I put him out of my mind? He's not real.

"You miss him?"

"What?" I snap my binder shut and glare at my baby brother. "No, of course not. I mean, miss who?"

"You know who. Come on, you were great together. I've never seen you so happy."

I slide the binder back on a shelf behind me. They've never looked so good. After a meltdown a couple days ago, I pulled everything off the shelves, tossed out anything that didn't belong, reorganized, and set it all back together again. It's my way of pretending I have control over my life. I don't, but my binders lie better than my heart.

"You don't know what you're talking about." I swivel my chair to face the filing cabinets behind me, a signal that he should get lost, but since when does Hudson listen to signals?

"I know more than you think I do," he says. He comes around the side of my desk. "I know he's undercover."

I spin back, eyes wide, accusing finger jamming into his chest. "You knew? You knew and you didn't tell me?"

Hudson explodes to his feet, backing away from me as I follow him to the double doors of my office. His hands come up like my finger is a gun. "He said he stays behind the computers most of the time. I figured he was like an accountant or something. I didn't think I needed to tell you."

I shriek and turn away from him. "He's not an accountant, Hudsie. Accountants don't carry automatic weapons."

I've stolen his thunder, silenced him by accident. After a moment, the knob on my door turns. "All I know is he was falling in love with you. Figured that was worth taking a chance on."

The words circle me, taunting my best sense on a dare. I turn to ask him for more, but he's gone.

※ ※ ※

Roman

"You look like death."

I try to laugh at Rick's stupid joke, but nothing happens.

"Funny, I feel worse than that."

"Pretty hung up on her, huh?"

Kennedy Cartwright is the last thing I want to talk about right now. I turn back to the screen. I've been working around the clock trying to decrypt the secret file I stole from *The Nightingale* computer. Nothing works. I need a secondary piece to unlock the encryption.

"You could let the analysts take a crack at that, see if they get anywhere," Rick says, motioning to the computer.

"It's keeping me busy."

"You need to get out. Go see your parents or something. I think you've lost ten pounds in a week."

"I don't want my mom to see me beat up like this. I can't

exactly explain it." I'm moving around better, but my face still holds the bruises from the raid.

"Then go for a walk. You need air. That's an order."

With an aggravated sigh, I press back from the computer, give him a mock salute and head out the door.

*** * * ***

Kennedy

Vic knows something's up. Since nine this morning, she's be placing plates of snacks, desserts, and appetizers on my desk. Normally, by now she'd be off to wherever my secretive sister disappears to, but she's staying close, claiming she needs to practice recipes.

She pitched an idea to dad last night, a circle of food trucks for the summer series, but he shot her down. It's not the first time. He's stuck in this old way of doing things. Food trucks are how the world operates now, but he calls them chuck wagons and makes jokes about chucking up everything he ate. Guy had one bad experience with a roach coach twenty years ago, and there's no dealing with him.

Between her disappointment and my broken heart, we're quite the pair. Glad Hudson's not around. His girlfriend Jill is the light of his life and both Vic and I agreed that we're throwing him in the nearest trough the next time he starts gloating. Misery loves company and loathes his happiness.

"He doesn't get it," Vic breezes back through the double doors with yet another plate, "it's where the money is. These aren't fly by night operations. It's another form of independence from the social norm."

She moves to set the plate in front of me, but between all her other creations, there isn't a square inch left. Vic frowns at me until I pick up a plate of deep fried something.

"You need to eat."

"You need to stop cooking." I pick up one of the balls and sniff it. "What is this?"

"Deep fried mac and cheese. I thought they'd do well at the concerts." She groans as if the next part will hurt. "In my booth, where the food gets cold, and I have to schlep back here to get refills like a snack bar attendant."

"You know dad's going to hate this."

"Yeah, I know." She sets her plate down in front of me. If I'm not mistaken it's a homemade waffle cone stuffed with fried chicken bits. "He wants the regular, nachos with cheese from a pump and hotdogs boiled in old water."

I pop the fried bit in my mouth and instantly melt with it. "Oh my gosh," I say without bothering to swallow. "This is amazing."

She smirks. "Just imagine if you ate it hot an hour ago when I brought it to you."

I set the plate on the file cabinet behind me. "I haven't been hungry."

"I noticed." She perches on the edge of my desk like this is about to be some counseling session.

"Don't start acting like you're the nosey one. We both know that's Hudson."

"I know my place, don't you worry," Victoria smiles, "but I am the one who's been through her share of bad decisions, so if you want to talk about it, I'm around."

"Same goes for me, you know. Dad's been getting to you. I can see it. Between his bad heart and your temper, I'm not sure who's going to kill who."

Victoria snags a popcorn chicken from the cone and shrugs. "I'm planning on going crazy soon, feel free to join me."

"Join you? I'm already there."

She moves to the door and pops it open. The smell of the fryer and something sweet catches me by the nose.

"You're not crazy," she says, hesitating in the doorway.

"Oh no?"

"No," she steps through before she says, "you're lovesick and won't admit it, close but not crazy."

The door clicks shut before I can throw anything. She's faster than Hudson, been around me too long, I suppose. But she's wrong. To be lovesick, you'd have to be in love. To be in love, I'd have to know the person I'm in love with. Roman is fictional at best, like any dream too good to be true, once it's over, he's best forgotten. No way will reality ever live up to what I thought we had.

* * *

Roman

It's suicide.

I know better.

I turn the knob anyway.

A flurry of smells accosts me as I step through the cottage door. The kitchen is a conglomerate of pots, pans, steam and smoke. Somewhere in the haze, Victoria pops up. Her mouth falls open in shock. I don't know what Kennedy's told her. For all I know, she's more dangerous than half Dark Fox's men. Her knife skills alone have me cautious.

"What are you doing here?" Victoria lingers on the 'you' of it all, as if anyone else in the world would be welcome, but not me.

"I wanted to see her," I say.

"She doesn't want to see you."

The curtains are drawn over the glass double doors to her office. I don't know if she's there, or if I'm wasting my time.

"I can't stop thinking about her."

"She's doing just fine without you."

"Please," I take a step toward the kitchen island, the same one where I thought of five ways to get to Kennedy, "I don't know what she's told you—"

"Nothing," Victoria says, picking up a knife. She lets it glide through a tomato with razor thin accuracy. "She hasn't said anything, but I've known Kenny her whole life. I know when she's hurting."

"I need to explain everything. If she had a chance to hear me out, maybe it'd be different."

"Maybe it'd be the same, except wounds would be reopened."

"Please," I set my hands on the counter, "tell me where she is."

Victoria drops the slices into a bowl of batter. After a swish of her hand, she retrieves them and slides them into a fryer. "She's our favorite, you know? Hudson, Dad, me, we all think she's the best of us. Me, I cut out of this place as soon as I could. I could live here, but I like having my own space, and my own life. But Kenny, Kenny sticks it out. She took over management when dad's heart started to give him trouble. She raised Hudson. She's the mom around here, so you can't expect me not to protect her a bit." She hands me the fried tomato slice on a napkin. "Tell me why I should help you out."

I set the napkin on the counter. With all the courage I have left, I draw in a deep breath. All I have left is the truth.

"Because I fell in love with her."

A slight twitch to her eyebrow is the only indication I have that I might have surprised her. She weighs it in her mind, presses her lips together, then yells, "Kenny, can you come here? I think I got the tartar sauce too spicy again."

She's been here the whole time. Does she know I'm here? Is she coming? I can't stop my racing mind. With sweaty hands, I run my fingers through my hair, and brush a palm over my unshaven face. Rick's right, I probably do look like death.

Sounds of movement come from beyond the door. The knob rattles. Soft strains of country music filter out as it cracks open, and then her voice.

"Why are you asking me? You know I'm a wimp when it comes to spicy stuff." She looks up, but all she sees is me.

※ ※ ※

Kennedy

My breath catches in my throat.

"Roman." It's my voice, but I know I didn't issue the command to speak. I search out my betrayer, but Victoria is already switching off burners and wiping her hands.

"You two should talk," she says with a squeeze to my arm. Uncharacteristically, she pulls me close and whispers in my ear, "Give him a chance."

I watch her leave, fully aware of how alone I am, and the man she chose to leave me with. The door clicks shut. I can't be this close to him. I walk to the opposite side of the island, only comfortable once I have a barrier.

"So, talk," I say.

"I miss you," Roman takes a step toward me, but I move back. His lips part as if it hurt him. "You haven't missed me?"

"I don't know you," I say, barely loud enough to be heard over the pots still simmering on the stove.

"You know me, Kennedy. You just didn't know everything."

"You used me."

"I followed orders."

"That doesn't make it right."

"No, it doesn't."

I wish he'd fight back, argue, so I could scream some obscenities and send him packing. The look of devastation on his face is more than I can bear. Mixed with the purple bruises on his left cheek and cut to his lip, I only want to pull him close and take care of him, but that would be a mistake.

"Who are you? Really? Is Roman Palermo even your name?"

"Yes," he says. "I used my own name to go undercover this time. It's been a nice change of pace."

"This time? This is normal for you then? The guns and fighting, and butterfly stitches?"

He looks away, careful to try to hide the emotion and pain. "I go undercover sometimes. People tell you more when they don't know you're a federal agent. Normally, I stay behind the computer, but things got sticky."

"That's why my brother thinks you're an accountant."

"I told him exactly what I just told you. He drew that conclusion on his own." Roman clears his throat. "I've tried not to lie, if possible."

"But this time, this sticky time, things changed?"

"I'm a trained agent. I don't like the field, but I can hold my own. Rick needed me out there." Roman takes a step closer. "*You* needed me out there."

"You could have told me," I stop myself, "or is this some, if you told me you'd have to kill me type situation?"

"Nothing like that," he's quick to set me straight, "but being undercover, you keep it close to the chest."

"Was any of it real?"

"All of it." He moves to come around the island, but I reverse back, keeping the distance between us like some childhood game. He stops, begging me with his eyes to let him closer. "I'm going crazy, Kennedy. I miss you. Let me show you who I am."

I've never been a skeptic, but I can't help it after what he's put me through.

"How on earth could you show me anything that would make me believe you?"

"I want to show you a part of me even the FBI doesn't have."

"You're not making any sense, Roman."

His lips press into a straight line. "I want you to meet my parents."

CHAPTER 20

Roman

She wouldn't ride in my car. Shouldn't surprise me, I guess. Not after all the lies I've told. I've broken her trust, but if I have to crawl through fire or beg her for the rest of my life, I'll do it.

Kennedy steps out of her sedan. I stuff my hands in my pockets. I've never brought anyone home before. Even if I were buck naked in my parent's driveway, I don't think I'd feel any more vulnerable than I do right now. She wants to know who I am, then this is the best way.

I reach for her hand, but she crosses her arms tight around her center. I stop her early. "My mom is gonna assume a lot by me bringing you here. I understand you need space, but I'm warning you that she'll probably have a wedding planned before we leave."

Kennedy's eyes narrow. "Why? Is that what she does when you bring girls home?"

Can't she see that she's stripped me down to the bone? Yet, she still tries to cut me.

"I've never brought anyone home. Not ever."

I jog up the steps, aware that Kennedy hasn't moved an inch. Six seconds tick by before she falls in beside me. She won't take my hand, but at least she's near enough to feel her warmth.

My mom's footfalls pound out the seconds until she'll pull open the door. I tack on one last word of caution. "They don't know what I do for a living. They think I'm a bookkeeper for a law firm."

That same distrust billows up in her eyes, but I hope she's also starting to see the way I'm trying to keep the people around me safe. The door pulls back and mom smiles ear to ear.

"Roman! I wasn't expecting you! What a delightful surprise!"

"Hi, Ma," I sink into her embrace, squelching the cries of pain from my aching joints. "We were in the neighborhood and thought we'd stop by."

Her eyes widen to disbelief. It's only then that she notices Kennedy. Her hands clap over her mouth to trap in the squeal of delight. They explode out and wide, capturing Kennedy before she has a chance to say a word about it. They rock back and forth, locked in a tight embrace I can't help but envy.

"Oh," she lets go of Kennedy long enough to squish her cheeks between her palms, "is she the one you were telling me about? Oh, I knew you'd find someone, Rome."

I set my hands on her arms, trying in many failed attempts to peel her from Kennedy. "Yeah, she's the one, Ma, but maybe you can introduce yourself before you manhandle her anymore."

She slaps my arm with good-natured love. "Well, if you were a gentleman, you would have introduced her already." Mom pushes the door wide. "Come in, come in. I'm Sylvia Palermo. Welcome to our home."

"Hi," Kennedy's voice is bashful and timid compared to my boisterous mother, "I'm Kennedy Cartwright."

"What a perfectly lovely name. Come right this way. I'll put on the iced tea and grab the photo albums."

She hurries into the next room and Kennedy shoots me a worried glance.

"Photo albums?"

I shrug. "You wanted to know who I am. She's the number one lady to tell you."

She starts to follow mom, but I set my hand to her lower back to lead her into the living room. I take heart that she doesn't slap me this time.

※ ※ ※

Kennedy

"Oh, here he is in the third-grade play. He was supposed to be part of the straw house, but we figured out early on he was allergic, so they put him as one of the brick house boys."

In the photo, a young Roman smiles from behind red paint smeared all over his face. I run a finger over the plastic protecting it. Strange to see him as a child. Before he became all about guns and protection and national security.

"He sneezed so many times in rehearsal, the director swore he would make a better big bad wolf." Sylvia points to the next picture, Roman still grinning but snot nosed and eyes red with allergies. "Poor kid. I think it kept him from a future in Hollywood."

I glance up at Roman from where I'm sitting with his mom on the couch. She points to another picture, but he smiles and my world spins. I don't know where to draw the line in my new reality. Is he the guy with the gun, or the sweet kid I'm seeing in pictures, but all grown up? Is it possible to be both?

"This was his awkward stage in high school. He had an awful time with acne, you see."

Roman rocks back in his chair, covering his face with his palms as I try not to laugh. He's come a long way from those years. Even through the acne and crooked smile, I see what he holds inside. His heart shines through, and even mad at him, I can't ignore it.

"I think he's still handsome," I say, making eye contact with him. "His true character shows in his smile."

I don't want to admit it, but sitting here, listening, looking at the pictures, it all shows me he's exactly who I thought he was. But even if I did know him, what about the rest? His ability to lie? His career? His double life? Do I let it go, or do I walk away knowing what I stand to lose?

"Oh, he is a good boy, you know." She turns the page. "See this? When he was thirteen, he helped out at the local sanctuary for birds. Came home covered in bird droppings, but he loved helping out. Oh, and this one. He used to help the old man across the street by mowing his lawn every other week. Old Hugh always tried to pay him but Roman told him it was good practice."

My heart warms at the stories, but I struggle with how to put it together.

"It's been nice having him working at the law firm." Sylvia turns another page. "He's around so much more now. We don't get to see his sister or brother that often. Roman is such a dear and tries to drop in a few times a week."

"I can tell he cares about you."

"That says a lot about a man, doesn't it?" Sylvia winks. "A guy who takes care of his mother will always take care of you."

"It's true," Roman says.

I don't acknowledge him, but Sylvia plows on just the same. "He's always been that way, overly protective, sacrificing for the greater good. Figured he be a cop or something, not a bookworm. Not to say I'm complaining. It's nice not worrying about him. Except," she looks up at him as if the thought just occurred to her, "what happened to your head this time?"

Roman sets his drink to the side table and gives her a tight smile. "A box of books fell off a top shelf. My fault really."

She continues with her stories, but I watch Roman instead. He hates lying to her, but obviously she can't handle the truth. As she said only moments before, he's protecting her, sacrificing what he wants for what she needs.

"How's dad doing today?" Roman's question jars Sylvia from her story.

"Oh, he's okay, I think. Pretty coherent. I'm sure he'd love to meet Kennedy."

She stands and sets the album in my hands before she exits down the dim hallway. Roman rises and takes a few steps toward me, cautious for my reaction. When I give him none, he slides in where he's mother was sitting.

"Learn anything?"

I chuckle a bit, looking at the picture of him in a tux with tails, no older than thirteen. "You've been playing the piano a long time it seems. I guess I thought it might be fake somehow, something they had you learn for your cover."

Roman waits a second before he says, "I'm the same guy you thought I was, but I can't sign you to a label." His touch tickles at the side of my face before he tucks my hair behind my ear. "If I could, I would."

Words hedge up in my throat, but before I can form a sentence, Sylvia beckons us from the end of the hall. Roman stands first and extends a hand to me. "Let me help you up. This couch eats people."

I take his invitation and let him pull me to my feet. We end only a few inches away from each other. Roman bends to kiss me, but I turn my face at the last second, giving him my cheek. Warmth burns my skin where his forehead falls against me.

"Come on." His whisper tickles my ear before he takes my hand and leads me down the hall. We pass more pictures of Roman, and others with his siblings. Funny to see how similar our families are. I swear I have the same sort of pictures in our hallway at home.

"Not too long," Sylvia says to Roman before she lets him in. "He's very tired today. I don't want to wear him out before he can eat something."

Roman gives her a quick nod and my curiosity peaks. His grip tightens on my hand, but I get the feelings it's about strength for him, not affection for me. Seeing his dad is hard. When Roman moves out of the way, I understand it.

"Dad, how are you feeling today?"

Roman's dad sits upright in the hospital bed. His gray hair is unkempt, though I'm sure Sylvia tried to brush it. Brown eyes move from his son to me, and back to his son.

"Who are you?" he asks in a croaking voice. "Where's Sylvie?"

"Mom's in the hall," Roman's grip tightens on mine again. "I'm Roman. Do you remember, dad? Do you remember me?"

His eyes narrow a bit, searching through the cloudy haze for something tangible. "I have a son named Roman. He's a good boy."

"Yeah, he is," Roman whispers, turning his face from me. Despite his best efforts, the tear is too hard to miss. "He misses you too, Gio."

His eyes are red and glassy when he looks at me, emotion too close to the surface to cover. "Kennedy, this is my dad, Giovanni Palermo. Gio, this is Kennedy."

Gio's eyes brighten. One trembling hand reaches out for me. I give it, feeling an action like that deserves acknowledgement. The muscles have deteriorated, leaving not much more than bone covered in thin skin. But despite that, his grip is true and connected, as if he needs me to know he's aware.

"I knew Kennedy once. But she's a might bit prettier, don't you think?"

"Yes, sir," Roman whispers, casting an appreciative glance my way.

"Is Roman coming today?" Gio asks me.

I turn to point out that he's right there, but Roman shakes his head quickly. He's traveled this path before.

"I'm sure he'll be here soon," I say.

"Roman!" Sylvia's voice carries through the small house. "Roman, I can't get this lid off, can you help me?"

He shoots me a look to ask my permission. I smile and nod. Roman wipes his eyes with the back of his hand and hides his sniffle until he's in the hallway.

"Do you know my son? Roman?" Gio asks me.

"Yes, sir," I tell him. "I know Roman very well."

His grip tightens on my hand again, as if he's struggling to cleave to this moment. With great effort, he pulls himself forward. Voice low, he whispers, "He's FBI you know. It's a big secret. Don't tell his mother. Roman told me the last time he was here."

"Oh? Yes, he told me too."

Gio sinks back into the pillows. "Then you know. You know how he helps people."

A fit of coughs take hold of his body, each one stronger than the last. Gasps of air suck into his lungs as if he might lose the battle at any second. I drop his hand and retrieve a cup of water with a straw. Gio allows me to put the straw between his lips, and he sips what he can before he falls back again.

"I'm proud of my son, proud of who he's become." Gio's dark eyes catch mine. "Can you tell him that? Next time you see him?"

"Yes, of course," I say between the cracks in my pending tears.

Gio's trembling grip finds mine, and I press my opposite hand over his cold skin. "You'd be good for him, I think. He needs someone kind like you. Caring and gentle. A soft place to land at the end of a hard day. Someone like my Sylvie."

I press my lips together to keep the emotion in. Footfalls echo in the hallway. Gio's eyes close, and his breathing evens until I know he's asleep. Roman pauses in the doorway before he enters.

"I'm sorry, mom needed me. I hope that was okay."

It's all I can do to nod. I wanted to know Roman, the real Roman, thinking it would make all this that much easier. But my heart is ripped in half, knowing what I'll have to give up.

❈ ❈ ❈

Roman

"Are you sure you won't stay for dinner? I have Stouffer's big enough for everyone."

I kiss the top of her head again. "I promised I wouldn't keep Kennedy away for long. She's busy with work."

Mom frowns and yet smiles at Kennedy at once. "I hope you'll come back again."

"I'll try," Kennedy says, but I can't tell if she's lying.

Once more she allows me to set my hand to her back to guide her out. The door shuts behind us, and she gives a quick swipe to her eyes. I follow her to her car, eager to know if any of this changed my standing.

"I'm sorry I left you alone. I probably shouldn't have—"

She waves me away with her opposite hand. "It was fine. He loves you so much."

It pricks my already wounded heart. "He doesn't know who I am anymore. Alzheimer's has taken that from him."

"But he does know," she says, "he told me all about your work in the FBI, and how proud he is of what you've become. He knows who you are, he just doesn't recognize you."

Forgettable face, that's my curse. It should help that he knows me, but the pain remains. Watching my father deteriorate and become a shell of who he once was has taken its toll. If I have to add losing Kennedy, my heart might give out. Because unlike my father, she'll *choose* to forget me.

"And you? Do you know who I am?" I ask her.

"Roman," her head begins to shake and my hope drops from my heart, "Roman, this was amazing, and they're great people, and yes, I get it, you're exactly who I thought you were."

"But?"

"But I can't live this life with you. I can't do guns and danger and wonder if you're coming home." Her hands press against my chest, running up toward my collar. "I'm not made for this. You need someone who can stay at your side, understand why you're doing this."

"I'll quit," I whisper, pulling close to her. "I'll become a bookkeeper. I'll be your bookkeeper." My lips find hers, and for a second, she gives in, kissing me back, giving back the hope she stole from me.

"You don't mean that," she says as she breaks the kiss. "You help people. You're good at this."

"I need you," I whisper against her neck. Her grip tightens as I plant kisses along the length. "I'd give it up for you."

Her hands press me back, pushing too much distance and sense between us. "No, I won't let you."

"Please," I smash my hands over her hair, kissing her deeply before I beg again, "Please, don't do this to me."

Tears well and fall over her cheeks. I brush them away with my thumb. Then when they fall too fast, I kiss them, tasting the salt and bitter pain in each one.

"We weren't meant to be, Roman. I should have listened to you from the start."

Suction breaks as her door pops open. The metal wedges between us. She pauses before she can sink inside.

"Goodbye, Roman."

CHAPTER 21

Roman

"Careful 'round him, he's in a foul mood," Rick says to the analyst, John, working with me.

"He's been in a foul mood for a couple weeks now, hasn't he?" John asks like I'm not five feet away.

"Girl done him wrong." Rick drops his volume. "I took him to the shooting range, I let him beat the crap out of me in some sparring matches, even blasted the country music for a while. Nothing's helping."

"If he takes down Dark Fox, that might do it," John says.

Rick has his doubts. "Time is about the only thing that will heal this kind of pain."

But I doubt even that. The pain hasn't lessened in two weeks. It might never let up.

The phone rings on the side table, but Rick grabs it before I have a chance.

"Yeah?" A pause fills the air until I fear it might explode. "You've got to be kidding me. That's not possible."

He has my interest all at once. Rick runs a hand over his almost non-existent hair. He's still talking but, on the far side of the room, I can't make out the words. He hangs up the phone and strings together four of his favorite curse words.

"They're out on bail. The whole lot of them."

"What?" My mouth goes dry. "Pedro Marquez?"

"Everyone." Rick kicks a chair. It clatters across the floor, punctuated by his cursing. "Said we didn't have enough evidence, says what we had was circumstantial. Judge threw out half of what we brought in, saying we gathered it illegally."

"They've got someone on the inside."

"Obviously, someone's been bribed, but what does that do for us?"

"More importantly, where are they going?" John says.

I turn to look at the squirrely nerd. "What do you mean?"

My intense stare scares him a bit. He twitches for a moment before he says, "I've been looking at their history. If a town gets hot, they cut ties, tidy up loose ends, and move on to a new place."

"Loose ends?" Rick asks. "What do you mean by that?"

The analyst shrugs. "Informants, dealers, heck, if they know we have these files Roman stole, we'll be at the top of the list."

His giddy optimism is misplaced, as if he's excited the whole crew is headed our way. Rick shoots me a quick glance before the orders start.

"We're pulling up stakes first. Shut down everything here at Santos Sound. I want every hard drive cleaned and scrubbed once you have the information sent off. We're gone within twenty-four hours, understand?"

It's protocol. Leaving like this is my normal. We need to be ready to move as soon as they move. We have to stay on their trail while it's hot. That means no time for goodbyes or explanations, not for my parents, and certainly not for Kennedy Cartwright.

※ ※ ※

Kennedy

"Hudson, have you seen Carly and Marco?" My typically small

voice echoes across the auditorium.

"No, last I saw they were doing mic checks."

I groan. The concert is set to start in less than four hours and losing the first singers before I can give them last minute instructions isn't a good omen. I jog down the stairs to the lowest level and take the exit off the side that leads to the backstage area. I smile at a few band members from *Last Summer Serenade* and stare into the darkness looking for someone, anyone, who might know where I can find Carly and Marco.

I should turn on the overhead lights. This place is creepy without them. Dim rays from the auditorium streak in, but the faint glow through the door isn't enough to illuminate the entryway, let alone under the stage.

A sound catches my attention. A can hitting the ground? Likely a beer can. We've kept a tight rule on alcohol and drug use since the start of the series, but I'm not naïve enough to realize some will find ways to break the rules.

"Hey, Marco, Carly, come out. I know what you're doing."

The can rattles across the floor. I shake my head. I'm younger than both of them, but you'd never guess it with this routine.

"Come on, guys. We just need to run through the line up one more time before tonight. Could you please get it together for a minute or two?"

Laughter echoes beneath the stage. They think I won't go in there? They've got another thing coming. I'm scared of spiders, snakes, and clowns, but the dark doesn't freak me out.

"I'm coming in," I call into the ether. In response, a second can rattles out and lands at my feet. I pick it up, frowning, and toss it behind me. "You guys are going to be lucky if I don't bump you from the entire line up."

The dark doesn't answer back.

Maybe I'm losing it. I've been going nonstop since...since meeting Roman's parents.

Since saying goodbye.

Since making a big mistake.

I saw on the news a couple weeks ago that they took them all in, the whole corrupt lot of scoundrels from *The Nightingale*.

Now with his case wrapping up, he'll be moving on, and I'll never see him again.

My fingers run through my hair, catching in a few places, but my nails on my scalp alleviate some of the tension. I thought if I threw myself into work it'd be enough.

I'd forget him.

I'd move on.

So far, no dice.

A quick glance at my watch says I'm behind schedule. No built-in buffer for wallowing in my feelings, let alone chasing down ghosts and performers beneath the stage. I have a four o'clock meeting with the lighting specialist to go over requests for tonight's lineup.

"Finish up whatever you're doing. I'll meet you on the stage in twenty." I raise my voice to carry into the black ether. I take a step to leave, but laughter echoes from beneath the stage. Harsh, wicked, jagged at the edges, verging on maniacal laughter. I take a step away. My fingers latch around my cell phone. I pull it free and unlock the home screen.

Feet shuffle and drag. The sound echoes around me, but I can't place the direction. Fear creeps in with the encroaching steps. I was wrong. That isn't Carly or Marco under the stage.

My contact list swirls in front of me.

I glide through the names until I hit his.

Roman.

I select the name, and the screen shifts.

The footfalls move, sticking to the shadows, but instincts tell me not to let them get behind me.

The auditorium door slams shut. The entire backstage area goes pitch black. A scream erupts from my throat, strangled, terrified. I'm locked in.

The laughter continues, bouncing off the walls until I can't tell the position.

Involuntary sobs burst from my chest. I'm trapped. He's getting closer. In the dark, I'm not safe, too disoriented to make my way out.

"Help!" I scream with all my air. "Help me!"

I can hear him breathing. I fling my hands out trying to strike at the phantom I can't see, but I come up with air, more terrified than before. I shrink back, trying to pull away from the danger.

"Help me!" My throat shreds under the strain. I draw in a breath amidst the sobs of fear. "Please someone help me!"

A tickle at my arm steals my breath. I jerk away, flashing the light of my cell's screen to chase the darkness. But I'm a matchstick in a cavern. Nothing but grey haze shines back at me.

Fingers wisp through my hair, like a phantom in a hallucination.

I scream.

I scream again.

"Please! Please help me!"

My feet break into a run, disoriented, backwards, unsure of whether I'm running for the door or running deeper into the abyss. The steel double doors rise up in my vision as I near them. The metal rod cools my hot hands. I grip it and shove with all my might. It won't move. I slam my body against it. A slip of air tells me I've managed to push it far enough that a crack has opened to the stage area. Pulling close to the gap, I smash my mouth to the only chance I have left. Cool air eases over my lips. Safety calls from the other side, if I could just get through.

"Help me! Please! Someone help me!" I pray my voice carries through the gap in the doors.

I look at my phone screen, hopeful that the call has connected.

Roman will hear me.

Roman will save me.

No Service.

I scream again, this time in defeat. An arm loops around my waist, another smothers my mouth with sweaty hands. With no other options, I bite down into their flesh with all my strength. My attacker flings me from his body. The light of my phone clatters in the opposite direction, sliding across the floor until the glow extinguishes. The ground slams against my shoulder, hip, and leg. I roll under the momentum until I finally give up.

Weak.

Exhausted.

Finished.

The pressure starts at my ankle, a hand working up my leg, over my hip, curving around my back until I feel his whole weight pressing down on me. An exhale flickers over my ear. Condensation from his breath gathers on my neck. My sobs are the only sound.

Until he whispers, *"Sing for me, Nightingale."*

Pain cracks my skull. Light flashes behind my eyes, and the world goes numb.

CHAPTER 22

Roman

Twenty minutes. I have twenty minutes to tell her goodbye. I'm lucky Rick is giving me that. Going by the local haunts for Dark Fox's crew, everything has been stripped. They're in the wind already, breaking protocol and skipping the steps for getting rid of loose ends. Maybe I should take comfort that we managed to scare them, but it puts unneeded pressure on an already tense situation.

I head for the cottage first, assuming she'll be in her office, but other than a few high school kids in server's uniforms, it's empty.

"Do you know where I can find Kennedy Cartwright?"

The shaggier of the two shrugs. "We're helping with the food, man. Everyone else is at the auditorium."

It takes everything in me not to beat directions out of him. His companion comes to his rescue. "You can't miss it. Everyone's headed there now. Follow the path past the barn, up toward the back forty. The concert is set to start soon."

"You the missing guy?" the shaggy one asks.

"Missing guy? No, I'm not one of the acts." I stop short of the door, curiosity peaked. "Someone's missing?"

"Yeah, they're looking all over. Can't start the show I guess until the head guy turns up."

Head guy?

Ace?

I find the path with ease. Just like the delinquents said, the crowd of people is moving as a body to the largest building at the back side of the property. I search the crowds for someone, anyone, I might know, but to no avail.

"Ticket, please?" Another teen accosts me at the front door of the auditorium.

I stretch on my toes to see inside, but the wall of people gives me nothing to work with.

"I don't have one. I need to find Kennedy Cartwright."

"No ticket, no pass," he says.

"Look, I'm not here for the show. I'm here to see Kennedy, Ace's daughter."

"You won't get by without a ticket, pal." He folds his toothpick arms across his chest and squares his jaw like it means something.

I dig into my back pocket, I'm sure he thinks I'm grabbing a wallet. Instead, I jam my badge into his face. "How about this, Junior? This enough of a ticket for you? Or are you looking to hinder a federal investigation?"

The couple behind me draws back, as if they might go down for being within cuffing range. At this point, I'll take anyone out if it means getting to Kennedy. I don't feel like myself. It's not like me to lose it, but my gut is screaming that something is horribly wrong. It's strange that I haven't seen her yet. My senses are drawn tight, nervous that there's more here than I know.

"Yeah," the teen opens the gate and welcomes me through, "go ahead. Last I saw, Ace is up by the stage. I think Victoria is there too."

"And Kennedy?"

He frowns. "I haven't seen her for a while. But I'm sure one of them can help you."

I don't bother to thank him. I brandish my badge, calling out, "FBI! Move!" as I push through the crowd shuffling to their seats. The crowd parts easily, scared of what I might do. It's an empty threat. If Rick finds out I'm misusing my badge, he'll hang me from the nearest tree.

"Roman!"

I spin, hoping it's Kennedy, but Victoria catches my arm.

"Do you have her?" There's hope, even pleading in her wide eyes. "Please tell me she's been with you."

"No, Kennedy's not with me. I was coming to tell her goodbye. What's going on?"

Ace Cartwright shoves up next to me, cantankerous as ever. "Kenny's missing. Can't find her anywhere. Not like her to miss something like this. Sound team said she never checked in with them either and that was three hours ago."

"Has anyone seen her in three hours?" My training tells me this isn't a typical missing person.

"Carly and Marco said they were supposed to meet her at four and she never showed. Carly said they were a few minutes late, but it's not like Kennedy to run off. She'd track them down if she had to. Where could she be?" Victoria rises up on her toes to search the crowd.

I look at my watch. Three hours. She could be anywhere in three hours.

"Where were they supposed to meet?" I lean close to Victoria to hear her answer over the throng.

"Backstage," she says. "I'll show you."

I ignore Ace's glare and follow Victoria through the crowd. She gains entry past the bouncer standing at the door, but the chaos extends to the backstage area as well.

"Kennedy!" Victoria yells. "Kennedy, are you back here?"

Something's not right. I grab Victoria's arm to pin her in place and dial Macroe's number. She picks up on the first ring.

"Yeah?"

"It's Palermo. Are you in the van?"

"Waiting on you, Rom-e-o."

"Run a trace for me, would you?"

Thankfully, she doesn't question me. I recite Kennedy's number from memory. In the background, the agent's fingers clack against the keys. Opening strains from the first act fill the air.

The crowd goes wild. No way would Kennedy miss this, not with all the work she's invested.

"You're right on top of it," Macroe says. "You want me to ping it?"

"Do it."

I hang up the phone, listening for the alert Macroe has triggered. It's nearly impossible in the din, but a faint ping resonates. Victoria catches sight of it first and retrieves it, crawling beneath a rack of chairs on the wall. Her face pales as she holds it out to me. The shattered screen confirms my fears.

Kennedy was taken by force.

"Get your family," I tell Victoria. "Meet me out front. I want to walk the area."

She nods, but fear hobbles her feet. I shove her forward, trying to get her moving. In cases like this, every second counts. I press through the crowd, knowing if someone subdued her backstage, they would have used a back door to get her out, not the front where they'd be seen by everyone.

The metal handle gives way, and the setting sun lights the horizon in orange and pink. I search the ground for signs of a struggle, or dragging, but the ground is clear. I start around the front, headed to meet her family. My phone buzzes in my hand. Without looking at the screen I click it though, hopeful that Rick is there and willing to help.

"Yeah, it's Roman."

"Ah yes, the piano man."

I stop dead in my tracks.

"Dante Alvero."

"Nice to talk with you, Agent Palermo. Wasn't sure I'd get through. Probably real busy where you're at right now."

"How would you know where I am?"

Victoria spots me from the front and motions for Hudson and Ace to follow. I walk away, shoving distance between us so I can talk. Pushing the speaker button, I click through to text Macroe.

"Trace the number calling me."

Alvero laughs at my words. "I'm like you, agent. I have eyes and ears everywhere. I trust by now you've found my songbird's phone?"

I hold up a finger to silence Kennedy's family as they pull close.

"Do you have her?"

"Of course, after all, she belongs to me."

Anger courses through my veins. "She doesn't belong to you, you psychopath. Let her go, and you won't be charged."

My frustrations amuse him. "Big threats for you. I'm only playing by your rules."

"My rules? What are you talking about?"

"You took something of mine and called it yours. I've taken something of yours and made it mine."

Realization dawns at once. "The files."

"Specifically, one. You stole my fox. I need it back."

Ace glares at me with hatred brimming in his eyes. If he could, he'd wring my neck for the danger I've brought on his family.

"What do you want?" I ask.

"I'm reasonable," Alvero says, "a trade for what the other owns will be sufficient for now."

"When and where?"

"Not so fast agent. I'll be calling those shots. I'll be in touch."

Ace snatches the phone from my hand. "Alvero, I'll shoot you in both kneecaps and leave you to die. You tell me where my daughter is right now!"

"Oh, Ace!" Alvero sounds close to giddy with excitement. "I'd hoped you caught wind by now. Careful of that heart. We'd hate to have something happen to you."

"You send her back or I swear no one will recognize your corpse, you hear me?"

"Ace, no one ever said harm would come to her. Follow my instructions and I'll be glad to send her back without harming a feather on my songbird's head."

"How do we know you have her?" Victoria breaks in front

of her father, grabbing my phone away. "How do we know she's alive?"

There's pause, a few words in the background and then the worst sound I've ever heard.

"Help me! Please, someone help me!" Kennedy's screams of terror cut right through me. A clean slap cuts off her voice until it fades away into soft tears.

Alvero comes back on the line with his last direction. "Be ready in one hour. Cross me and the bird will be in bits."

Three beeps indicate the end of the call. I stare at the phone, unsure of how to proceed. The file is key evidence against Alvero and Dark Fox. Giving it away would be like letting them go. But at the same time, we can't use the files without the encryption key. What good is a lock without a key?

My thoughts are jarred by Ace's grip on my jacket. "What's it gonna be, Mr. FBI? How are you getting my daughter back?"

I shake him off, shoving him back into Hudson's arms. "We'll take care of it. That's what we do."

"Like this?" Ace asks. "You had them, and now they have her. Is that how you're going to take care of it?"

"Daddy," Victoria puts her hand on his shoulder, "this isn't Roman's fault."

"He got her wrapped up in this mess, didn't he?"

"She's been going to *The Nightingale* long before Roman came to town," Hudson says. "She didn't tell you because she knew you wouldn't approve."

Ace shakes his kids off and levels his finger at me. "I don't care what they say. I'm holding you responsible. You bring my daughter back, you hear me?"

I agree, but in the back of my mind I worry that bringing her back might mean a body bag.

CHAPTER 23

Kennedy

Thoughts churn like those old-time lollipops mom used to buy us at the state fair. The colors swirled together. Then the lollipop twisted the swirls. My mouth waters just thinking about one. It sounds amazing. Cherry and pineapple, maybe grape, or lemon. Anything to get this taste out of my mouth. What is it? Feels like the week I spent at camp and forgot my toothbrush. Or the time I fell from the swing set and knocked out my front teeth.

Blood.

Metallic tang and a swollen lip. I try to open my eyes, but the left won't cooperate. Even through my right eye, the world is hazy. I move to rub the sleep away, but my hand jerks in place. Panic wells up in my heart.

"I wouldn't move too much," a man says to my left. "You're not in a position to hold your own weight just yet."

I follow the voice, but through the haze in my eyes, I see nothing more than an outline. Tall, broad shouldered, dark suit and tanned skin.

I open my mouth to speak but nothing comes out. A snap from my left clicks. I hear footfalls across a hollow floor. Fingers grip my chin, but before I can pull away, water floods my mouth. I gulp the water, spilling half of it down my front. The trickles run over bare skin into crevices.

I recoil.

I'm not wearing my own clothes.

Squinting my bad eye, I focus on my legs. Sequins wink up at me. Far too elegant for what I'm enduring.

A strapless dress.

They changed my clothes.

Did who knows what, while I slept unconscious.

Revulsion churns my stomach.

"Who are you?" My hoarse whisper grates on the air.

The figure turns away from me, as if he won't answer, but his voice trails through the air, a perfect juxtaposition of refinement against my haggard appearance.

"That is of no concern to you, but if you must know, those in my circle call me Dark Fox."

"What do you want with me? Why am I here?" Speaking the words lights my throat on fire. I want to collapse to the ground, but my body remains upright.

"I'm afraid you've become a nuisance we can't afford any longer. Your risky relationship with federal agents outweighs even my employee's morbid fascination with you. I ordered a bullet between your eyes, but Dante thought up this scheme. Two birds, one stone." His laughter is musical, more refined from what I would expect from a man of his caliber. "Birds, excuse the pun. You're quite the little songbird, aren't you? I was impressed at Dante's party."

"I don't understand." My knees buckle, and I feel hands for the first time. Someone stands behind me, keeping me upright, forcing me to remain still, as if collapsing to the ground might disrespect the boss.

"No, you wouldn't. The honest answer is far too simple. You're caught in the middle. This war goes back decades. Players in a game won by more than cards. We had a truce. But it looks as though those days are over. Too bad. That's when the innocent die. Children paying for the sins of their fathers, that's all this is. But," his feet echo down a set of stairs, "rejoice because your death will mean sustained life for my empire. Quite the noble sacrifice, Miss Cartwright."

I follow the shadow of his figure, moving far away until a sliver of light betrays a door, and he's gone. The hands at my back release me, and I collapse to the floor.

* * *

Roman

"I don't understand," I repeat myself back to Rick. "We know Dante has her. We know we could stick him with an abduction rap as well as who knows what else, but you're not willing to consider it?"

He stands outside the van, arms crossed over his chest, unwilling to budge an inch. "Are you new around here? The standard line won't change. We don't negotiate with terrorists. Not even when it's the girl you've got a crush on."

"She's a civilian, Rick. She's only wrapped up in this because of choices we made, yours and mine. Her blood is on our hands. We have to get her."

Rick shakes his head, pressing his lips tight. "It's not that simple. If you were talking about a raid, maybe. But you want to trade valuable intel. What kind of precedent would we be setting?"

"Valuable intel? It's half a file. It's nothing to us without the encryption code. Who cares?"

"They do, Palermo. That's what's got me." Rick's jaw tightens, shifting side to side. "If they're this desperate to get it back, don't you think we have something more than useless information? I can't risk that on the life of one girl. We have agents scouting out their locations, as least the ones we know about. They just cleared *The Nightingale*. We're in the waiting game right now. I know it's frustrating, but there's nothing else we can do."

He makes me want to scream. I slam my open palm against the van. Pain lights up my system. The swell of adrenaline subsides, leaving me with a sick calm in the face of destruction.

"There has to be something we can do. I refuse to stand by and let her die."

"When that call comes in, we'll make a counter plan. Follow protocol. That's all we have left."

Rick turns on his heel and climbs back into the van. I lean back, smacking my head repeatedly against the window, hoping to knock free some loophole, some tidbit I've never thought of.

I scoured the entire auditorium. Searched the perimeter. With all the foot traffic, it was impossible to see a trail of any kind. With two men they could have easily carried her to a waiting vehicle. But in broad daylight?

Spotting him in the distance, I flag Hudson down. He jogs toward me, eyes wide with hope.

"Did you hear from her?"

I hate squashing his optimism, but I need his instincts instead. "Not yet. Tell me about this event. Do you do everything? Or do you bring in sub-contractors?"

"We do almost everything, I guess we contract a few things out."

"Like what?" My impatience speeds my words. "What specifically would apply to the auditorium?"

Hudson shakes his head like he's never going to pass this test. "I'm not sure, that's Kennedy's world. I know we have a sound guy, but he's been with us for years. I help him out in the booth. He's taught me a lot, and he's like seventy. No way could he take Kennedy. And the lighting guys bring in some stuff, but most everything is already here. That's why they like working with us."

"What about food? Catering of any kind? I'm looking for anyone who would be carrying large chests, or a bag big enough for —" I stop before I can say body.

Tears gather in his eyes. The sun has set. Trauma is always harder in the dark.

"Victoria takes care of the food," Hudson swallows his emotion the best he can. "I can't think of anyone—"

"I didn't do the food this time." Victoria comes up beside her brother. "Dad and I got in a battle a couple days ago. He went around me and hired caterers."

"Where are they?"

Victoria shrugs. "I swear I saw the van pull up, but I've been looking for them for a couple hours, and I haven't found them anywhere." Horror dawns in her eyes. "Do you think they took her?"

"What kind of caterers kidnap a person?" Hudson's voice cracks under the stress.

"The kind who aren't dealing in food." I take him by the shoulders. "There's a chance your sister is still here, on the ranch. They might not have risked taking her very far. Is there somewhere quiet they could hold her?"

Before he can answer, my phone rings. I slam my hand against the van window until Rick sticks his head out. I hold up my phone and motion for everyone around me to stay quiet. I click through the call and switch to speaker.

"This is Roman. Who am I speaking to?"

"Pedro Marquez," he answers, but I'd know his squirrely little voice anywhere.

"What are your demands?"

"We told you our demands. We want the file back in exchange for the girl. What you need to know is our directions. The directions you're going to follow, or we'll blow your little girlfriend into a hundred bits."

He's baiting me, trying to get under my skin, but he's a low rung nothing, which means Dante is making his break and leaving Pedro to clean up. Rick whirls his finger in the air, telling me to stretch it out, the trace must be working.

Ace steps in next to his daughter. Victoria sets a hand over her father's arm for comfort. I hate letting them hear this. If I'm going to stretch the phone call, I'll have to dive into details no family member should ever hear.

"How'd you get her out, Pedro? We know you posed as caterers, but I can't find van tracks by the auditorium. You must have gotten sly. Expected something a little heavier handed from the likes of you."

"She's small. Fits perfect in an ice chest, long as you break a few things to jam her in."

Her father's lip trembles at the thought. My own rage kindles in my chest but betraying my calm would only aggravate the situation. I have to keep the power on my side.

"Then what? Carried her across the field like a picnic?"

"Just about. She's pretty as a picnic, but I don't have to tell you that, do I, Agent Palermo?" Wicked laughter crosses the line. "Got her looking real good in this little number right now. Strapless, slit up the leg. You seen her body yet? Real treat, I assure you."

I stare at the phone, contemplating every way I want to kill this guy. I can't let him rattle me, but the helplessness of the situation is more than I can bear.

"You wanna hear from her? I can make her sing good." Pedro says something away from the phone. Screams light up the line, indistinguishable sounds except to know the voice who made them.

"You like that, Palermo? You want some more?" Another command in Spanish brings on a torrent of Kennedy's screams. They're torturing her. The scream winds into my brain, twisting like a knife until I can't think, breathe, or function.

I palm my phone, holding it close to my lips. "So help me, Marquez, I will kill you. I will cut you myself, if that's what it takes. Don't lay a finger on her!"

"Oh? A finger? You mean like this?"

Her voice floods the phone. I'm unable to escape the sound of her wailing.

"Roman! Roman! Please! Help me, Roman! Stop! Stop!"

I understand Kennedy's screams this time.

I sink to my knees.

Her sobs choke out to gasping breaths and pitiful wails of

pain.

Pedro's voice comes back over the line, "One hour, shipping yard on the outskirts of town. Hand the flash drive to the parking attendant and he'll give you the name of the cargo hold. Try anything stupid, and we'll blow the whole yard."

The line falls dead. I drop my phone, falling forward to my palms to catch my breath. It's my fault. Her life is in my hands, and I've killed her.

"We got the trace," Rick yells from the van. "He's at that shipping yard outside town. We need to move."

My training takes over. Feelings pack into tiny boxes, compartmentalized where I won't have to deal with them. All that remains is the rage.

"Wait," Hudson catches my arm, "he's not there. It's a trap. You're walking into a trap."

"It all adds up, kid. Now, I gotta act on it."

Hudson won't let go. "I'm telling you. You didn't hear what you thought you heard."

"I heard all of it, kid. It was agony, but now I have to do something about it."

"You *think* you heard it," he blocks my path. "I've worked with the sound guy, remember. I know a recording when I hear it. They recorded her, and now they're playing it back to manipulate you."

Ace steps in behind his son. "I agree. The sound echoed differently than his voice. They're in two different locations."

"Palermo! Let's go!" Rick yells again.

"Where's the catering van?" Ace asks. "I checked security tapes. It came in, but it hasn't left. I have guys out searching the property right now."

"You think she's here?"

"I know she is," Ace says. "You can either run off to whatever trap they've laid, or you can trust instincts of people who know a bit more about the players. I've dealt with the likes of Dante Alvero. Not like him to shoot straight like this. He's always looking for an upper hand, a backroom deal if he can get one."

"He's obsessed with her," Victoria points out. "That's what Kennedy told me. Dante wanted to own her. If he can get her and take out the FBI agents tracking him, why wouldn't he try?"

"Now, Palermo!" Rick screams from the van.

Against my better judgement, I turn to face Rick. "Wait, sir, I have other intel."

His face glows red with frustration. "I gave an order. You'll follow that order, do you understand?"

"Even if I think you're going in blind, walking into a trap?"

"We're working on the counter plan. Fall in line Roman or face the consequences."

For as much as I have a one-track mind with Kennedy, Rick has had a single focus for Dark Fox since the beginning. He won't listen to reason. I draw in a breath, glancing back at her family once before I solidify my decision.

"I'm staying here, sir."

Rick shakes his head in disbelief. His hands ball into clenched fists and then release.

"Your funeral, Roman."

The van rocks as he jumps inside and slams the door shut, extinguishing the only light besides the moon. Seconds later, the van lumbers out of sight.

* * *

Kennedy

Blood drips from the corner of my mouth. In the beginning, it was a couple drops, but I fear it's a stream now, pooling and overflowing. Sweat drips from my head, over my chest, down my arms. The heat blurs my thinking worse than the pain.

"Tell me, songbird," Dante pulls close until he's pressed against my frame, "what do they know? How much did they uncover? Did they find the roster? Do they know the players?"

"I don't know," I say again. It's the same answer. I have nothing to give him. If I had something, I'd tell him. "I'm just a talent scout."

Dante's nose bores into my neck, condensation from his breath gathers on my skin. I pull back. His backhand catches my cheek, knocking me to the ground once more.

"You're mine now, did you know that? You belong to me." His fingers lace into my hair, dragging me to my feet, ignoring my cries of pain before he whips me to the ground again. "Mine to do whatever I please, until you no longer please me."

I clasp my hands together, bound at the wrists and push back to standing.

I could run.

If I could find my way out.

The world blurs once more as Dante plants a foot into my back and shoves me to the floor again. My face grates against the slick surface, burning and crying out for relief.

"I didn't tell you to stand yet. You'll learn to follow my commands, or there will be consequences."

Feeling the defiance well up in my chest, I push to standing once more, stumbling as the world tips in my limited vision.

"I'd rather die." I spit on the ground before me, a mixture of saliva and blood.

Even in the dim light, I watch his eyes narrow until a sick smile twists over his features.

"Don't worry, that can be arranged as well."

CHAPTER 24

Roman

"They found the van." Ace yells across the field. "They found it on the far side of the property."

"Tell them to pull back. We can't risk anyone seeing them and taking it out on Kennedy."

Ace sets the phone to his ear, doling out directions to his employees. I review the recording of my last phone conversation that I received from our analyst, John.

"Right there," Hudson stops the tape and reverses it. "Listen. She's screaming, but there are other sounds as well." His fingers roll over the switchboard, thankfully eliminating her screams and enhancing the rest.

"Play it back now," Victoria leans closer, staring at the screen as though it will give us answers.

Hudson plays back the ambient noises captured in the recording. To my untrained ear, the sound is nothing more than wind through the trees, but Hudson's eyes light up.

"That's a dove. Did you hear it, Vic?"

"Definitely," she says. "But he wouldn't risk the old barn. Harley would be making noise if he were in there."

Hudson presses his lips tight. "That only leaves the old auditorium. Doves have been roosting in the crawlspace up above."

"There's another one?" I check the clip in my gun and slam it back in. "Where is it?"

"Other side of the property." Victoria rises with me. "It's much smaller than this one. Been abandoned for nearly a decade. No one goes in there. The place has to be in total disrepair. Dad's talking about tearing it down."

Hudson bites his lip hard. "Kenny goes in there. That's where she pretends to be a star. She doesn't know that I know that. I followed her a couple times. She's been fixing it up. Lights still work. Recording equipment is still functional. It could have made these recordings easily."

Instantly, I know the building he's talking about. I found him dancing with a girl when I was snooping through the warehouse, but it's not like I got a good handle on the layout.

"Tell me about the basic structure." I motion for them to follow me. "How many entrances? How many exits? Hiding places? Anything you can think of?"

"It's basically a movie theater. One hallway in, and a large room with seats and a stage. There's an attic with vents to prop up, and a control room. Entrance is in the front, plus an emergency exit off the auditorium behind the stage curtains, but it has an alarm." Victoria pulls on a jacket to combat the dropping temperatures. "It doesn't have a backstage area like this one, but there is a crawl space under the stage for storage with access from the top."

Hudson breaks off, headed for the main house. Victoria calls after him, "Where are you going?"

"I'm getting my gun, and yours too. We're going after Kennedy."

I raise my hands, stepping in front of Victoria. "No, that's not happening. I can't allow you to put your life at risk. This is my op, and I won't have you—"

A rifle cocks behind me. I whirl to stare at Ace Cartwright ready for action.

"Let's get something straight here, Mr. FBI. You're lucky we're letting you tag along. This is a family matter, on family land to boot. You want to come up with a plan, we're glad to hear it, but you're not calling the shots, not with my daughter."

* * *

Kennedy

The haze burns off, wicked in its release. I groan from the pain. Time has no meaning. Dante could have taken me hours ago, or maybe days. Pain blurs those lines as well as my vision. Sweat drips and mixes with the blood on my skin.

"Get up." Dante jerks me to my feet again. I stumble forward but he yanks me back like a ragdoll. "Stay where I put you. It's especially important that you follow my commands."

My hands come loose. On instinct, I rub the raw flesh, sore from the tight ropes. But seconds later, Dante steals them back. A zip tie catches my skin, cutting into the vulnerable tissue. Weight drags my arms down as he sets a device on top of them. Red glows back at me, like an alarm clock from my childhood.

"Stay close," Dante whispers. His lips press against my forehead. I recoil, trying to move away, but I'm anchored to the boards beneath me. I jerk the rope and metal clanks. His footsteps move away, thumping down the stairs, echoing out to the darkness. A hinge creaks and a door slams. The sounds register in my memory, but cloudy.

Overhead, speakers blare feedback. I cringe, unable to cover my ears with my bound hands anchored to the floor. The overhead lights flash.

No, not overhead lights.

A spotlight.

Dead centered over the top of me.

My surroundings gel in an instant, too many nights spent on this exact stage. I know where I am, and my stomach drops. No one will think to look for me in the abandoned auditorium.

My one eye adjusts to the light. My dress clings to my figure, dabbled in blood from my injuries. But my hands come into view, and my horror triples.

Tied to my wrists, ready, armed and waiting, a clock stretches over my forearms with a block of c-4 sandwiched between. A rope anchors me to the handle of the trap door on the stage. Like a lamb for slaughter, I have no escape.

Dante's voice booms over the empty auditorium as he steps down the stairs to the seats below. "We could have been so good together. But Dark Fox doesn't allow loose ends."

My body trembles with fear. "Please, don't do this."

Dante shrugs as if he's tossing out leftovers. "It's done, but I'll tell you what. You sing me something. That way you go out with a bang."

Despair brings my chin to my chest, breaking under the pressure of it all.

I'm going to die.

It's over.

"Sing!" Dante's command bounces off the walls. I shake my head, unwilling to give him any satisfaction. "Sing, or I end this right now!"

I lift my gaze, stare out to where he's perched in a center seat, four rows up, boots on the seat in front of him, crossed at the ankles. He shakes what I have to assume is a detonator in his hand. I'm nothing more than a puppet for his entertainment.

"SING!"

* * *

Roman

"You any good with that thing?" I ask Hudson as we close in on the old auditorium.

"I bet I'm better than you," he says. "How many guys you shot?"

I cast him a quick glance. "How many guys *you* shot?"

He frowns. "No guys, just ducks, a few rabbits, and one mountain lion last year."

Kid's making a point. Ducks take tracking and calculation. Rabbits are fast. Mountain lions are determined to kill you, and it's do or die, no hesitation. I let the subject drop.

"I'm going in the front. You wrap around the back."

"Dad and Vic have the exits covered from the tall grass back there."

I hope they're at least as talented as my seventeen-year-old shadow.

"Don't shoot anyone if you don't have to. If you do, go for a leg, shoulder, or arm. I don't need you having your first kill today."

"Kill or be killed, isn't that the saying?"

"Just stay alive," I tell him. "There's a chance Dante is in there alone. Keep your cell on you."

"You ready?"

"Recon only, you understand?"

Hudson gives me a quick nod and drops into his knees, following my advice to stay low to the ground, but fast. We move through the dark without a sound. A guard pops up from behind the corner, illuminated by the rising half-moon.

The flash from his muzzle catches my attention. I shove Hudson to the ground and take the shot. The guard groans and collapses. A second crops up in my vision on the opposite side. I take aim, but a rifle fires from the hill. The guard falls to the ground, unmoving.

The building remains still. Hudson flashes a thumbs up to his family from the grass.

"Vic took state in a rifle competition three years in a row. She's pretty accurate."

"Good thing."

I signal to move out. Brush smacks against my leg. It's too hard to see what I'm walking into in the dark, but I keep my sights down the barrel of my gun. Faint strains from the concert still catch the wind. A whole world outside this one that has no idea danger lurks on their doorstep.

We meet no more resistance along the way. I motion for Hudson to guard the entry and hope his family can pick off any extra intruders before they get to him. Remembering the building, I should be able to enter, clear the hall that leads to the main room, and steal a peek inside the auditorium. I pull back the door, clearing the front hall first. Using my foot to brace the sound, I let the door fall shut behind me.

Heat from the day swelters inside. With no windows, and hardly any doors, there's no escape from the temperatures. I push forward, gun up, searching for any sign of life. A faint glow emanates from the doorway ten feet ahead. I don't want to walk in blind. That sort of thinking could get not only me killed, but Kennedy as well.

Steeling my nerves, I start forward, but the next sound stops me dead.

Her voice.

Though trembling, though ragged, I'd know it anywhere. Staying close to the wall, I ease until my view to the auditorium opens up through the open main entrance. She's right where she belongs, under the spotlight, but just like Pedro promised, she's in a dress I've never seen. My guts churn over the abuse she might have endured. I'm about to pull back when I catch sight of it. Strapped to her wrists is a timer. That maniac strapped a bomb to the woman I love.

My heart surges forward, ready to take on any danger inside to save her life, but training pushes me back. Protocol dictates calling for backup and notifying my superior. I reverse without a sound, clinging to the fact that she's still alive.

Hudson catches the door, pulls it back, and waits with expectance. "Well, is she in there?"

"Yeah," I pull out my cell, moving away from the building, "but it just got complicated."

"How so?" Hudson trails after me like a puppy. "Let's go get her."

"She's wired," I say, hoping it translates. His lost expression tells me I have to clarify. "He strapped a bomb to her. I don't know where he is, or what he's planning, but he has the upper hand in this situation."

I press Rick's name on my phone as Hudson launches into his tirade of how stupid I am and what a waste of time this is.

"Palermo," Rick's fury has only deepened, "you've got a lot of nerve calling me."

"I found her," I say, hoping it will dissipate the anger, "she's here on the far side of the ranch."

"You got eyes on her?"

"I did. She's wired."

"Any hostiles inside?"

"Couldn't see, sir. You're walking into a trap. Circle back."

"I don't take orders from you. How do we know she's not in on it? Maybe she's bait to lure you away? Maybe they're storing her? We're set to take down the whole organization in ninety seconds. You expect me to abort because you saw a pretty girl?"

"I'm telling you, they set you up."

"We turned in the fake drive. We're on the way to the storage container, Trojan horse style. They won't know what hit them. Trap or not, we're coming out of this on top. Consider yourself relieved of duty, Palermo."

The phone falls, but Rick didn't cut the call. Sounds of pounding feet fuzz up the receiver. Gunfire rattles over the line, but I have no way of knowing which side has fired. Shouts of alarm, screams of anguish, and cries for help widen Hudson's naïve eyes. A deafening explosion shatters the air, not only through the phone line, but through the ground we stand on in violent vibrations.

The phone falls from my grasp.

They're gone.

I'm alone.

Kennedy needs me.

CHAPTER 25

Roman

"I can't disarm a bomb, Hudson. We have to call it in to the locals, get a bomb squad out here."

"What kind of FBI agent can't disarm a bomb?"

"Most of us," I snap back. My entire team was slaughtered seconds ago. I don't have the patience for his assumptions. "You have to go through extra training."

"What's the hold up?" Ace pushes back the last of the brush and stops beside us. "Is she in there or not?"

"She's in there, and he's too chicken crap to go after her," Hudson says, pointing to me. "She's wired."

Ace's eyes widen. "There's a bomb?"

"Yeah," I run my fingers through my hair, trying to catch hold of my mind and the situation. "I don't know bombs, and I'm fairly sure my entire team got blown sky high. Including our bomb tech."

Ace clears his throat. "I can do it."

"What?" I look up to see if he's bluffing, but the old rancher's eyes are steady. "You can disarm it? How? How on earth do you know about—"

"US Army. Served four years. Someone was always trying to blow us up. Served me well to learn how to kill one of those things. Not to mention, you work on a ranch long enough, and you pick up some knowledge about wiring."

"You willing to risk her life on that knowledge?"

He narrows his eyes as he stares me down. "You think I'd be offering if I weren't. Let's get this done."

"Dad," Victoria set her hand to his shoulder, "your heart, I don't think you can take this."

"You worry about getting your sister out. That's all that matters, you hear me?" It's Ace's word that carries the family. Victoria backs down and the patriarch looks to me. "What's the plan?"

I'm not a leader. I'm a pawn in the battle. I receive commands and execute them, but these three Cartwrights need me to step up and take over.

"Like Vic said," I steal the family name for her, "he's obsessed with her. If it's Dante in there, he's got her on the stage performing for him while he's in the center. He'll have a remote detonator. We'll have to time it perfectly."

"I'll take Vic with me," Ace says, "I'll strip the alarm on the emergency exit door and enter from the wings on the stage."

"No," Victoria says, "Roman needs me to shoot. I'm climbing up top, going in through one of the vents on the roof. I have an idea."

* * *

Kennedy

Music has never tortured me. It's always been my liberator. But my voice strains and cracks. Dante threatens the detonator every time I drop a note. My heart can't take this abuse.

"Just do it!" I scream mid-song. "Just hit it. You'll take us both out. No way will you survive."

A grin curls over his slippery cheeks. "I planned for that, darling. I have thirty seconds to make my way out. That's hardly even a quick jog. These walls will contain the blast—and the mess you'll make."

I have no tears left. The saltwater stings the wounds anyway. My shoulders shake with silent sobs no one will ever hear.

"Sing for me," Dante leans forward in his seat, "sing me one last song."

"Concert's over."

His voice jerks my head up. Roman fills the entryway to the main room in the auditorium. A gun tight in his grasp, he levels it at Dante, still sitting in the center seats. Like a stalking predator, Roman slips closer by the second. As if expecting it, Dante laughs.

"Did you feel that thunder a minute ago? Who knew FBI agents would make such a ripple in the pond? I have to say I'd hoped you'd gone up with them."

"You're under arrest, Dante. Disarm the bomb. Let the girl go. I'm taking you in." He crosses at the base of the seats, headed for the stairs, pulling closer to Dante at the center of the room.

Dante's laughter increases. "Such bold words from you. Didn't know you had it in you." He lifts that detonator over his head. "I'll be glad to drop it, but you should know, this model came with a bonus dead man's switch. If I drop it," he mimics the explosion with his hands.

"Roman, get out of here!" I shout from the stage. "It's not worth it."

Dante smirks in my direction. "Smart girl. There's no way to win this one."

The FBI agent slinks closer, climbing the stairs, first level, second level, never taking his eyes off of his target. "You're gonna disarm that bomb, Dante."

"Not likely."

PSSSTTT

I pry my eyes away from the showdown and search the darkness of the wings. Hudson motions for me to join him. Dad's crouched on the ground, waiting. I shake my head, motioning to the rope securing me to the floor.

"I'm gonna give you until three," Roman says, holding my

captor's focus.

"You won't risk it," Dante says. "You shoot me, and we all die."

"You think you hold all the cards with that switch," Roman shakes his head, "But all I have to do is keep you in here with me. You're not looking to die today. Disarm the bomb, Dante."

"Tell you what, I'll count for you, because it's an empty threat." Dante holds up his hand and counts down. "Three, two, one."

A shot shatters the silence. Dante pulls his hand back in, clutching it to his chest. Blood pools where the bullet has torn through the flesh. Roman's gun hasn't moved. He never fired. He has a second shooter. Fear flashes in Dante's eyes before his arrogance takes over.

"I'd rather die in here then rot in prison."

"It's an option," Roman says, voice level as his gun. He moves into position, third level, even with Dante. "Three, two..."

"You wouldn't think to—"

A shot breaks through his words, not waiting for the final count this time. Dante grabs his leg, screaming, sinking to his knees. Metal grates metal as the shooter jams the bolt back and ejects the shell.

"Vic!" Roman shouts to rafters. "At least wait for the count."

Dante spews threats, curses, and death upon us all. "You asked for this."

The detonator falls from his hand and clatters to the ground. In the next second, Dante raises his gun to shoot Roman. Roman's gun fires in rapid succession. Dante's body falls beneath the seats and out of sight. Hudson hurries my dad across the stage to my side.

"Ace! Can you do it?" Roman yells from the center seats.

My father grabs my wrists, twisting until he can see the housing. The clock ticks down.

00:29

00:28

00:27

"I don't know," Dad yells back at him. "Get Vic and Hudson out of here."

* * *

Roman

00:25

Victoria scrambles down from where she was perched, rifle in hand.

00:24

00:23

The clock ticks down without any regard for our lives.

"Can you do it or not, Dad?" Hudson holds Kennedy's hands steady, knife ready.

00:21

00:20

00:19

"I don't know. It's been a long time."

The confidence her father displayed earlier is vanishing in the face of blowing his daughter to bits.

"You guys gotta get out!" I scream at them. "Go! Now!"

00:17

00:16

"I'm doing it, Dad" Hudson flicks his knife open and slices the zip tie securing the bomb to Kennedy's wrists. He saws through the rope that secures her to the stage. Once free, he shoves her into her father's arms, but there's no time for celebrating. Jerking the handle on the trap door, Hudson drops the bomb into the storage unit below.

00:11

00:10

The tiny door slams shut.

"Run!" Hudson screams.

I jump the cloth seats, counting the last seconds in my mind. I rush through the auditorium exit into the hallway. Gripping the door, I slam it shut. Ace and Hudson wheel an ancient lighting unit in front of the door.

"Go!" I push them forward, trailing behind them.

3

2

1

The blast wave slams me against the wall. A high-pitched wail rings in my ears, unrelenting and blinding with pain. Walls shake and cripple. I collapse to the ground, air knocked from my lungs, leaving me gasping. Shockwaves rip through my body. I crawl forward, glass and cement chunks cutting into my arms. Debris falls from the ceiling. I drag myself over the floor.

"Watch out!"

I don't know who screamed it, but it's half a second too late. A beam collapses on top of me, pinning my legs. I struggle hard, panic caving in around me with the rest of the building. I can't get free. Every movement is more painful than the last.

Hands link with mine, dragging and pulling. Muffled shouts and commands hedge up around me. I scream in agony as I'm jostled free. The ground, caked with cement and wreckage, shifts to cold earth and dewy grass as I am dragged free of the old auditorium. I collapse against the soil, moaning, but strangely happy for the pain that tells me I'm alive.

Insistent hands roll me on my back. I recoil my arm, positive it's broken. Hudson pats down my frame. I bat him away with my good arm, hoping for one moment's peace.

Ace's face floods my vision. "Your shoulder is dislocated!" He's yelling, but I can barely hear him. "I'm gonna set it."

"No, don't!" I try to say the words, but my lungs are coated in debris and dust. Without listening, Ace pulls me against him. Fire rips through my body as he jams my shoulder back into place. I collapse again, searching in my delirium for the one thing that matters.

"Where's Kennedy?" I cough until I gasp for air. "Where's Kennedy?"

Ace leans over me again, sizing me up. "Why should I tell you?"

I'm too tired to think of a lie. Too tired to give an excuse. I only have one answer left in my delirium.

"Because I love her."

I cling to consciousness, but it slips away and takes me with it.

CHAPTER 26

Roman

Five days in the hospital.

Four days back east facing my consequences from superiors.

Two days staying with mom and lying my butt off about why I can't hear her very well. Dad seemed to know. For the first time in a long time, he recognized me. Maybe because I'm finally acting like myself.

Two more days to argue with myself about seeing her, because technically she told me to keep my distance. But that was before I rescued her from a psychopath.

Ten minutes parked at the front of her driveway, trying to get the courage to drive in.

Twenty-three seconds before Hudson accosts me outside the house.

"Whatcha doing here, Roman?"

"Good to see you too, kid," I say. "You doing okay?"

He shrugs. "The ringing stopped by day two. How about you?"

"Comes and goes. It was quick thinking to throw the bomb in the storage locker. Probably saved my life since it contained some of the blast."

"You know, just trying to be a hero like you. You got us all outside the building before the blast hit."

Small talk has never been my forte.

"Is she home?"

"She's around." Hudson's non-committal answer only tightens my nerves.

"You think she'll see me?"

"Never know until you try, I guess." He points to the path that leads to the cottage.

Of course, she's working. I start that way, slower than normal, but I ditched the cane six days ago. Hudson's voice catches me before I get too far.

"I'm pulling for you, man."

It's something, though I don't know if he'd still say it if he knew the news I'm bringing. Ten steps down the path I regret ditching the cane. My leg aches where the beam caught me. Looking to the south it's not hard to spot the construction crew working on the old auditorium. Knocking it down, or building it up, I can't tell, but if I had to guess, I'd wager Ace would flatten it and salt the earth.

A sharp whistle splits the air. My nerves go raw, reaching for a gun that isn't there. But Ace's laughter slows my racing heart.

"Still a little on edge?" Resting on a bench under a tree, the Cartwright patriarch cocks an eyebrow. Pieces of his rifle cover the table in front of him.

"Can you blame me? Last time I was here I was nearly blown to bits."

"Not bits, maybe halves or quarters. How's the leg?"

"Sore. But I'll recover." I motion at his gun and cleaning supplies. "Were you expecting me?"

"Happy coincidence." Ace tries to keep his features tight, but a smile tugs at his eyes. "Vic never cleans these after she shoots. Always expects her dad to clean up her mess. You'd think they'd grow up."

Looking down the sights, he adjusts one side before he checks it again. I chew on my words, knowing I have one chance to make things right with him.

"My dad taught me to shoot when I was a kid. Did you teach your kids?"

Ace draws in a breath and lets it out with a rumble from his chest. "Sure tried. Vic, she picked it up real fast. She was out hunting with me by the time she was seven. And Hudson, he's got bravery, and a little talent. Whole lot more luck."

"And Kennedy?"

Ace laughs to himself. "Kenny, she's not one for violence. She's like her mama. Tender, careful, cautious." He eyes me over the gun. "She's not made for danger."

"I know." That truth has been eating away at me for days. "I never meant—"

"That girl was in over her head long before you ever showed up," Ace raises a hand to stop me, "I told her to stay away from that club and what does she do? She makes it her typical Thursday night. In reality, Roman, having you around was the best thing that ever could have happened to her."

For once he used my name. I do my best to hold his stare, even when it feels like it's burning right through me.

"You mean what you said? You fell in love with her?"

"Yes, sir." Where that puts us, I don't know, but it feels good to admit it.

"You swear you'll always put her first? You'll keep her safe?"

"I swear." I shake my head. "I don't know if any of it matters. Last we talked, she wasn't real keen on seeing me again."

Ace locks the barrel back into the housing, a sly grin plastered on his face. "You know how women are, one second they want one thing, and the next minute it's a new darn thing. Never know unless you talk to her, I wager."

"And you, sir? You didn't seem happy about someone my age dating your youngest daughter. You're not gonna shoot me in the back if I start out for that cottage? Hudson has informed me you have pigs, and no one will ever find a body."

A full belly laugh seeps from Ace's chest. "That boy, he's too much like his father. Whole lotta talk. We sold the pigs two years ago. No, I've never shot a man in the back, and I'm not planning to start today."

"What if she wants to—"

"If she wants you, if she decides she can handle this life you're choosing," Ace's thick shoulders bounce once, "I won't stand in the way of love and her happiness. Kennedy has always been mature beyond her years. I guess this shouldn't surprise me."

The bench groans as he pushes back. Without another word, he heads for the house. I draw in a breath and blow it out between tight lips. Approval from her father is one thing, approval from Kennedy is another.

I start off on the path again, my limp more pronounced than before. I've gone over what I want to say a hundred times and in a hundred different ways, but the variables are too vast. Every step closer to the cottage is a tick down to her final answer on the subject, and my heart won't relax knowing what might be coming.

I count to ten outside the cottage before I turn the knob and step inside. The kitchen smells like a bakery at peak hours. Victoria must be stress cooking to take the edge off. Every counter boasts a sweet of some kind. Cupcakes, macaroons, cookies, candies, I wouldn't be surprised if she's single-handedly given her family diabetes.

"Roman?"

Kennedy's clipboard clatters to the ground. I hurry to grab it for her, but she stoops first and pins it in her hands.

"I wasn't expecting you. I figured you were—" she looks away before she finishes, "gone."

"I was back in the area. I wanted to check in on you."

Not a total lie.

The bruises haven't faded, but she's managed to lessen them with makeup. Her left eye is open again, albeit still puffy. Red tinges her wrists, but at least they aren't bleeding. Despite all that, she's still the most beautiful woman I've ever laid eyes on.

"I'm managing. Trying to get back into things." She motions to her open office door. "We had a wedding last weekend. I had to let Vic run things. She chased a bridesmaid around the pond for insulting her food. I figured it was time to get back to it. Ready or not."

I crack a smile imagining her sister bearing down on some sorority brat. "I'd run if Vic got mad at me too." I step closer. She doesn't move away. I take it as a positive sign. "You look good, Kennedy."

She turns her cheek away from me as if to hide. "You lie well, Roman. I almost believed you." She crosses my path to move to the kitchen. "You want a cookie or something? Victoria has been stressed about something. She won't tell me anything, other than to say she's making some big decisions. I took a load down to the homeless shelter yesterday, just to return and find she'd at least doubled what I'd donated."

A cookie doesn't interest me, only her, but I don't know where I stand. I rest my hands against the island for support, frustrated that once more she's put it between us.

"I'm sorry for everything that happened, Kennedy. If I could go back and do it all again, I'd do it differently."

Her hand floats over the cookies, passing up the chocolate dipped one for a vanilla crème. Her shoulder shifts, a mini shrug, as if she isn't sure she wants to commit to it.

"I wouldn't."

* * *

Kennedy

"What?" Roman starts to come around the island but thinks better of it. "What'd you say?"

"You said you'd do it all differently." I catch my healed lip between my teeth before I let it slip out. "I wouldn't."

"You wouldn't?"

"No." I stack a few chocolate chip cookies before I knock them over. "I mean, that's how we got to this point, isn't it? If I changed something, we might not end up here."

"Where's here?"

Yesterday I discovered I can smile without pain again. I'm happy to show him my trick.

"Back to you thinking of five ways to cross this island to get to me."

"Six," he says. "Thought of a new one. But might not work with all these cookies and my busted leg."

"Save it for another day, I guess." I change the subject, needing answers of my own. "Are you leaving?"

It's a loaded question, I think. Roman shakes his head, but not because his answer is no. "I went back east, faced the music, so to speak. Got dressed down for involving civilians on an op. Took a lot of heat over that."

"I'm sorry." I move around the corner of the island, lessening the distance. "I hope you didn't get fired because of me."

"No," he pauses like he can't believe his answer, "they promoted me. I have my own team."

"So they lectured you, and then gave you a raise?"

"A lot like sitting in a cold pool, then jumping in the hot tub. Shocking, but at least it wasn't the other way around."

"You're leaving then?" It hurts to say it out loud when my heart hoped otherwise.

"No."

"You turned it down?"

"No." Roman takes a step closer. "They want me here. Pedro and the others escaped in the aftermath of the explosion. Dark Fox hasn't left the area. With Rick gone, I'm the only one with experience dealing with the Dark Fox organization. They want me here."

"Here?"

"Here," he says. His hand catches mine, brushing over the skin, waiting for my reaction. When I take his hand, his breath stills.

"Before," Roman says, "what were you saying about not changing us?"

I apply pressure to my grip, pulling him closer. "I was saying that when you look down the barrel of a gun or watch a clock tick off the seconds until you die, you start to reconsider your life decisions."

Roman draws in a slow breath. "Like what?"

I can't look at him. Not yet. Not when this could still go sideways.

"I'm not good at this way of living, Roman. I'm not made for it. It doesn't come naturally to me like it does for you."

"I know." His grip falters, heavy with disappointment.

I take the final step and stare up at him through my lashes. "But maybe you could teach me."

Roman's eyes widen with surprise. "What?"

"I mean," I grin to lighten the mood, "if *Victoria* can shoot a bad guy, maybe I'm tougher than I think. Besides, I heard a rumor about you."

"What kind of rumor?"

He's watching my lips like primetime television. I catch the bottom one between my teeth and revel in the way he draws me closer.

"Vic said you told daddy something before you passed out, something about the way you feel for me. I guess I was wondering if it was true."

Roman swallows hard, fear and wonder mixed up in his expression. "And what if it is? What would you say about that?"

I can't draw him out any further in this torture. "I love you too, Roman."

"You're saying," his gaze drops to my lips before it returns to my eyes, "you're saying you still want to be with me? You don't want to move on and forget we ever met?"

"Forget you, Roman?" I lose myself to his kiss before I whisper, "Not possible," against his lips.

The End.

A SNEAK PEEK:

The Unbelievable Queen of Hearts

Cartwright Ranch-Book 2

CHAPTER 1

Victoria

He's here again. Mr. Twenty minutes to close, always orders a number five, hold the pickles, sits at the center table and stares. He's gorgeous, so I don't mind when he takes his normal spot while eating his usual. In my mind, I call him Mr. Number Five for short. He's said maybe sixteen words to me in seven visits, but his eyes are speaking volumes. Too bad I'm not fluent in that language, whatever it is.

The number five is a chicken sandwich, waffles for the bun, slathered in a special sauce that I refuse to disclose a single ingredient from—strictly eat at your own risk. It's not my most popular item in the trailer, but his consistency is messing with my statistics at this point.

Tattoos peek out from the edges of his sleeves, only a couple totally visible on his forearms. He keeps his sandy blonde hair short, clipped close to his scalp, likely so he doesn't end up with helmet hair. I figured out three visits ago that he's the one with the black motorcycle parked at the perimeter of the food truck court.

I saw a coyote up close and personal once, popped up in the field while I was waiting for Kennedy to finish a consult with a bride. We locked eyes, and for a moment, I know it considered eating me.

That's what I see in him.

Hunger.

That's not my fault. The number five he's devouring has more than enough food. I'm not stingy. I get the feeling food has nothing to do with whatever I see smoldering in his eyes.

I'd wager he's as dangerous as that coyote too. I've lived my share of adventures, and I can smell reckless nights and fearless abandon rolling off him in waves. Once upon my last life, I would have thrown myself at that kind of future. I know better than to chase any of that now. I put those days behind me.

He's never spoken to me, other than to order. Catching his eye, the left side of his mouth hooks into a crooked grin. Mr. Number Five winks, and blood rushes to my cheeks. I turn away from the window, quick to busy myself with closing down the trailer for the day. A text goes off on my phone. In the security of the back of my food trailer, I retrieve my cell from my apron.

"Don't be late. I promised Roman a nice, normal, family dinner."

Kennedy and her boyfriend. It's been about four months that they've been together. Roman is older than I am, but I think Dad is finally coming around. Doesn't like it but tolerates their relationship because Roman's as clean cut as they come, not to mention he dotes on my sister like she's the queen of freaking Sheba.

The sun rises and sets on those two lately. Like the whole earth has been blessed for their love. I'm cynical by nature and not feeling the sunshine and glitter side of it, but to each their own. I've never felt a connection like theirs, so who am I to judge?

I'm glad Kenny's got some freedom, really, I am. She's spent too long pulling the family along, bearing all the responsibility. She deserves this happiness. She's performing at a few local shows on the weekends, chasing her dreams, and everyone encourages her. So, I'm happy for her, but I'm happy with a side of jealous to go with it.

Two years ago, I came back from culinary school for good. I'm the first to admit that I have a past and a reputation around here. I came back with every intention of putting that behind me, showing everyone in this town, my family, and even myself, that I'm not the same person anymore. Never thought it would be such an uphill battle. People have a hard time shaking their preconceptions. They hang on to the past tighter than they should, but I've done my best despite it all.

I've been catering weddings at Kennedy's side since I came back. It's great. It's reliable. It's what's expected of me if I want to be a Cartwright. But I'm itching for something more. Something that belongs to me outside the Cartwright name. I started looking into food trucks about five months ago, all the freedom of my own restaurant, but without the heavy upfront startup costs. Freedom to travel, freedom to change, just plain freedom on every angle. After two years of walking the Cartwright line, it has a certain appeal to it.

I mentioned the possibility of a food truck to Dad a few times, but he hit the ceiling. Man doesn't like change. He said it wasn't a real job. It's a fad. It won't last. There was more, but I stopped listening when I knew the answer was no. I'm not one to stay down for long, and if he wasn't willing to help, then I knew I could do it myself.

I opened Fried Wildflower three months ago with every penny I'd saved from the weddings I've been working at the ranch. Couldn't afford a whole food truck, but taking after my dad, I won the truck and food trailer in a backroom poker match. Back when I was a kid, Dad used to show me card tricks. We played poker late into the night until Mom got after us. I never stopped learning. By the time I was twelve, I could hustle even the most seasoned players when they came by to see Dad. He warned me no good would ever come of it. He probably never guessed I'd get my stake the way he won his. Probably thought I gave it up. No such luck. Some apples don't fall far from the tree.

Like mom always said, "God gives you talents, so you better use them." Might not be exactly what she was talking about, but I made it work for me. I heard about the poker game, gathered up enough for the buy in and let the cards fall where they may. When the keys to the trailer and truck hit the table, I knew it was fate. I knew it was a risk, I knew I probably shouldn't, but for a chance at the future I wanted, it was worth the gamble. When I had the makings for a royal flush in my hand, minus one card, I held my breath. When that card came in the next round, it became my destiny fulfilled. After my big win, I swore I was done with cards, but the itch remains. Maybe it always will. But I'm different now. I need to show everyone I'm responsible, not reckless like before. That's my plan with Fried Wildflower, show everyone what I'm capable of on my own.

A few hundred fried chicken and waffle sandwiches later, and I'm actually making rent on a place in the court. It's not easy making my schedule work with all the weddings and events out at the ranch, but I made it through our busy season while still making a profit at the trailer, and that's saying something. My family relationships took a hit with my dual lives, that's for sure, but the ranch is slowing down again, and I'll make it up to everyone.

Fried Wildflower isn't much right now, I know that. One day I might make enough to see a little more space than my one-room tiny apartment in town. One day, Dad is going to see that I can make this work. One day, I'll tell them everything, and they'll be proud of me. But, then again, my life has always been a long list of 'one days'. I've learned to look forward to a better future to endure the trials of the present. Nothing, good or bad, lasts forever. But meanwhile, I'm hiding this side game from everyone.

I shoot Kennedy a snarky text saying I'm coming home early because I know how cranky her old man gets when we keep him up late. I'm sure she'll fire back with a zinger of her own. I switch off the fryers. A quick cursory glance later, I notice Mr. Number

Five hasn't moved even though his basket is empty. Typically, that's all I find at the end of the night, an empty basket with a few wildflowers tucked into the wax paper liner. But this time, he's sticking it out.

I wash what I can and pack the rest up, knowing I'll have plenty to do at home, but after a solid day like today, I don't mind. I run through the checklist for closing. All the normal cleaning, wiping down, stacking trays, taking inventory of the food I have left, and packing what I'll need to take with me by the door. I lean toward the front window until I sneak a peek at my visitor.

Still there.

I snap back out of view before he spots me. This is it. He's finally worked up the guts to talk to me, and here I am at the end of a shift, covered in grease and syrup and smelling like smoke.

Oh yeah, that's a love connection, right?

"Hey lady!" a voice yells from the window. "You open?"

The voice is far too young to belong to my mysterious stranger, but not young enough to be endearing. Last thing I want at the end of a shift is a bunch of teen punks making trouble.

I wipe my wet hands on my apron and step back to the window. "Sorry, closed up for the night."

Three young men stare back at me, one with a gold tooth marring up his warped smile. They're nothing but trouble. I've seen them hassling other food truck members for leftovers, spare change, anything they can get their mitts on, because heaven forbid, they actually work.

"You sure you don't got nothin'?" The gold-toothed one asks. "It'd be in your best interest to give over a few tidbits for rent."

"This a shake down?" I ask. Looks like someone wants to own the block. "I pay my rent fine, and not a penny is for brats like you."

"Well, this is our territory, and your trucks are impeding on our work, so it seems it like you ought to give up a little payback, waffle lady." He leans closer, squinting his eyes and giving me his best tough guy impersonation. "You don't want any trouble, do you, lady?"

I draw in a deep breath, considering my options. I don't want to deal with these little idiots, but if I back down or give in today, it'll only be worse tomorrow. Still, I groan internally knowing it might make me late for Kennedy's barbeque.

"Get out of here before I call the cops." I slam the window shut and paste the closed sign with a thump against the glass. If I'm going to make Kennedy's barbeque on time, I don't have a spare minute for wannabe thugs. Their voices fade after a few minutes. Likely I'll have to deal with them again, but at least for today it's done. I gather up the trash and unlatch the back door to the trailer. I toss the first bag out and then the second before I step down.

Pain lights up my head. Two bodies smash against me, throwing me back against the fiberglass wall. I jerk my arm free, but the punk collects it again, sneering at my struggle. The one with the gold tooth weighs a knife in his hand. Twisting from one side to the other with a flick of his wrist.

"See, we could have walked away with just a bite to eat, but now that you've disrespected us, we're gonna need something more from you."

Anger wells in my throat. A knife complicates things, but it doesn't change the fact that the only way to deal with bullies is to stand up to them. Being raised as Dad's oldest has its benefits. I know how to defend myself. I relax my arms, letting the twerps think I've given up. The leader steps closer, smiling like he's won. "You know what I'm thinking I'd like, waffle lady?"

I don't wait to hear his answer. Exploding with all my strength, I strike out with a kick to the front, catching him directly in the stomach and doubling him over. The knife falls from his grip. In the confusion, I jerk my right arm free and punch the opposite goon in the nose, just like Dad trained me. He screams and falls back. I whip around, striking the third with a backhanded slap, but he catches my arm and twists it behind me.

"Hey!" Mr. Number Five moves to intervene, but I shoot him a glare that halts his steps. This is my fight.

With a shove, the brute holding me throws me forward. The momentum rolls me twice before I stop. My pride propels me from the ground, and I dust off my clothes. Gravel drips from my arms. The bigger one swings, but I stay low like Dad taught me. I slam my palms into the teen's chest and shove him back. He crashes into his buddy, still coughing on the ground.

To my left Mr. Number Five watches the whole ordeal, no longer sitting but standing and ready. His eyebrows up come up. "You need some help?"

"I'm fine!" Little punks probably just needed to be shown a thing or two.

"Are you sure? They keep coming."

"Butt out!" I yell at the stranger. They're nothing I can't handle. I'm not like Kennedy, I don't need some muscle-head coming to rescue me.

A scream behind me brings my attention around. The ringleader rushes me, rage burning in his eyes. I spin, catching his arm, and twisting it behind his back, another one of Dad's tricks, but his thick comrade recovers, pulling me back, arm wrapped around my throat.

My feet go out from underneath me as he drags me. I cough, wheeze, and slam my palms against his arm. No matter how hard I twist, I can't free myself. Black edges in on my vision. A lightheaded bliss enters my mind.

An impact shakes my body seconds before I crash to the gravel. Air fills my burning lungs. I gag, cough and try to find my feet again. I stand in time to see Mr. Number Five throw the leader to the ground.

"Get out!" Mr. Number Five yells. "Little boys playing at thugs. Run, before I do worse."

They're moving before he finishes the sentence, scrambling away like field mice on mowing day. I rub my palm over my throat, still feeling the pressure there. I pull myself back to standing. My head spins at the motion. I lean forward, hands catching my legs to breathe deep and stop myself from falling.

"You okay?" Mr. Number Five asks.

"Yeah," my head bobs without looking up, "I had them on the ropes there."

"Sorry to get in your way," he says, not moving any closer. "Turning blue was an interesting strategy."

I can appreciate a little dry humor to chase the reality away.

"Freaks people out." I shrug like this is some weekly occurrence despite my shaky nerves. "Sometimes they drop you and run away."

"Wasn't working this time."

I straighten and twist my head side to side to stretch my neck. "No, you've got it all wrong. I figured his favorite color was blue. He thought he'd strangle me until he got to the right shade."

That same crooked grin presses into his cheeks, but the concern remains in his eyes. "You sure you're okay?"

There's not much to say. This is part of the gig. I'm usually the last one to close, the last one to leave, the one who wants that last dollar, so I make a good target.

"I'm glad you stuck around a little later this time, that's all."

His mouth twists as he thinks on my words. "I was hoping to get your name, maybe your number, if you're feeling generous."

"Why should I give you either?" I motion to where my attackers ran off. "You were content to watch me drown from what I can tell."

"Hardly. I offered to help, but you turned me down." He spins, pointing to the other ten food trucks in the circle. "Not to mention, I didn't see any of them coming to your rescue either."

"They're closed."

"Not the falafel guy. I saw him peek out his curtains."

"Fine." I raise my eyebrows. "I won't give him my number either."

I turn to gather my trash from where I left the bags, but his voice catches me.

"Just your name then?"

My feet hesitate.

Stupid feet.

"Victoria," I say without turning back to face him. "My name is Victoria Cartwright."

Plastic rustles in my grip as I grab my forgotten trash and start for the dumpsters. I don't know why I gave him my name. County like this, name like mine, he'll have my number by the end of the day. I barely contain my smirk. Maybe that's my endgame, see how bad he's willing to work for it.

"Good to meet you, Vickie. My name's Maverick."

I glare over my shoulder, standard protocol for anyone who profanes my name.

"It's Vic, or Victoria, never Vickie."

Maverick winks. "See you tomorrow, Vickie."

* * *

Maverick

"Hey Romeo, you strike out again?" Greg yells from across the yard.

I tuck my helmet under my arm and head for the house. "Why should I tell you anything?"

"Inquiring minds want to know, brother."

I know better, likely him and the rest of the guys have money riding on it. If they can bet on something, they will.

"No number yet."

Greg lets out a whoop and behind him Tim swears out loud. "I thought you had it this time. Please say you at least talked to your dream girl."

"Yeah, we talked," I say. "Even got her name."

Greg sets down the axe and stops splitting wood for a minute. "Well, at least that's progress. I mean, at this rate you might have her number by Christmas."

They mean well, but they haven't met this Victoria Cartwright before. The way she carries herself, regal like a queen, but down home like apple pie sitting in a window. She's the complete package, and you don't rush a sweet find like that.

"Come on," Tim picks up his axe and takes a swing at the stump. "What's her name? Maybe we know her."

I consider keeping it to myself, like treasure I ain't willing to share, but Tim's right, they might have information for me.

"Victoria Cartwright," I tell them.

Greg starts laughing like I've said some joke. Tim shakes his head and walks back to the steps. "A Cartwright girl? You sure set your sights high, boy. And you picked The Queen of Hearts, of all the rotten luck."

I turn to leave, but Greg's voice calls me back. "They're legend around here, Mav. Ace Cartwright knows everyone and everything in this county. The man is made of money, and his kids are everything to him. You're not getting anywhere near that girl with Ace involved."

"She doesn't have a mind of her own?"

Greg and Tim exchange a look before Greg says, "Out of all of them, Victoria's got her own ideas about life, sure, but I still don't think she'd go against Ace. Not these days. Not since she moved back. She's all reformed and whatever."

"She used to be wild or something?" I don't have to ask to know it's true. Even if I hadn't seen her fight, it was there in her eyes, like a caged tiger dying to get free.

"You picked the right one though." Tim whistles low. "She's gorgeous."

I don't like him talking about her that way, not that I have much to lay claim to. "You said this county. Does that mean she lives around here?"

Greg laughs again. I'm thinking about smacking that smirk off his face when he says, "Cartwright Farm is about five miles from here."

"Sounds like I should meet our neighbors sometime." I turn to leave again, eager to change from my work clothes and grab a quick shower.

"Pedro called, says he has work for us. You interested?" Greg calls after me.

I wave him off. I'm exhausted. Last thing I want is to get mixed up in that riffraff.

This summer, fall in love with

The Unbelievable Queen of Hearts

THANK YOU FOR READING

The Unforgettable Queen of Diamonds
If you enjoyed the book, please consider leaving a review at Amazon.com or Goodreads.com

Contact or Connect:

Facebook: Nellie K. Neves Author

Instagram: Nellie K. Neves Author

Twitter: Nellie K. Neves Author or @NellieKatie

Email: Nelliekneves@gmail.com

Website:

www.nellieknevesauthor.com

Never miss a new release. Avoid FOMO (Fear Of Missing Out) and join the mailing list. You'll learn about upcoming events, new releases and gain access to content that won't appear anywhere else.

OTHER BOOKS BY THE AUTHOR

Sentry 6 Duo

Nightwatch

Falcon

Lindy Johnson Mystery Series

Caskets & Conspiracies

Saddles & Sabotage

Sparrows & Sacrifice

Fables & Felonies

Babysitters & Bodyguards

Lighthearted Romance

Pre-Approved Identity Theft

Set to Simmer

Christmas with Granny McPherson

© 2020 Nellie K. Neves
All Rights Reserved.

The Unforgettable Queen of Diamonds © 2020 by Nellie K. Neves. All Rights Reserved.

All rights reserved. No part of this book may be reproduced in any form or by any electronic or mechanical means including information storage and retrieval systems, without permission in writing from the author. The only exception is by a reviewer, who may quote short excerpts in a review.

Cover designed by Nellie K. Neves

Photo Credit: Analise Benevides

This is a work of fiction. Names, characters, businesses, places, events and incidents are either the products of the author's imagination or used in a fictitious manner. Any resemblance to actual persons, living or dead, or actual events is purely coincidental. While the cities or places listed in the novel may real places, all companies, people and events are fictitious and products of imagination.

Nellie K. Neves

Visit my website at www.nellieknevesauthor.com

Printed in the United States of America

First Printing: June 2020

Made in the USA
Columbia, SC
26 August 2022